'Do remind me,' she said scathingly.

'That's what Deventer would have had in mind, I believe. It will do to begin with.'

'Hypocrite!' Felice spat. 'As if you care a damn what Lord Deventer has in mind.'

'That's the wildcat. Now we begin to understand one another. Now, come here.'

She remained rooted to the spot, glaring at the darkening windows.

'Come here, Felice.'

Trembling inside, she went to him, dreading what was to come and fearful that her inevitable response would mock at all she had been asserting. 'No,' she whispered. 'Please don't.'

His hand reached out and slipped round to the back of her neck, drawing her lips towards his.

Juliet Landon lives in an ancient country village in the north of England with her retired scientist husband. Her keen interest in embroidery, art and history, together with a fertile imagination, make writing historical novels a favourite occupation. She finds the research particularly exciting, especially the early medieval period and the fascinating laws concerning women in particular, and their struggle for survival in a man's world.

Recent titles by the same author:

THE MAIDEN'S ABDUCTION

A MOST UNSEEMLY SUMMER

Juliet Landon

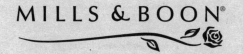

MILLS & BOON®

Chapter One

Lady Honoria Deventer shaded her eyes against the strengthening pale green rays that streamed into the best bedchamber at Sonning House. By her side, Lord Philip Deventer quietly opened the window, blowing a brittle winter cobweb into the garden below, where already a fuzz of new green covered the untidy plots.

Their joint attention was focussed on a tall and slender figure who stood motionless in the early sunshine, her dark mass of silky hair piled untidily on top of her head, her back curving into a neat waist without the support of whalebone stays. And though her face was turned from the house, her mother had guessed at its expression of sadness.

'What is wrong with her these days?' she whispered. 'So angry. So quiet.'

'She was not so quiet yesterday morning when she boxed the gardener's lad's ears, was she?' her husband replied.

'He was tipping birds' eggs out of their nests to

feed the cat. He deserved it. But she was never so severe until recently, Philip. Perhaps I should find her a new tutor.'

'She'd be better off with a husband. A home. A few bairns.' The typically brusque response sent a shadow across his wife's face, which naturally he missed. His great hand wandered across her distended stomach, anticipating the gender of the new bulge, the first of a new strain of Deventers. Their combined families, eleven of his by his late wife and seven of hers by two previous husbands, would total nineteen by summer.

Lady Honoria nestled into him, covering his hand with her own. 'But she has a home here…' she turned her face up to him, suddenly unsure '…doesn't she? She's only nineteen, dearest, and she's always been good at managing a household. Until we moved here to Sonning,' she added as an afterthought. Lord Deventer's household had not appreciated her expertise.

'Well then, she can go down to Wheatley and manage *that*.'

'What d'ye mean?' Lady Honoria slowly turned within his arm, puzzled by his tone. 'To Wheatley Abbey? There's no one there, dear.'

'Yes, there is. Gascelin will be there now, after the winter break. He sent a message up last week. There'll be plenty of room for her in that big guest-house, and she can make a start on the rooms in the New House ready for our move. We could be away from here in the autumn, if they both get a move on.'

His new wife turned away, glancing at her daughter's lovely back with some scepticism. 'You cannot be serious, Philip. I know you and Felice haven't got to know each other too well yet, but I'll not have her packed off down to Hampshire on her own to work with that man. There'd be trouble.'

'Yes,' Lord Deventer replied, unhelpfully, 'but that man, as you call him, is the best surveyor and master builder this side of the Channel. Brilliant chap. And anyway, Hampshire's only the next county, love, not exactly the other side of the world. She can always come back if she finds the task too daunting.' He braced himself for his wife's predictable defence of her beloved and only daughter.

'Daunted? Felice? Never! But *he's* not the easiest man to work alongside, is he? You know what a perfectionist he is.'

Lord Deventer had chosen Sir Leon Gascelin for just that quality and was only too well aware that the last thing he would appreciate would be someone like young Lady Felice Marwelle getting under his feet. However, there were ways of overcoming that problem.

'Well,' he said, 'so is she, for that matter, and heaven knows the place is big enough for her to keep out of his way. He won't want much to do with a lass like her. He was after Levina again when I last heard.'

'Levina! Tch! Half the court is after Levina.' Hearing the amusement in his voice she quickly closed the window against his impending laughter. 'You'll send a message to prepare the best rooms for her? She'll be comfortable, Philip?'

'Of course she will, love,' he said, bending to kiss her downy neck. 'I'll send a man down today. She'll be in her element.'

'Today? So soon?'

'Yes, love. No time like the present, is there?'

If only the daughter had been so pliable.

The daughter, Lady Felice Marwelle, had surprised her stepfather by an unusual co-operation verging on enthusiasm over a means of escape that had occupied her mind almost incessantly in recent weeks. But her expectations of the comfort promised by her mother were dashed against the large stone gatehouse leading to Wheatley Abbey through which a large and untidy building site was framed.

The elegant but sour-faced steward held his ground, clinging to his staff with one hand and the wide spiked collar of a mastiff with the other. 'I received no orders from Sir Leon about a visit,' he said. Though his tone was courteous, his finality might have dismayed most of those present.

But the young lady astride the bay mare was remarkably steadfast, giving back stare for stare from large brown eyes rimmed with thick black lashes, beating down the watery pale ones that time had faded. 'That has no bearing whatever on the fact that I am here, now, with thirty members of Lord Deventer's household and a fair proportion of his possessions,' she replied, coolly. 'And in Sir Leon's absence you may take your orders from myself, Lady Felice

Marwelle, Lord Deventer's stepdaughter. Is *that* good enough for you?'

'Lady,' the steward bowed stiffly, 'I beg your pardon, but the fact is that Sir Leon—'

'The fact is, steward, that we have been on the road for two days, at the end of which I was assured there would be lodging in the guesthouse available to us. Are rooms available or not?'

In truth, she was beginning to doubt whether the guesthouse would be the most suitable place to stay, after all, for although the fourteenth-century complex of buildings appeared to be more than adequate, they were far too close to the building site for comfort.

It was inevitable, of course, that any reconstruction work on this scale would cause some considerable mess, and although the abbey's original stones were being re-used, the sheer scale of the undertaking had turned the whole of the abbey precinct, once so well kept and peaceful, into a waste land. The large area between the gatehouse, guesthouse, abbey church and its old monastic buildings were stacked with stone and timber, scaffolding and hoists, with mounds of grit and sand, with the lean-to thatched sheds of the masons, carpenters, plasterers and tilers.

Most of the workers had finished for the day, but a group of grimy and wide-eyed young labourers hung round to see who would win the argument, Thomas Vyttery, steward, or this saucy young lass on the bay mare. They gawped at her and her two maids appreciatively until their attention was diverted by the steward's impressively muscular mastiff that suddenly noticed, through the legs of the lady's horse, two grey deerhounds almost as large as donkeys, standing passively but with bristling crests and lowered heads. Taking him by surprise, the mastiff wrenched itself out of the steward's grasp and fled for the safety of home with its tail between its legs, leaving the steward without his main prop.

'My lady, may I be permitted to suggest that, before you make a decision'—he was nothing if not formal—'you take a look at the inn in the village of Wheatley. You would have passed it on your way to the abbey. It's quite…'

Lady Felice was not listening. She was looking over to the right, beyond the church, towards a group of ancient stone-built dwellings that must once have been used by the monks for eating and sleeping before the terrible years of the Dissolution had driven them out. The message that Lord Deventer had received last week from his master builder and surveyor, Sir Leon Gascelin, had said that some of the rooms in the converted abbey would soon be ready for furnishing. Surely those must be the ones he meant.

'Those buildings over there. That must be Lord Deventer's New House, I take it?'

The steward did not need to look. 'The men are still working on that house, m'lady, and Sir Leon himself will be moving into the old Abbot's House within the next day or two.'

'Mr…?'

'Thomas Vyttery, m'lady.'

'Mr Vyttery, hand me the keys to the Abbot's House, if you please.'

The steward's voice quavered in alarm. 'By your leave, lady, I cannot do that. I shall be dismissed.'

'You will indeed, Mr Vyttery, if you refuse to obey me. I shall see that Lord Deventer replaces you with someone who knows more about hospitality than you do. Now, do as I say.' She held out a hand. 'No, don't try to remove any of the keys. I want the complete set—kitchens, stables, the lot. Thank you.'

In furiously silent remonstration, the impotent steward turned away without another word. Behind Felice, the cavalcade of waggons, carts, sumpter-horses, grooms and carters, cooks and kitchen-lads, household servants and officials lumbered into motion, creaking and swaying past the building site through ruts white with stone chippings and lime.

The fourteenth-century Abbot's House was on the far side of the abbey buildings within the curve of the river, far removed from the builders' clutter and larger than Felice had imagined. There were signs of extensive alterations and additions, enlarged windows and a stately carved porch with steps leading up to an iron-bound door.

Sending the carts, waggons and pack-horses round to the stableyard at the rear, Felice handed the large bunch of keys to her house-steward, Mr Peale, whose meteoric rise to the position had been effected especially for this venture. Still in his early thirties, Henry Peale took his duties very seriously, ushering his mistress up the steps into a series of pine-panelled rooms with richly patterned ceilings of white plaster that still held the pungent aroma of newness. In the fading light, it was only possible for them to estimate the rough dimensions, but the largest one on the first floor would do well enough for Lady Felice's first night, and the rest of the household would bed down wherever they could.

It was testimony to the young lady's managerial skills that a household, quickly assembled from her stepfather's staff at Sonning in Berkshire, so soon worked like a well-oiled machine to unload whatever was necessary for their immediate comfort and leave the rest on the carts until they knew where to put it. There was no question of assembling the lady's bed, but when the candles and cressets were lit at last, the well-swept rooms held a welcome that had so far been denied them. So much for her stepfather's assurances of comfort, she muttered to Lydia, her eldest maid.

'We'll soon have it ship-shape,' Lydia said, drawing the unpinned sleeves over her mistress's wrists. 'But where's Sir Leon got to? Wasn't he supposed to have been expecting us?'

'Heaven knows. Obviously not where Lord Deventer thinks he is. More to the point, what's happened to the message he was sent?' She stepped out of her petticoat, beneath which she had worn a pair of soft leather breeches to protect her thighs from the chafing of the saddle. 'You and Elizabeth take the room next door, Lydie. I'll have the hounds in here with me.'

Perhaps it was these vexed questions that made her come instantly to life long before dawn and respond with a puzzled immediacy to her new surroundings. To investigate the moonlight flooding in broken ripples through the lattice, she crossed the room to the half-open window, watched by the two sprawling hounds. The scent of wood-ash hung in the air and in the silence she could hear her heart beating.

The moonlit landscape was held together by an assortment of textured greys that there had been no time for her to remember as trees or groups of sleeping water-fowl. A cloud slid beneath the moon reflected in the glassy river below and, as she watched, a series of counter-ripples slid across the water, chased by another, and then another. Across on the far side where the darkness was most dense, a disturbance broke the surface and, even before her eyes had registered it, she knew that it was a boat, that someone who rowed on the river had been caught by the moon. Then the boat disappeared, towing behind it a wide V of ripples.

Wide awake, she pulled on her leather breeches and her fine linen chemise, tucking it in and hurriedly buckling on the leather belt to hold them together. Then, without bothering to look for her boots, she commanded the hounds to stay and let herself silently out of the room. The wide staircase led down to the passageway where the front doors were locked and bolted. They were new and well oiled, allowing her to exit without attracting the attention of the sleeping servants. She was now almost directly below her own chamber window and only a few yards from the riv-

erbank that dropped to a lower level, dotted with haw-
thorns and sleeping ducks.

She followed the river away from the Abbot's
House in the direction of the boat, her bare feet making no sound on the grass. She kept low, putting the
trees between herself and the river, passing the kitchens and the tumbledown wall of the kitchen garden
and eventually finding herself on a grassy track that
led to a wooden bridge and from there to the mill on
the opposite side.

A small rowing boat was tied up below the bridge
and, as there was no other, she assumed it to be the
one she had seen, suggesting that whoever had left it
there was probably in the mill. The miller, perhaps,
returning from a late night with friends?

The owls had ceased their hooting as she retraced
her steps, the moonlit abbey now appearing from a
different angle, the great tower of the church rising
well above every rooftop. Rather than return by exactly the same route, she was drawn towards a gap in
the old kitchen-garden wall that bordered the track,
its stones paving a way into the place where monastic
gardeners had once grown their vegetables. It was
now impossible for her to make out any shape of plot
or pathway, but she picked her way carefully towards
the silhouetted gables of the Abbot's House, brushing
the tops of the high weeds with her palms.

A slight sound behind her made her jump, and she
turned, ready for flight, only her lightning reaction
saving her from a hand that shot forward to grasp at
her arm. She felt the fingers touch the linen of her

sleeve, heard the breath of the one who would hold her, and then she swerved and fled, leaping and bounding like a hare without knowing which part of the wall ahead held the means of her escape.

She was tall, for a woman, but her pursuer's legs were longer than hers and she was forced to use every device to evade him, swerving and zig-zagging, ducking and doubling, hoping by these means to make him stumble. But it was she who stumbled on the rough ground that had not been cultivated for some twenty years or more, and that hesitation was enough for the man to catch her around the waist and swing her sideways, throwing her off-balance. She went crashing down into a bed of wild parsley and, before she had time to draw breath, his weight was over her, pressing her face-down into the weeds and forcing an involuntary yelp out of her lungs.

That was all she allowed herself, knowing that to reveal her identity might make her a greater prize than she already was. Let him think her a servant, a silly maid meeting her lover. It was not until he spoke that she realised how she must have appeared.

'Now, my lad, that was a merry little dance, eh? Let's introduce ourselves then, shall we? Then you can answer a few questions.' The voice that breathed softly into the back of her neck was nothing like a common labourer's, nor did he seem to be out of breath, but more like one who had enjoyed the chase, knowing he would win. He eased himself off her shoulders to kneel lightly astride her hips. 'Your name, lad?' he said.

Felice clenched her teeth, waiting for the persuasive blow to fall. This was something she had not
reckoned on. Her face was deep in the shadow of long
stalks and feathery leaves where the moonlight could
not reach, her cheek pressed against the night-time
coolness of the earth, which was to her advantage as
soon as she felt his response to her silence.

'All right, lad, there are other ways.'

His hands were deft around her waist, searching her
lower half for weapons and hesitating over the soft
fabric of the chemise tucked into the belt. 'Hey!
What's this, then?' he said more softly. Slowly, his
hands moved upwards, spanning her back, his fingertips already well out of bounds. The next move would
be too far.

Taking advantage of his shift in position, Felice
twisted wildly, flailing backwards with one arm to hit
hard at the side of his head with a crack that sent a
wave of pain through her wrist. It took him by surprise, and although he was quick to recover his balance, it gave her the time she needed to roll beneath
him and to push hard with one shoulder, using every
ounce of force she could summon.

He swayed sideways but caught her again before
she could free her legs from his weight, and then she
fought madly, desperately, knowing that her boy's
guise was not, after all, to be her safety. In panic, she
tore at his shirt and sleeveless leather jerkin, missing
his face but raking his neck and forearms and finally
sinking her teeth into the base of his thumb as he
grabbed at her wrists. She felt him flinch at that, giv-

ing her yet another chance to twist away, kicking and beating, desperate to be free of him.

She rolled, lashing out, but he rolled with her, over and over through the spring growth of chickweed and willow-herb and she was sure, without seeing his face, that he was actually enjoying her efforts, even while being hard pressed to contain them. At last she was stopped by an ancient half-buried wheelbarrow, and she lay, panting and exhausted, in an embrace so powerful that it hurt her ribs, immobilised by strong legs that encircled hers, her back against his chest and her wrists held fast beneath her chin by one of his hands.

She felt his chest shake in silent laughter while his free hand took her heavy plait and slipped the ribbon off the end, combing her thick hair loose with his fingers and letting fall a silken sheet of it across her face.

'There now, my beauty. Shall we stop pretending now. Eh? Fleet of foot and sharp of claw and tooth. That's hardly a lad's way now, is it? You're going to tell me who you are, then?'

Her resolve to remain silent wavered while her mind sought a quick answer to the question of his intentions; whether he would have as many qualms about violating a noblewoman as much as a village lass. Yet there was something about his persistent interrogation that suggested some other purpose behind his violent pursuit. Surely he would not have chased a lad with such ferocity if he'd had only rape in mind.

But having discovered he held a woman, would he now change his purpose?

Panic, anger and dread screamed through her mind and left a sickly void at the pit of her stomach, for now his hand had come to rest upon the large silver buckle of her belt, loosening the thong in a leisurely mockery of her weakness.

'No,' she whispered, writhing. 'No…please!'

The hand stopped, but the voice was smiling. 'No? No, what? You're not going to tell me who I've captured? Are you a moon-spirit, perhaps?'

'No,' she whispered again. Having broken her silence, it seemed necessary now to insist. 'Let me go. Please.'

He spoke teasingly against her ear, his words touching her. 'Then I require some kind of proof that you're mortal, don't you agree? Do you have any suggestion of a harmless nature? Nothing too… irreparable?'

Holy saints! What was he talking about? Suggestions of a harmless nature? Nothing irreparable? Angered, obdurate, she remained silent, now becoming aware of the throbbing in her wrist. She tried twisting to bite at any part of him, but his hand tightened its grip as she writhed, his free hand gently easing the linen chemise from the safety of her breeches.

She stopped, again paralysed with foreboding.

'So, tell me who sent you here. Who are you working for?' His hand was still, waiting on the bare skin of her midriff, and when she again refused to answer, he shifted slightly, settling her sideways against him and wedging her head into his shoulder with one iron forearm.

Looking back on this episode, she was to wonder why she had not screamed, why she had suddenly been aware of her heart fluttering instead of beating, or why the dread had suddenly become tinged with a shade of illicit excitement. It was dark, she was to excuse herself later, and she had not been able to see when his mouth covered hers, and then all proper maidenly resistance was obscured by longings that had lain dormant over the long dark months of autumn and winter, waiting to be rekindled.

It was no excuse, of course, but it would have to serve in the absence of anything more persuasive. What was more, it was the certainty that she would never again encounter this stranger on any level that freed her mind and body to his direction. If she had believed, even for the space of one second, that they would ever meet again, she would have killed him rather than give what he took so expertly, what she gave without further protest.

She was not inexperienced, but this man was a master, claiming her mind, her total participation from start to finish. She was hardly aware when his hand moved upwards to capture her breasts and to explore them in minutest detail while his lips held hers in willing submission, suspending all resistance with cords of ecstasy. She moaned and pushed against him, feeling the brush of his hair on her eyelids, his warm hand caressing and fondling, her own hands now freed and hanging numbly out of harm's way, allowing him free access.

In the far distant reaches of her mind, a comparison stirred and settled again, dimly reminding her to take, while she had the chance. So she took, greedily and unsparing, surprising him by her need that, had he known it, had never before reached these dimensions. How could he have known what part he was playing in her desperation?

Responding immediately, he tipped her backwards on to the cool dark bed of greenery and lay on her, whispering to her like a voice of conscience that she must think...think. Unbelievably, he told her to think what she was doing.

It was a familiar word to her, one which she had not thought to hear again in this connection, and the senses that moments before had been submerged beneath a roaring storm of emotion now emerged, chilled and shaking, drawing her attention to the prickly coldness at her back and the pale shocked stare of the moon. Tears blinded her, shattering the white orb into a thousand pieces.

'Let me go,' she whispered yet again. 'Let me up now, I beg you.'

'Who are you? Tell me, for pity's sake, woman.'

She turned her head away, suddenly shamed by his limbs on hers, his hand slowly withdrawing, leaving her breast bleak and unloved. 'No, I'm nobody. Let me go.' The tears dripped off her chin.

His sigh betrayed disappointment and bewilderment, but there was to be no return to the former roles of captor and captive. He rolled away, lying motionless in the dark as Felice scrambled unsteadily to her feet and hobbled away with neither a word nor backward glance, wincing at the pains that now beset her like demons, clutching her chemise in both hands.

She could not know, nor did she turn to see whether he followed, nor did she know how she found her way out of that vast walled space and through the stone arch that had once been closed off by wooden gates. All she knew was that, suddenly, it was there, that the rough ground had changed to cobbles that hurt her feet unbearably, and that she used the pointed finials on the rooftop to show her where the Abbot's House was.

Predictably, Lydia scolded her mistress on all counts, especially for leaving the two deerhounds, Fen and Flint, behind. 'Whatever were you thinking of, love?' she whispered, anxious not to wake young Elizabeth. 'Why didn't you tell him who you were? He could have been somebody set to guard the site at nights. Here, hold your other foot up.'

Shivering, despite the woollen blanket, Felice obeyed but felt bound to defend herself. 'How could he be? All those who work here would know of our arrival. He'd know who I was, wouldn't he? But he didn't guess, and that shows he's a stranger to the place. Ouch! My wrist hurts, Lydie.'

'I'll send Elizabeth to find some comfrey as soon as it gets light. Now, that'll have to do till we can have some water sent up. Into bed, love.'

Bandaged and soothed and with a streak of dawn already on the horizon, Felice gave in to the emotions that surged uncontrollably within her, awakened after their seven-month suppression. She had shared her heartache with no one, though faithful Lydia had been aware of her relationship with Father Timon, Lord Deventer's chaplain and Felice's tutor, and of the manner of his death. Now this stranger had forced her to confront the pain of an aching emptiness and to discover that it was, in fact, full to overflowing.

The revelation had both astounded her and filled her with guilt; what should have been kept sacred to Timon's memory had been squandered in a moment of sheer madness. Well, no one would know of that deplorable lapse, not even dear Lydia, and the man himself would now be many miles away.

But try as she would to replace that anonymous ruffian with the gentle Timon, the imprint of unknown hands on her, ruthlessly intimate, sent tremors of self-reproach through her aching body that were indistinguishable from bliss. The taste of his lips and their bruising intensity returned time and again to overcome all comparisons until, once again, she sobbed quietly into her pillow at the knowledge that *that* memory also would have to last for the rest of her life.

By first light, the servants were already astir under the direction of Mr Peale and Mr Dawson, the clerk of the kitchen from whom Lydia had obtained buckets of hot water. Elizabeth, a blonde-haired, scatterbrained maid of sixteen and the apple of Mr Dawson's discerning eye, had been sent off to find some comfrey for Felice's bruises while Felice herself, examining her upper arms and wrists, found exactly what she expected to find, rows of blue fingertip marks that were visible to Lydia from halfway across the room.

'Merciful heavens, love! I think you'll have to tell Sir Leon of this when he returns,' she said. 'It's something he ought to know about.'

'By the time Sir Leon Gascelin returns,' Felice replied, caustically, 'this lot will have disappeared.' She stirred the water in the wooden bucket with her feet, enjoying the comfort it gave to her cuts and scratches. 'And by the sound of him,' she went on, 'my wellbeing will probably be the last thing on his mind.'

'Lord Deventer said that of him? Surely not,' said Lydia, frowning.

'Not in so many words, but the implication was there, right enough. Keep out of his way. Don't interfere with his plans. And above all, remember that he's the high and mighty surveyor to whom we must all bow and scrape. Except that he's not available to bow and scrape to, so that gives us all time to practise, doesn't it? Pass me that comb, Lydie.' Thoughtfully, she untangled the long straight tresses, recalling how it had recently been undone by a man's fingers. 'I should wash it,' she mumbled.

A shout reached them from the courtyard below, then another, a deep angry voice that cracked across the general clatter of feet, hooves, buckets and boxes. Silence dropped like a stone.

Another piercing bark. 'Where, exactly?'

The reply was too quiet for them to hear, but Lydia mouthed the missing words, pointing a finger to the floor, her eyes wide with dismay.

'That doesn't sound like the steward,' whispered Felice.

Lydia crossed to the window but she was too late, and by the time she reached the door it had been flung open by a man who had to stoop to avoid hitting his head on the low medieval lintel. He straightened, immediately, his hand still on the latch, his advance suddenly halted by the sight of a stunningly beautiful woman sitting with her feet in a bucket, dressed in little except a sleeveless kirtle of fine linen, half-open down the front. It would have been impossible to say whose surprise was the greater, his or theirs.

'Get out!' Felice snapped, making no effort to dive for cover. If this was a colleague of the miserable steward, Thomas Vyttery, then his opinion of her was of no consequence. Yet this man had the most insolent manner.

He made no move to obey the command, but took in every detail of the untidy room as he bit back at her. 'This is my room! *You* get out!'

It took a while, albeit a short one, for his words to register, for the only other person who could lay claim to the Abbot's House was Sir Leon Gascelin, and he was known to be away from home.

The man was tall and broad-chested, the embodiment of the power that she and Lydia had facetiously been applauding. His dark hair was a straight and glossy cap that jutted wilfully out over his forehead in spikes, close-cropped but unruly enough to catch on the white lace-edged collar of his open-necked shirt. Felice noticed the ambience of great physical strength and virility that surrounded him, even while motionless, and the way that Fen and Flint had gone to greet him with none of the natural hostility she would have preferred them to exhibit in the face of such rudeness.

He caressed the head of one of them with a strong well-shaped hand that showed a scattering of dark hairs along the back, while his straight brows drew together above narrowed eyes in what might have passed for either disapproval or puzzlement.

Felice's retort was equally adamant. 'This house belongs to Lord Deventer and I am here by his permission. As you see, I am making no plans to move out again. Now, if you require orders to bully my servants, I suggest you go and seek Sir Leon Gascelin, my lord's surveyor. That should occupy your time more fruitfully. You may go.' Leaning forward, she swished the water with her fingertips. 'Is this the last of the hot water, Lydie?'

Lydia's reply was drowned beneath the man's icy words. 'I don't need to find him. I *am* Sir Leon Gascelin.'

Slowly, Felice raised her head to look at him through a curtain of hair, the hem of which dripped with curving points of water. She had no idea of the picture of loveliness she presented, yet on impulse her hand reached out sideways for her linen chemise, the one she had worn yesterday, gathering it to her in a loose bundle below her chin. Promptly, Lydia came forward to drape a linen sheet around her shoulders.

'Then I have the advantage of you, Sir Leon,' Felice said over the loud drumming of her heart. 'I was here first.'

'Then you can be the first to go, lady. I require you to be out of here by mid-day. My steward tells me that you call yourself Lady Felice Marwelle, but Lord Deventer never mentioned anyone of that name in my hearing. Do you have proof of your relationship to his lordship? Or are you perhaps his mistress with the convenient sub-title of stepdaughter?' He looked around him at the piles of clothes, pillows, canvas bags and mattresses more typical of a squatter's den than a lady's bedchamber. 'You'd not be the first, you know.'

Outraged by his insolence, Felice shook with fury. 'My name, sir, is Lady Felice Marwelle, daughter of the late Sir Paul Marwelle of Henley-on-Thames who was the first husband of my mother, Lady Honoria Deventer. Lord Deventer is my mother's third husband and therefore my second stepfather. I am not, and never will be, *any* man's mistress, nor am I in the habit of proving my identity to my stepfather's boorish acquaintances. His message would have made that unnecessary, but it appears that *that* went the same way as his recollection that he had a stepdaughter named Felice. He assured me that he sent a message three…four days ago for you to prepare rooms in the guest…' She could have bitten her tongue.

'So you decided on the Abbot's House instead. And there was *no* message, lady.'

'Then we share a mutual shock at the sight of each other, for which I am as sorry as you are, Sir Leon,' she said with biting sarcasm. She felt the unremitting examination of his eyes which she knew must have missed nothing by now: her swollen eyelids, her bruises, her soaking feet, all adding no doubt to his misinterpretation of her role. Defensively, she tried to justify herself whilst regretting the need to do so. 'I chose this dwelling, sir, because I am not used to living on a building-site, despite Lord Deventer's recommendations. Whether you received a message or not, I am here to prepare rooms in the New House next door ready for his lordship's occupation in the autumn. And I had strict instructions to keep well out of your way, which I could hardly do with any degree of success if our two households were thrown together, could I? Even a child could see that,' she said, looking out of the window towards the roof of the church. 'Now will you please remove yourself from my chamber, Sir Leon, and allow me to finish dressing? As you see, we are still in the middle of unpacking.'

Instead of leaving, Sir Leon closed the door behind him and came further into the room where the light from one of the large mullioned windows gave her the opportunity to see more of his extreme good looks, his abundant physical fitness. His long legs were well-muscled, encased in brown hose and knee-high leather riding boots; paned breeches of soft brown kid did nothing to disguise slim hips around which hung a sword-belt, and Felice assumed that he had stormed round here immediately on his return from some nearby accommodation, for otherwise it would have taken him longer to reach an out-of-the-way place like Wheatley.

'No,' he said, in answer to her request. 'I haven't finished yet, lady. You'll not dismiss me the way you dismissed my steward yesterday.'

Instantly, she rose to the bait. 'If your steward, Sir Leon, knows no better than to refuse both hospitality and welcome to travellers after a two-day journey, then it's time he was replaced. Clearly he's not up to the position.'

'If Thomas Vyttery is replaced at all, lady, it will be for handing you the keys to this house.'

'That was his only saving grace. The keys remain with me.'

'This is no place for women, not for a good few months. We've barely started again after winter and there are dozens of men on the site,' he said, leaning against the window recess and glancing down into the courtyard below. It swarmed with men, but they were her servants, not his builders. 'And I have enough trouble getting them to keep their minds on the job without a bevy of women appearing round every corner.'

'Then put blinkers on them, sir!' she snapped. 'The direction of your men's interest is not my concern. I've been sent down here to fulfil a task and I intend to do it. Surely my presence cannot be the worst that's ever happened to you in your life. You appear to have survived, so far.'

'And you, Lady Felice Marwelle, have an extremely well-developed tongue for one so young. I begin to see why your stepfather was eager to remove you to the next county if you used it on him so freely, though he might have spared a thought for me while he was about it. He might have done even better to find you a husband with enough courage to tame you. I'd do it myself if I had the time.'

'Hah! You're sure it's only *time* you lack, Sir Leon? I seem to have heard that excuse more than once when skills are wanting. Now, if you'll excuse me, my feet are wrinkling like paper, and I *must* hone my tongue in private.'

It was not to be, however. Enter Mistress Elizabeth bearing a large armful of feathery green plants, her face flushed and prettily eager. Without taking stock of the situation in the chamber or sensing any of the tension, she headed directly for her mistress and dumped the green bundle on to her lap. 'My lady, look! Here's chervil for your bruises. There's a mass of it in the old kitchen garden. There, now!' She looked round, newly aware of the unenthusiastic audience and searching for approval.

Felice looked down at the offering. 'Chervil, Elizabeth?'

'Comfrey, Elizabeth,' said Lydia. 'You were told to gather comfrey.'

'Oh,' said Elizabeth, flatly.

'You have injuries, lady?' said Sir Leon. 'I didn't

know that.' His deep voice adopted a conciliatory
tone that made Felice look up sharply, her eyes suddenly wary.

'No, sir. Nothing to speak of. The journey yesterday, that's all.' In a last effort to persuade him to
leave, she stood up, holding out the greenery to Lydia
and taking a thoughtless step forward.

She went crashing down, tipping the bucket over
and pitching herself face-first into a flood of tepid
water, flinging the chervil into Sir Leon's path. He
and Lydia leapt forward together, but he was there
first with his hands beneath her bare armpits, heaving
her upright between his straddled legs. Then, to
everyone's astonishment, he lifted her up into his
arms as if she weighed no more than a child and stood
with her in the centre of the room as the two maids
mopped at the flood around his feet.

Felice was rarely at a loss for words, but the shock
of the fall, her wet and dishevelled state, and this
arrogant man's unaccustomed closeness combined to
make any coherent sound difficult, her sense of helplessness heightened by her sudden plunge from her
high-horse to the floor.

His hands were under her knees and almost over
one breast that pushed unashamedly proud and pink
through the wet fabric; his face, only inches from
hers, held an expression of concern bordering on con-
sternation. He was watching her closely. Inspecting
her. 'You hurt?' he said.

She peered at him through strands of wet hair,

shaking her head and croaking one octave lower. 'Let me go, sir. Please.'

He hesitated, then looked around the room. 'Where?' he said.

'Anywhere.'

For a long moment—time waited upon them—their eyes locked in a confusion of emotions that ranged through disbelief, alarm and, on Felice's part, outright hostility. It was natural that she should have missed the admiration in his, for he did his best to conceal it, but she was close enough now to see his muscular neck where a long red scratch ran from beneath his chin and disappeared into the open neck of his shirt. His jaw was square and strong and his mouth, un-smiling but with lips parted as if about to speak, had a tiny red mark on the lower edge where perhaps his lover had bitten it in the height of passion. His breath reached her, sending a wave of familiar panic into her chest, and as her gaze wandered over his features on their own private search, he continued to watch her with a grey unwavering scrutiny, noting her bruised wrists before holding her eyes again.

Her gaze flinched and withdrew to the loosely hanging points of his doublet that should have tied it together; the aiglets that tipped each tie were spear-heads of pure gold. One of them was missing. She took refuge in the most inconsequential details while her breath stayed uncomfortably in her lungs, refusing to move and gripped by a terrible fear that seeped into every part of her, reviving a recent nightmare. She fought it, terrified of accepting its meaning.

His grip on her body tightened, pulling her closely in to him, then he strode over to the tumbled mattress where she had lain that night and placed her upon it, bending low enough for his forelock to brush against her eyelids. He stood upright, looking down at her and combing a hand through his hair that slithered back into the ridges like a tiled roof. Without another word, he picked up the grimy doeskin breeches she had worn in the garden, dropped them into her lap and strode past the sobbing Elizabeth and bustling Lydia and out of the room, without bothering to close the door. They heard his harsh shout to someone below them, and the two deerhounds stood with ears pricked, listening to the last phases of his departure.

Mistress Lydia was first to recover. 'For pity's sake, Elizabeth, stop snivelling and help me with this mess, will you? What's that you're fiddling with? Let me see.'

'I don't know. I found it under the chervil in the kitchen garden.' She held out her palm upon which lay a tiny golden spear-head with a hole through its shaft.

Lydia picked it up, turning it over in the light before handing it to her mistress. 'An aiglet,' she said. 'Somebody lost it. Now, lass…' she turned back to Elizabeth '…you get that wet mess off the floor and throw it out. Plants and men are rarely what they seem: that chervil is cow-parsley.'

Chapter Two

The unshakeable determination that Felice had shown to her early morning visitor regarding her occupation of the Abbot's House now collapsed like a pack of playing cards, and whereas she had earlier brushed aside Lydia's suggestion that they might as well return to Sonning, it now seemed imperative that the waggons were loaded without delay.

'We can't stay here, Lydie,' she said, still shaking. 'We just can't. Send a message down to find Mr Peale.'

Mistress Lydia Waterman had been with Felice long enough to become her close friend and ally and, at five years her senior, old enough to be her advisor, too. She was a red-haired beauty who had never yet given her heart to any man to hold for more than a week or two, and Felice loved her for her loyalty and almost brutal honesty.

'Think what you're doing, love,' said Lydia, businesslike. 'That's not the best way to handle it.'

Felice winced at the advice, given for the second time that day. 'I *have* thought. That was him!' she whispered, fiercely. 'This is his missing aiglet that Elizabeth found. He's a *fiend*, Lydie.'

Lydia lifted a dense pile of blue velvet up into her arms and held it above Felice's head. 'Arms up,' she said, lowering it. 'Losing an aiglet in the kitchen garden doesn't make him a fiend, love. And he didn't arrive here until now, so how could it have been him who chased you? Last night he'd have been miles away.'

'If he was near enough to get here so early he couldn't have been far away, Lydie. He must have been snooping while they believed he was away, looking for something…somebody. And I recognised the voice too, and the way he looked at me. I know that he knows. He wanted to humiliate me.'

'All men sound the same in the dark,' said Lydia, cynically. 'But he picked you up out of the water fast enough.'

'And he pretended to believe that I was Lord Deventer's mistress, too.'

'Perhaps he really believed it. His lordship's no saint, is he? It was an easy mistake to make, with him not recognising the name of Marwelle. Turn round, love, while I fasten you up.'

'I don't care. We're not staying. We can be away tomorrow.'

'No, we can't,' Lydia said with a mouthful of pins. 'Tomorrow's Sunday.'

Lydia's pragmatism could be shockingly unhelpful,

yet not even she could be expected to share the torment that now shook Felice to the very core. The knowing stranger she had presumed would take her secret with him to the ends of the earth now proved to be the very person whose antagonism clearly matched her own, the one with whom she would not have shared the slightest confidence, let alone last night's disgraceful fiasco.

He would misconstrue it, naturally. What man would not? He would believe she was cheap, a silly lass who needed reminding to think before she allowed a man, a total stranger, to possess her, hence his whispered warning that should more typically have come from her rather than him. Oh, yes, he would revel in the misunderstanding: she would see it in his eyes at every meeting unless she packed her bags and left.

It was a misunderstanding she herself would have been hard-pressed to explain rationally, a private matter of the heart she had not discussed even with the worldly Lydia, for Father Timon had not been expected to know what it was frowned upon for priests to know, and his role of chaplain, confessor, tutor and friend had progressed further than was seemly for priests and maids of good breeding.

Timon Montefiore, aged twenty-eight, had taken up his duties in Lord Deventer's household soon after the latter's marriage to Lady Honoria Fyner, previously Marwelle, and perhaps it had been a mutual need for instant friendship that had been the catalyst for what followed.

Friendship developed into affection, and the affection deepened. As her mother's preoccupation with a new husband and a young step-family grew, Felice's previous role as deputy-mistress of their former home became redundant in Lord Deventer's austerely regimented household. Rudderless and overlooked by the flamboyant new stepfather, Felice had drifted more and more towards Timon, partly to remove herself from Lord Deventer's insensitivities and partly because Timon was always amiable and happy to see her. He had been exceptional in other ways; his teaching was leisurely and tender, arousing her only so far and no further, always with the promise of something more and with enough control for both of them. 'Think what you're doing,' was advice she heard regularly, though often enough accompanied by the lift of her hand towards his smiling lips and merry eyes.

She had discovered the inevitable anguish of love last summer when Timon had caught typhoid fever and her stepfather had had him quickly removed from his house to the hospice in Reading. Forbidden to visit him, Felice had been given no chance to say farewell and, during conversation at dinner a week later, she learned that he had died a few days before and was already buried. Lord Deventer was not sure where. Did it matter? he had said, bluntly. Until then, Felice had not known that love and pain were so closely intertwined.

Since that dreadful time last summer, no man's arms had held her, nor had any other man shared her thoughts until now. Her terrible silence had been explained by her mother as dislike of her new situation, exacerbated by talk of husbands, a remedy as painful as it was tactless to one who believed her heart to be irrevocably broken.

The usual agonies of guilt and punishment had been instilled into Felice from an early age and were now never far from her mind without the courteous priest to mitigate it. The replacement chaplain had been stern and astringent, not the kind to receive a desperate young woman's confidences, and she had been glad to accept any means of escape from a house of bitter-sweet memories upon which she had believed nothing would impose. But last night's experience had suggested otherwise in a far from tender manner, and her anger at her heart's betrayal was equal to her fury with the shiftless Fate who had plucked mockingly at the cords that bound her heart.

'Out of the frying-pan, into the fire' was a saying that occurred to her as she went about the first duties of the day, now demurely dressed in a blue velvet overskirt and bodice that set off the white under-sleeves embroidered with knotwork patterns. Black-work, they called it, except that this was blue and gold. Her hair was tidily coiled into a gold mesh caul at the nape of her neck almost as an act of defiance to the man who had warned her of his men's easily deflected attentions. At home, she would have worn a concealing black velvet French hood, yet she had never been overly concerned by prevailing fashions and saw no reason to conform now that there was no one to notice. That dreadful man had seen her at her worst; whatever he saw now would be an improvement.

The first floor was thronged with men carrying tables, stools, chests and cupboards and, in her chamber, several of the carpenters were erecting the great tester bed and hanging its curtains. The ground floor was the servants' domain, containing the great hall and steward's offices, but the top floor covered the length and breadth of the building, a massive room flooded with light from new oriel windows that reflected on to a magnificent plasterwork ceiling. Knowing that these additions were the result of the surveyor's vision, Felice tried hard to find fault with it, but came away with grudging admiration instead. It was no wonder he had been irked by her takeover.

She visited the kitchens across the courtyard next, but came close to being trampled underfoot by lads carrying boxes, baskets, pans and sacks; so, to give her feet some respite, she headed for an area at the back of the Abbot's House that gave access into the derelict square cloister. Here at last was peace where, in the enclosed warmth, the kitchen cat poured itself off a low wall at the sight of Flint and Fen and disappeared into the long grass.

Shelving her thoughts about how to make a dignified return home, she sat with her legs stretched out between the stone columns that topped the low wall, her eyes unconsciously planning a formal garden with perhaps a fountain in the centre. Not that it mattered;

she did not intend to stay. She removed her shoes to inspect the soles of her feet in valuable privacy.

The deerhounds nosed about behind her, so their silence went unheeded until, sensing their absence, she turned to check on them. Their two heads could not have been closer beneath the hand of the tall intruder who stood silently in the shadows on the church side of the cloister, watching her.

Her heart lurched, pounding with a new rhythm, and she turned away, throwing her skirts over her bare ankles, pretending an unconcern she was far from feeling. She snapped her fingers, angrily and called, 'Flint! Fen! Come!'—by no means sure that they would obey but reluctant to turn to see.

The hounds returned to her side but they were not alone, nor had they obeyed her command but his, and she knew then that, like the steward deserted by his mastiff, she would never again be able to rely on them for protection. Angered by their inability to tell friend from foe, she snapped at them, 'Lie down!'

Sir Leon was laughing quietly at this calamity as he came to sit on the wall just beyond her feet and, as she began to swing them to the ground, he caught one ankle in a tight grip, making her flight impossible. 'No, lady,' he said. 'We have some unfinished business, do we not? A moment or two of your time, if you please.'

'Be brief, sir. And release my foot.'

She did not need to look at him to see that he had already started work, for he had discarded his doublet and now wore only the jerkin over his shirt, the sleeves of which were rolled up to expose well-muscled forearms. A deep V of bare chest showed in the opening, and his boots were powdered with stone-dust. Unhurried by her command, his hand slid away and spread across his knee. 'Well?' he said, tucking away the remnants of a smile.

She frowned at him, puzzled. 'Well, what, sir?'

'I'm allowing you to state your case before I state mine, Lady Felice Marwelle. And you need not be brief.'

'Nevertheless, I will be. You will be relieved to know that I intend to return to Sonning within the next few days.' She spoke to a row of purring pigeons on the angle of the wall behind him, disconcerted by his close attention, his attempted dominance even before words had been exchanged.

'Is that all?'

'Yes.'

'Then you've changed your mind about staying.'

'Yes,' she snapped. 'Don't ask me why. It's what you wanted, isn't it?'

'You changed your mind to please me?'

Her mouth tightened. 'No. It pleases *me*.'

'Then I'm sorry to disappoint you. I must reject your decision.'

'What?' She frowned, looking at him fully for the first time. 'You're in no position to reject it. I've already made it.' His eyes, she saw, were grey and still laughing.

'Then you can unmake it, my lady. You'll stay here and complete the task Lord Deventer set for you.'

Rather than continue a futile argument, Felice's response was to get up and leave him, but her body's slight message was deciphered even as it formed, and her ankle was caught again and held firmly.

'Ah, no!' he said. 'I'm aware of your aptitude for bringing discussions to an abrupt conclusion but really, you have to give them a chance to develop occasionally, don't you think so? Now, what d'ye think your stepfather will say when you tell him you haven't even seen the place yet?'

Riled by his insistence and by his continued hold on her ankle, she flared like a fuse. 'And what d'ye think he'll say, Sir Leon, when I tell him of the disgraceful way I've been received? Which I will!'

This did not have the effect she hoped for, no sign of contrition crossing his face. 'About mistaking you for one of his mistresses, you mean? That jest will keep him entertained for a month, my lady, as well you know. And if he'd intended to send a message to warn me of your arrival…'

'To *warn* you? Thank you!'

'…he would have done. Clearly he had no intention of doing so.'

'Why ever not, pray?'

'Because he knew damn well he'd have to look for another surveyor if he had. He knows my views about mixing work and women.'

Felice bent to clutch at her leg and yank it bodily out of his grasp, swinging her legs down on to the long grass. 'Then there will be three of us pleased, sir. There is nothing more to discuss, is there?'

'Correction. There'll be two of us pleased. You'll stay here with me.'

She sat, rigidly angry, with her hands clutching at the cool stone wall on each side of her. 'Sir Leon, I am usually quite good at understanding arguments, but when they are as obscure as yours I'm afraid I need some help. Explain to me, if you will. If you are so disturbed about having women near you, why have you suddenly decided that I must stay? I can only conclude that you must need to please Lord Deventer very much indeed to sacrifice your principles so easily. Do you need his approval so much, then?'

He allowed himself a smile before he replied, revealing white even teeth. 'Certainly I do. He pays me, you see, and the sooner this place is lived in, the sooner I can move on to others. I'm in demand, hereabouts.'

'Not by me!' she muttered under her breath. 'Barbarian!'

'Still sore?' He lowered his tone to match hers, catching the drift of her mind.

It was a mistake she regretted instantly, having no wish to discuss those terrible events, neither with him nor with anyone. Forgetting her shoes, she was quicker this time, managing to reach the centre of the overgrown quadrangle before her wrist was caught and she was brought to a halt. She shook off his grip and whirled to face him in a frenzy of rage.

'Don't touch me!' she snarled, her eyes blazing like coals. 'Don't *ever* lay a finger on me again, sir, or I swear I'll…I'll *kill* you! And don't think to dictate to

me where and when I go. You are not my guardian.'
She turned her back on him deliberately, but had no
idea how to get out of the quadrangle without climbing shoeless over the low wall. Her heart thudded in
an onslaught of anger. She hesitated, feeling the sharp
tangle of weeds on her sore feet. There was an un-
canny silence behind her.

'You'll need these to get out of here, my lady.' His
voice came from where they had been sitting.

She knew he referred to her shoes but still she hesitated, wondering if it was worth risking more pain to
her feet. The cloister walkways were littered with rubble.

'Come on,' he said, gently. 'We're going to have
to talk if we're to work together.'

'We are *not* going to work together,' she snapped.
'I want nothing to do with this place. I'm going
home.'

'You'll need your shoes, then.'

She turned and saw that he was sitting on the wall
again with one leg on either side, holding up her
shoes as bait. 'Throw them,' she said.

'Come and collect them.'

She looked away, then approached, eyeing his
hands. She reached the wall just as he dropped them
over on to the paved side, beyond her reach. 'Don't
play games with me, Sir Leon. I'm not a child,' she
snapped.

'Believe it or not, I had noticed that, but I'm determined you shall conclude this discussion in the
proper manner, my lady, whether you like the idea or

not. Now, please be seated. I am not at all disturbed by the idea of having women near me, as you see. Actually, it's something I'm learning to get the hang of.'

She knew he was being ridiculous. Any man who could move a woman so quickly and with such mastery was obviously no woman-hater. 'You have a long way to go,' she said, coldly. 'About twenty years should be enough.'

The smile returned. 'That's better. We're talking again. Now, my lady, I shall show you round the New House and we can discuss what's to be done in the best chambers on the upper floors. The lower one…'

'Sir Leon, you are under a misapprehension. I have already told you…'

'That you are not staying. Yes, I heard you, but I have decided that you are. If Deventer has entrusted you with the organisation of his household here at Wheatley, and to furnish his rooms, then he must think highly of your abilities. Surely you're not going to throw away the chance to enhance your credit with him and disappoint your mother, too? They would expect some kind of explanation from you. Do you have one available?'

'Yes, sir. As it happens, I do. I intend to tell them that you are impossible to work with and that our intense dislike of each other is mutual. Indeed, I cannot help feeling that my stepfather guessed how matters would stand before he sent me here, so I shall have no compunction about giving him chapter and verse.'

'Chapter *and* verse?'

'You are detestable!' she whispered, looking away.

'And you, as you have reminded me, are a woman, and therefore you will hardly be deceived by my very adequate reasons.'

'Not in the slightest. Nor would a child believe them.'

'Then how would it be if I were to inform your parents of what happened last night?' he said, quietly.

She had not been looking until now, but the real intention behind his appalling question needed to be seen in his eyes. He could not be serious. But his expression told her differently. He was very serious.

'Oh, yes,' she whispered, her eyes narrowing against his steady gaze. 'Oh, yes, you would, wouldn't you? And if I told them you were talking nonsense?'

'Whose word would your stepfather take, d'ye think? Whose story would he *prefer* to believe, yours or mine? I could go into a fair amount of detail, if need be.'

She launched herself at him like a wildcat, her fingers curved like claws ready to rake at his cool grey eyes, his handsome insolent face, at anything to ruffle his intolerable superiority and to snatch back the memories he should never have been allowed to hold.

Her hands were caught and held well out of harm's way and, if she had hoped to knock him backwards against the stone column, she now found that it was she who was made to sit with one at her back while her arms were slowly and easily twisted behind her.

His arms encircled her, his face close to hers, and once again she was his captive and infuriated by his restraint. 'And don't let's bother about talk of killing me if I should lay a finger on you because I intend to, lady, one way or another. You threw me a careless challenge earlier. Remember?'

Mutely, she glared at a point beyond his shoulder.

'Yes, well I've accepted it, so now we'll see how much skill is needed to tame you, shall we?'

She was provoked to scoff again. 'Oh, of course. That's what it's all about. First you pretend to be concerned with duty, yours and mine, and then you try threats. But after all that, it's a challenge, a silly challenge you men can never resist, can you? How pathetic! What a victory in the eyes of your peers when they hear how you took on a woman single-handed. How they'll applaud you. And how the women will sneer at your hard-won victory. Did you not know, Sir Leon, that a man can only make a woman do what she would have done anyway?' She had never believed it, but it added some small fuel to her argument.

'Ah, you think that, do you? Then go on believing it if you think it will help. It makes no difference, my beauty. Deventer sent you down here with more than his new house in mind, and somewhere inside that lovely head you have some conflicting messages of your own, haven't you, eh?'

Frantically, she struggled against him, not wanting to hear his percipient remarks or suffer the unbearable nearness of him again. Nor could she tolerate his trespass into her capricious mind. 'Let me go!' she panted. 'Loose me! I want nothing to do with you.'

'You'll have a lot to do with me before we're through, so you can start by regarding me as your custodian, in spite of not wanting me. Deventer will approve of that, I know.'

'You insult me, sir. Since when has a custodian earned the right to abuse his charge as you have abused me?'

'Abuse, my lady? That was no abuse, and you know it. You'd stopped fighting me, remember.'

'I was exhausted,' she said, finding it increasingly difficult to think with his eyes roaming her face at such close quarters. 'You insulted me then as you do now. Let me go, Sir Leon. There will never be a time when I shall need a custodian, least of all a man like you. Go and find someone else to try your so-called skills on, and make sure it's dark so she sees you not.'

'Get used to the idea, my lady,' he said, releasing her. 'It will be with you for as long as it takes.' He picked up her shoes and held them by his side. 'Fight me as much as you like, but you'll discover who's master here, and I'll have you tamed by the end of summer.'

'A most unseemly summer, Sir Leon, if I intended to stay. But, you see, I don't. Now, give me my shoes.' She would have been surprised and perhaps a little disappointed if he had obeyed her, yet the temptation to nettle him was strong and her anger still so raw that she would have prolonged even this petty squabble just to win one small point. As it turned out, the victory was not entirely hers.

'Ask politely,' he said.

'I'll be damned if I will! Keep them!'

Her moment of recklessness was redeemed by voices that reached them through the open arch that had once been a doorway, the way she had entered. Lydia and Elizabeth were looking for her. 'My lady?' they called. 'Where are you?'

'Here,' she called back. 'Elizabeth, ask Sir Leon prettily for my shoes, there's a dear. He's been kind enough to carry them for me.' Without another glance at her self-appointed custodian, she held up one foot ready for its prize. '*Such* a gentleman,' she murmured, sweetly.

It was better than nothing. But she could not bring herself to elaborate on the scene to Lydia, who was not taken in by Sir Leon's stiff bow or by her mistress's attempt at nonchalance, her blazing eyes and pink cheeks.

'We're staying, then,' said Lydia, provocatively.

'Certainly not!' Felice told her, surreptitiously probing along her arms for more bruises. 'We're getting out of here at the first opportunity. Why?' She glanced at her maid's face. 'Don't tell me you'd like to stay.'

'Well…' Lydia half-smiled '…I've just discovered that he has a very good-looking valet called Adam.'

'Oh, Lydie! Don't complicate matters, there's a love.'

Another reason for Felice's reserve was that her discord with Sir Leon had now acquired a sizeable element of personal competition in which the prize was to be her pride, a commodity she was as determined to hold on to as he apparently was to possess. Removing herself from the field of contest would indicate that it was probably not worth the fight, leaving him to be the victor by default. And naturally, he would believe her to be afraid of him.

Perhaps even more serious was his threat to make Lord Deventer aware of their first encounter from which she had emerged the loser. While her stepfather would undoubtedly clap his surveyor on the back for taking advantage of such a golden opportunity, not to mention his night-time vigil, she herself would be severely censured for such conduct, irrespective of its initial purpose. The thought of Lord Deventer's coarse laughter brought waves of shame to her face enough to make any castigation pleasant by comparison. He would find her a husband, one who was more concerned about the size of her dowry than her reputation.

As for Sir Leon, any man who could use such an intimate and enigmatic incident as a threat was both unprincipled and despicable; he must know that that alone would be enough to keep her at Wheatley. Still, there was nothing to stop her making him regret his decision, though she expected that future encounters would be both rare and brief. Except to Lord Deventer, the man had absolutely nothing to recommend him.

The news that men had been seen traipsing through the kitchen garden had intrigued her until she discovered at suppertime that they had been repairing the gap in the wall by the side of the river path. And when she had asked by whose orders—it was, after all, in her domain—she had been told it was by Sir Leon's.

She might have let the matter rest at that; it would not do to display an inexplicable curiosity. But in the comforting darkness of her curtained bed, the soft images of the previous night took unnatural precedence over the day's conflicts and would not leave her in peace. It was as if, in the darkness, they were beyond regret. She had now seen the man with whom she had been entangled and, although hostile, it was not difficult for her to recall the way he had held, caressed and kissed her, nor to remember how her own body had flared out of control before the sudden quenching of prudence. In the dark, shame did not exist.

With only the moon to watch, she took Flint and Fen quietly downstairs out of the front door and round through the kitchen courtyard to the back of the house, the reverse of last night's frantic journey. At the entrance to the garden she stopped, confronted by the derelict place washed by moonlight where dear Timon's memory had been cruelly disturbed by one insane moment of bliss, the like of which she had never known with him. Was it because of his absence? Her longing? She thought not, but no one need know it. She need not admit it again, even to herself.

One of the deerhounds whined, then the other, both

suddenly leaving her and bounding up the overgrown path into the darkness. Incensed by their preference for rabbits rather than her, she took a step forward, yelling into the silvery blackness, 'Flint! Fen! Come back here, damn you!'

They returned at the trot, ears flattened and tails flailing apologetically, but shattering her reminiscences and making her aware of their absurdity. 'Come!' she said, severely. 'Stupid hounds.'

This time, her return was unhurried and more thoughtful.

Had the next day been any other but Sunday, there would have been a good chance of avoiding the cause of her sleepless moments, but church-going was never an option unless one intended to attract the disapproval of the vicar and his church-wardens. Furthermore, as a close relative of the abbey's owner, Felice had a duty to attend.

She had had her hair braided and enclosed by a pearl-studded gold-mesh cap that appeared to be supported by a white lace collar. Over her elegant farthingale she wore a light woollen gown of rose-pink, a soft tone that complemented the honey of her flawless skin. As the early morning mist had not yet cleared, she wore a loose overgown of a deeper pink lined with grey squirrel, and she assumed Sir Leon's long examination of her to be approval of her outfit. But, as she had feared, she was given no choice of where to sit, the better benches being at the front and the church already well-filled. So his, 'Good morrow,

my lady,' had to be acknowledged as if all were well
between them.

Fortunately, there had been no time for more. The
vicar, a lively and well-proportioned middle-aged
man, was nothing like the sleepy village priest she
had half-expected, and it was not until after the service when introductions were made that Felice discovered he was married to the lady who had been
sitting beside her.

'Dame Celia Aycombe,' Sir Leon presented the
lady, 'wife of the Reverend John Aycombe, vicar of
Wheatley.'

Knowing of the new queen's objections to married
clergy, Felice was surprised. Those who defied the
royal displeasure usually kept themselves quietly busy
in some isolated village which, she supposed, was
what the Aycombes were doing. She had been equally
surprised to see that Sir Leon's unwelcoming steward,
Thomas Vyttery, had been assisting the vicar, and to
discover that he also was married.

Dame Celia introduced the woman who had been
sitting next to her and who had been craning forward
in perpetual curiosity for most of the service. 'Dame
Audrey Vyttery,' she said to Felice, who saw a
woman nearing her forties who must in her youth
have been pretty when her eyes and mouth had still
remembered how to smile. She was slight but over-
dressed, and spangled with brooches and ribbons almost from neck to toe. Whereas the plumpish con-
tented figure of Dame Celia held only a pair of leather
gloves and a prayer book to complete her outfit, Dame

Audrey fidgeted nervously with a pomander on a golden chain, an embroidered purse, a muff, a prayer book and a quite unnecessary feather fan. Acidly, she enquired whether Felice was to stay at Wheatley permanently and, if so, would she remain in the Abbot's House? She had understood Sir Leon to be moving in there.

Catching the direction of the enquiry, Felice put her mind at rest while speaking clearly enough for Sir Leon to hear. 'No, Dame Audrey. Certainly not. Indeed, I'm making plans to leave soon. This is merely a brief visit to check on progress for Lord Deventer.' Surprisingly, she thought she detected something like relief in the woman's eyes, but Dame Celia was vociferous in her reaction to the news.

Her pale eyes widened in surprise. 'Surely not, my lady. This will be May Week, when we have our holy days and games. You'll not return before we've given you a chance to see how we celebrate, will you?'

'Of course she'll not!' The answer came from halfway down the nave where the energetic vicar approached them in a flurry of white. Billowing and back-lit by the west door, he bore down upon them like an angelic host. 'She'll not, will she, Sir Leon? No one leaves Wheatley during the May Day revels, least of all our patron's lovely daughter.'

Sir Leon, who appeared to find Felice's denial more entertaining than serious, agreed somewhat mechanically. 'Indeed not, vicar. I've already told her she must stay.'

'Good…good.' The vicar beamed. 'That's settled, then.'

'Then you approve of May Day revels, vicar?' Felice said.

'Hah! It makes no difference whether I approve or not, my lady. They'd still do it. I believe half the fathers and mothers of Wheatley were conceived on May Eve. Swim with the tide or drown, that's always been my motto, and it's stood me in good stead, so far, as you can see. I keep an eye on things, and so does my good lady here, and we baptise the bairns who're born every new year. That's probably why the church is so full. Now, have you seen the new buildings yet, my lady? A work of art, you know.'

'Not yet, sir.'

'Be glad to show you round myself, but the master builder must take precedence over a mere clerk of works.' He grinned, glancing amiably at Sir Leon.

Sir Leon explained the vicar's mock-modesty. 'The Reverend Aycombe is also my clerk of works for the building-site, my lady. Both he and Mr Vyttery hold two positions as priests and building officials.'

'Priests?' said Felice. 'Mr Vyttery is a priest?' She stared at Dame Audrey who simpered, icily.

'Oh, yes,' she said. 'May hasband was sacristan here at Wheatley Ebbey. Augustinian, you see. All the manks were priests.'

Felice nodded. If she was to be obliged to stay here, she had better learn something about the place. 'Of course. And you, vicar? You were at the abbey, too?'

'Abbot, my lady,' he beamed.

Not only married priests, but married monks. And Timon had told her more than once that it could never be done, that he was already courting danger by celebrating the Roman Catholic Mass in private which was why no one must know of his whereabouts. But, of course, he had been concerned for her safety: recusants were fined quite heavily these days.

It was later that morning as she passed through the courtyard behind the Abbot's House that Felice noticed something odd which she could not at first identify. The yard was always emptier on Sundays, yet the stables had to be cleaned out, even on the sabbath, and it was not until she remembered yesterday's bustle of men and furnishings that she realised what was missing. The carts. The waggons.

'William,' she called to the head groom. 'What have you done with the waggons?'

William came towards her, leading a burly bay stallion. 'Waggons, m'lady? Sent 'em back to Sonning yesterday.'

'*What?*'

Unruffled, the man rubbed the horse's nose affectionately. 'Gone back to Lord Deventer's. Sir Leon's orders. He said you'd not be needing 'em. He wants the stable space for his own 'osses. This one's his.' He pulled at the horse's forelock.

'Did he, indeed? And how in heaven's name shall I be able to return home without horses and waggons? Did you ask Sir Leon *that*?'

'Yes, m'lady,' William replied, not understanding

her indignation. 'He said you'd be able to manage, one way or another, but there wasn't room for Lord Deventer's 'osses and his, too. He sent 'em all back, sumpter 'osses, too.'

'And the carters? He sent them back?'

'Only a few. He says the rest can stay and work here.'

'But carters don't do any other work, William. They cart.'

'Yes, m'lady. That's what they'll be doing for Sir Leon.'

'No, they will *not*!'

After quite a search of the New House and several missed turnings, she found the high-handed and mighty surveyor by crashing into him round a corner of one of the narrow pannelled passageways. He did not retreat, as she would have preferred him to do, but manoeuvred her backwards by her elbows until she sat with a thud upon a window-seat in the thickness of the wall.

'You certainly have a way with entrances and exits, my lady,' he said, smiling down at her. 'But I'm flattered by your haste to find me.'

'Don't be!' she said coldly, standing up again. 'Why have you removed my waggons and horses and appropriated my carters?'

He leaned an elbow on the top edge of the wavy-wood panelling and stuck his fingers into his thick hair, holding it off his forehead as if to see her better. 'Did you need them urgently?' he said, disarmingly.

'That is not the point. They were mine.'

'Yours, were they? Ah, and I thought they belonged to Deventer.'

'Don't mince words, Sir Leon. I needed them for my return to Sonning. You knew that.'

'Then you have a short memory, my lady, since we are not mincing words. I've already told you that you'll be staying here at Wheatley, and therefore the waggons and horses will be required by Deventer for his own use. Don't tell me you've forgotten our understanding already.'

'There is no *understanding*, Sir Leon. There never will be any understanding between us, not on any subject. And I want my waggons back. You have taken over my stables and my carters; do you intend to take over my kitchens next, by any chance?'

Languidly, he came to stand before her, easing her back again on to the window-seat, resting his hands on the panelling to prevent her escape. 'Not to mince words, my lady, I can take over the entire Abbot's House any time I choose, as I intended to do to clear the guesthouse for renovation. Would you prefer it if I did that sooner instead of later? We could pack in there quite cosily, eh?' He lowered his head to hers.

She gulped, her chest tightening at the new threat which she knew he was quite capable of carrying out, even at his own expense. 'No,' she whispered. 'But...'

'But what?'

'I...I did not agree to stay here. I *cannot* stay...in the...in the...'

'In the circumstances?'

She breathed out, slowly. 'Yes.'

'You are referring to our first meeting?'

She nodded, looking down at her lap and feeling an uncomfortable heat creeping up towards her ears.

'Which you find painful to recall?'

He was baiting her. 'Yes,' she flared, 'you know I do or you'd not insist on dragging it into every argument.'

His face came closer until he needed only to whisper. 'Then why, if it's so very painful, did you return to the garden last night, lady? To relive it, just a little? Eh?'

She looked into his eyes for a hint of laughter but there was none to be seen, only a grey and steady seriousness that gave nothing of either enjoyment or sympathy for her chagrin.

'Well?' he said.

'How do you know that?'

'I was there. I saw you.'

'The *hounds*…?'

'I sent them back to you.'

'I went to…to look at the wall. You had it repaired.'

'In the *dark*? Come now, lass, don't take me for a fool. You couldn't keep away, could you? You had to go to remind yourself or to chastise yourself. Which? Do you even *know* which?'

Goaded beyond caution, she broke the barrier of his arm and pushed past to stand well beyond his reach, panting with rage and humiliation. 'Yes, Sir Leon, I do know exactly why I returned, but never in a thousand years would you be able to understand. Of course,' she scoffed, 'you believe it was for your sake, naturally, being so full of yourself and all. But it was not, sir, I assure you. It was *not*. Did you believe you're the first man who's ever kissed me?'

She noticed the slight shake of his head before he answered. 'On the contrary, lady. I am quite convinced that I am not the one who lit the fire that rages inside you, and I also know that you are feeding it on some resentment that threatens to burn you up. Which is yet another reason why you'll be better down here at Wheatley doing what Deventer expects of you rather than moping about up in Sonning with little to do except think. Or are you so eager to continue wallowing in your problems unaided?'

'My problems, as you call them, are not your concern, Sir Leon, nor do I need anyone's aid either to wallow or work. And I'm stuck here with no transport, thanks to your interference, so what choice do I have now but to stay?'

'Less than you had before, which was what I intended.'

'You are insufferable, sir.'

'Nevertheless, you will suffer me, and I will tame you. Now you can go.'

'Thank you. I was going anyway.' She stalked away, fuming.

That prediction at least was true, though she missed the smile in his eyes that followed her first into a dark cupboard and then into a carpenter's bench and a pile of wood-shavings.

'Where the devil *am* I?' she turned and yelled at him, furiously.

His smile broke as he set off towards her.

'Come,' he said, laughing.

Chapter Three

Although the notion had taken root in Felice's mind that she might have to stay at Wheatley Abbey after all, Sir Leon's high-handed tactics hardly bore the hallmarks of subtle persuasion. Added to their disastrous introduction, it was this that made her almost wild with anger and humiliation to be so brazenly manipulated first by Lord Deventer and then by his surveyor. It was almost as if they saw it as some kind of game in which her wishes were totally irrelevant. As for his talk about taming her, well, that was ludicrous. Men's talk.

'Tamed, indeed!' she spat. 'You've bitten off more than you can comfortably chew, sir!' She threw a fistful of bread scraps to the gaggling ducks, scowling approvingly at their rowdiness.

Her companion on the afternoon stroll was Mistress Lydia Waterman, whose insight was heart-warming. 'Take no notice, love,' she called from further along the river's edge. 'You know what they're like. They

have to be given a sense of purpose. We could do
worse, though, than be stranded in a place like this,
and at least you have plenty to do. Just look at it; it
must have been swarming with monks twenty years
ago.'

To one side of them the river cut a tight curve that
enclosed the abbey on two sides before disappearing
beyond the mill into woodland. Where the grass and
meadowsweet had recovered from the builders' feet,
creamy-white elder blossom drooped over ducks,
geese and swans that jostled for food. They launched
themselves into the water in dignified droves as Felice's two deerhounds pranced towards them.

Wheatley Abbey had been left in ruins for twenty
years after the English monasteries were closed and
their wealth taken by the present queen's father,
Henry VIII. But the villagers had won permission to
keep the church for their own use while the rest of
the abbey buildings had been bought by Lord Deventer whose programme of rebuilding had already lasted
two years. During that time, his talented thirty-year-
old surveyor had restored and converted first the Abbot's House and then the New House, which had once
been the monks' refectory, dormitory and cellarium.
The enclosed cloister still awaited attention, and the
guesthouse, which at present stood apart from the
other buildings, was being used as Sir Leon's offices
and some of the masons' accommodation. There was
still plenty to be done, but work on the New House
was almost complete: courtyards, kitchens, stables

and smithy, storerooms and dairy had all been rebuilt from the monks' living quarters.

Even the church had had to adapt to the religious changes of the last twenty turbulent years. The young Queen Elizabeth was more reasonable than her forebears in her dealings with religion, but even she was not immune to pressure from her councillors to take a harder line with those who found the changes too difficult to accept, like Felice's mother, for instance. Lord Deventer himself cared little one way or the other but had taken on the young chaplain, Timon Montefiore, for the sake of his staunch Roman Catholic new wife who saw no harm in breaking the law every day of the week while relenting for an hour or two on Sundays, just to avoid being fined.

Felice and Lydia strolled along the river's edge in silence in the direction of the village and a wooden bridge under the dense white candles of a chestnut tree. A familiar figure came from the opposite side, joining them midway over the green swirling depths where a rowing boat was tied to one of the bridge supports. A clutch of small children fished with excited intensity, calling to Dame Celia as she crossed.

'They've been doing that for centuries,' she smiled. 'I did it myself when I was a wee child, though never on a Sunday.'

'You lived here as a child?' Felice said. 'I didn't realise.'

Slowly, they meandered along the opposite side of the river away from the thatched rooftops that appeared through the trees. Dame Celia pointed the way she had come. 'Down there,' she said, 'at the end of the village. You'd have passed Wheatley Manor the other day as you came through. My parents owned it, but now my brother and his family live there. John and I have the priest's house on the Wheatley estate.'

'So you went away to be educated, Dame Celia?' said Felice.

'With the nuns at Romsey until I was fifteen. It's only a few miles away. But it was closed down at the same time as Wheatley and everyone was turned out. I was fortunate in being able to come home, but the nuns and novices had a much harder time of it.'

They sat on a log that had recently been felled, its stump still oozing with sticky resin. Lydia sat on Dame Celia's other side. 'Then you didn't consider taking vows?' she said.

'Not I!' Dame Celia laughed. 'You see, John had been abbot of Wheatley only a year when the abbey closed. He was the youngest ever. And I had returned home to live when he took the post as chaplain to my parents, and as vicar at the church here. No one had better qualifications for those jobs than the former abbot. So that's how we came together.'

Felice's heart skipped a beat. Chaplain and employer's daughter. 'Did your parents approve?' she said.

Dame Celia's comfortable face crumpled in amusement. 'Certainly not, my lady. But John was given a goodly pension and he was very persuasive. But it was a very unsettled time, you know, with all the changes. At first, the former monks and nuns were allowed to marry; priests were even allowed to marry their former mistresses and concubines. Then the young King Edward decided they were not, and we swung from being Catholic to Protestant twice in the space of four reigns, m'lady, and it left everyone a bit troubled. Especially people like Dame Audrey and her Thomas.'

Felice recalled the steward's bejewelled wife, her sadly pretty face and her pseudo upper-class accents. 'Oh,' she said. 'Was Dame Audrey at Romsey Abbey, too?'

'She was a young novice when it all came to an end. Audrey Wintershulle, she was then, a very pretty girl.'

'But then she married the sacristan. Why was that so troublesome to her?'

'Well, you see, they were unfortunate because Thomas had been appointed only a few months before the date was set for the abbey's closure so he received only a small pension, barely enough to live on, so he took the job of chantry priest here at the church to say prayers for the dead. But then when the young King Edward came to the throne, all the chantry chapels were abolished and the money used for other purposes, schools and such-like. So poor Thomas was out of a job again. Then when the abbey was eventually sold off to Lord Deventer, Thomas was taken on as steward to oversee the property and maintain it. No one else could have done that better than Thomas; he knows the abbey like the back of his hand.'

'But what did he do for a living between times,

Dame Celia? Surely he couldn't live off his pension alone?'

'John helped him out,' the dame said. 'He's been so good to them both.'

But on such a small pension, Felice wanted to ask, why did he take a wife? Especially one with such extravagant tastes. Surely the vicar's assistance didn't stretch as far as jewels and furs, did it? There was more she would like to have known about the strangely matched Vyttery couple, but she had no wish to pry. Instead, she turned her attention back to the vicar's wife who appeared to have suffered few financial problems, for all her simplicity of dress.

'And does your husband approve of all the alterations to the abbey?' She looked across the river to the New House of pale grey stone, solid and glittering with tiers of windows that only the very wealthy could afford in such quantity. It sat at an angle to the Abbot's House next door, dwarfing it by its sheer bulk and magnificence.

'Oh, John is very adaptable,' said Dame Celia. 'He's had to be with so many changes. But, yes, he admires Sir Leon's work. They've always got on well together.'

'They've known each other long?' Felice's question was casual, though she doubted whether it would deceive the motherly lady at her side.

'Only over the time they've been working together. Sir Leon's been responsible for several abbey conversions in the south. He'll never be short of work. Everyone thinks very highly of him.'

'Of him, or of his work? Isn't he somewhat difficult to work for?'

Dame Celia smiled and laid a gentle hand on Felice's pink sleeve. 'Men like him hate any interruption to their work, m'lady. They can only think of one thing at a time, not like we women. One has to humour them to keep the peace.'

Felice and Lydia laughed, having harboured the thought many times but not heard it said out loud by the wife of a former monk. 'Who does the little boat belong to, Dame Celia?' said Lydia. 'The one tied to the bridge back there.'

'It's the smith's. His cottage is next to the inn, very close to where the boat's tied up. He works the mill near the Abbot's House.'

'He works there?' Felice queried. 'I thought that's where the miller worked.'

'Yes,' Dame Celia smiled. 'Smith *is* the miller. That's not a cornmill, you see, but a water-powered forge used for the estate. It's easier for him to carry his heavy things in a boat from one bridge to the other.'

'Does he work at night?' said Lydia, brushing the mossy bits off her gown. 'We thought we heard the paddles going.'

'He works hard at his drinking,' the dame said, firmly. 'He doesn't have far to go for that. Have you seen inside the New House, yet?'

The idea of dispensing with Sir Leon as tour guide appealed to Felice almost as much as the idea that she could annoy him by her independence, and this was enough to hasten them across the bridge by the mill towards the great flight of stone steps that led to an impressive porch and an unlocked door.

The mansion that had seemed, only a few hours ago, to resemble a rabbit warren now spread from the front entrance in shining newness across pine floors, intricately plastered ceilings, panelled and painted walls, floor-to-ceiling windows and a marble chimney-piece that no one could have missed. It was while they stood in awe, taking in the grandeur of the carved staircase, that voices penetrated a heavy door behind them only seconds before it opened.

Felice tensed as she recognised one of them, and her quick turn to examine the coat-of-arms above the fireplace gave Dame Celia the chance to greet the men with far more geniality than Felice could have done.

'Sir Leon…John…and *Marcus*! Well, what are *you* doing here?'

Half-turning, Felice watched from a distance as her two disloyal deerhounds made a fuss of Sir Leon, and the newcomer named Marcus greeted Dame Celia with a familiar kiss to both cheeks. He was, she thought, probably a year or two younger than Sir Leon and of slighter build, but dashingly well set-off by an immaculate suit of honey-coloured velvet and satin, by white linen, lace, gold buttons and braids. His face was lean and good-humoured, almost handsome, his hair curled in a carelessly arranged fair mop that fell into heavy-lidded blue eyes. His manner exuded a gentle charm that contrasted immediately with Sir Leon's dark dynamism and animal grace.

His greeting to Dame Celia over, the man called Marcus made a beeline for Felice that forestalled any introduction, taking her by surprise with a bow and one hand placed over his heart. 'Ah, lady!' he sighed. 'If you would consent to marry me, here and now, we can use this good priest here, and yonder chapel, to unite our souls without delay. Now, tell me you consent or I shall go away and die.'

She was spared the need to find a suitably frivolous reply by Dame Celia's husband, the Reverend John Aycombe, who boomed cheerily, 'Argh! Take no notice of him, my lady. He'd embarrass the queen herself, he would. Get a grip on yourself, man. You can't go about scaring ladies like that.'

'He can, sir,' Sir Leon said, wearily. 'He does it all the time. Lady Felice, allow me to present to you a boyhood affliction…er, friend. Marcus Donne of Westminster. He'll be going home tomorrow.'

'He's wrong, my lady, as usual,' said Marcus Donne. 'I've no intention of going home for quite some time, I assure you. How could I go now?' He took her offered fingertips, kissing them with such protracted ardour that she was bound to pull herself free, laughing.

'Marcus Donne,' she said. 'A poet, of course.'

'Poet, playright and artist, my lady. And suitor to your hand.'

'Correction,' said Sir Leon, drily. 'He's a limner. Forget the rest.'

Mr Donne adopted an expression of exaggerated anguish. 'All right, I'm a limner and I came here expressly to paint your portrait, my lady. Will you sit for me, or will you break my heart with a refusal?'

'The latter,' Felice said, still laughing at his absurdity. 'Paint my maids instead. Here's Mistress Lydia, for you.'

The banter continued over Lydia's colourful beauty while Sir Leon came to stand by Felice's side. 'Well,' he said, 'having made a remarkably sedate entry, you may as well allow me to show you round.' He followed the direction of her eyes. 'He's only just arrived.'

'Delightful,' she murmured, purposely ignoring his invitation. 'Such charming manners. What a welcome change.'

'Don't get carried away,' he replied. 'He puts on that performance for every woman, old or young, plain or pretty. He won't do for a husband.'

'That's not something that occupies my thoughts these days, Sir Leon. But thank you for the warning. It will make his flirtations all the more piquant.'

'Go ahead, but remember to take them with a hefty pinch of salt.'

'And you'll warn him about me, no doubt.'

'Naturally. I shall make him aware of our understanding.'

'Which I shall deny, sir.' She turned her scowl into a quick smile as the two Aycombes caught her eye.

'You'll deny it at your peril,' Sir Leon replied. Giving her no time to respond in the same vein, he turned to the others. 'Good. That's settled, then. A conducted tour to take stock of progress so far. This way, ladies and gentlemen, if you please.'

Inwardly seething at his continued provocation, Felice took Lydia's arm in a gesture intended to unite them against Marcus Donne's attempts at separation. It was while they were examining the beautifully carved pews in the small private chapel that Felice and Lydia, straying near the pulpit, noticed a battered leather chest upon the steps by the communion rail. They recognised it as one that had come from Sonning on one of the carts two days ago.

'It'll be the spare Latin bibles and altar plate that my mother wants out of the way,' Felice said.

Lydia agreed. 'And it'll not be needed here, either. I'll get someone to come and move it. It can go in the cellar for now.' But then the intention was put out of mind at the appearance of Adam Bystander, Sir Leon's tall good-looking valet who, having heard that Lydia was here, came to stake his claim before the notorious Mr Donne could do the same.

Lydia's interest in Adam was already established, being one of the reasons for Felice's decision to reconsider returning to Sonning. Lydia's ability to forget about men was the cause of much heartache; in fact, most men of her acquaintance would have agreed that her forgetting was too highly developed for her own good—certainly for theirs. It would be a pity, Lydia had said to Felice, to be rushed into a forgetting that would be premature, even by her standards.

The reason why the leather chest faded from Felice's memory was remarkably similar, for she now had to delude Marcus Donne into believing that she found him interesting, the Aycombes into believing that she was admiring every detail of the New House, Sir Leon into thinking that she was quite unmoved by his handsome presence and herself into believing that she was not watching him when, in fact, she was. It required all her concentration, especially as Adam Bystander had now weeded the willing Lydia away from her side.

However, the leather chest had also been noticed by the observant surveyor who, when his guests had been escorted away from the New House, returned for a closer examination. He found it to be unlocked, its stiffly studded lid at first unwilling, its contents unremarkable; bibles in the forbidden Latin, a linen altar-cloth spotted with iron mould, a priest's white surplice and a box of polished beechwood with a silver carrying handle.

He lifted it out on to a pew and sat down beside it, recognising it at once as a travelling box which priests had needed to celebrate mass before such rites were forbidden. The inside was lined with dark red leather, the contents still bright: a small silver chalice and plate, a crucifix, a candlestick, a rosary and a small leather-bound bible with a marker of old parchment still in place. The personal bible of a priest.

Angling himself towards the light, he opened the book to examine the fly-leaf and found the inscription in faded grey ink, the style bold and artistic. 'Timon

Montefiore'. The bookmark was even more interesting, for instead of some biblical quotation or the owner's initials, it was intricately decorated with the letter *F*, with pierced hearts, arrows, teardrops, bolts of lightning, thorns and every conceivable symbol of passionate love that the owner could have contrived. What was more, it marked the beginning of the Song of Solomon made up of verses metaphorically comparing spiritual love to earthly love in an unmistakably erotic manner.

'Well, well,' Sir Leon breathed. For some moments, he held it while he explored the implications and then, on intuition, he turned to the back of the bible and found between the black end-papers a lock of silky dark brown hair tied with a fine gold thread. As if he had known it would be there, he stroked it with his thumb, feeling its softness. Then he replaced it and closed the book.

'So, that's what it's all about,' he whispered. 'And what happened to you, Father Timon? Did Lady Deventer discover your secret passion, perhaps? Dismissed, were you? No, of course not, or you'd have taken this with you, wouldn't you? Death, then? Was that it?'

Without any clear idea of what he intended to do with it, he replaced the contents and closed the lid of the leather chest, carrying the priest's sacrament box back to his room in the guesthouse.

Marcus Donne lay full-length upon his friend's bed, idly leafing through one of Sir Leon's notebooks of architectural drawings. He barely looked up as his friend entered and closed the door. 'Lovely,' he said. 'Amazingly lovely.'

Sir Leon placed the beechwood box on the floor beneath his table and then removed the book from Marcus's inquisitive fingers. 'Yes,' he said, 'I know she is. So why have you decided to come here now, of all times? Did your nose lead you to the scent of woman, or have you no work to do these days?'

Marcus swung his legs off the bed and stretched upwards with a smile. 'I told you. I'm between commissions.'

'You said that because John Aycombe was there. Now, what's the real reason? You're in hiding again, I take it.'

'Your man put my bags next door. Is that all right?'

'Yes. But tell me or I'll have them slung into the river.'

Marcus remained unperturbed by the threat. 'Well, I was in London, and a certain possessive husband took a dislike to me.' He grinned.

'Yes, husbands can get tediously possessive, I believe. So you were painting the lady's likeness, I suppose, and you couldn't concentrate. Is that it?'

'Well, she couldn't, either.' He and Sir Leon had known each other since they were boarded out at the London home of the late Queen Mary's Comptroller of the Household, during which both young men had made excellent connections. Being unlike each other in temperament, they had retained a brotherly friendship over the years and this was not the first time that Marcus had sought his friend's hospitality at Wheatley in order to lie low for a month or two. 'Oh,' he said, 'it'll all die down. And I can paint the glorious lady while I'm here, just to keep my hand in.'

'Just to keep your hand in what, exactly? Paint her, if she'll let you, but no more than that, my friend, or you'll be off back to London before your jealous husband has had time to forget your handiwork.'

'Whoo...oo! Steady, lad! What's all that about, eh? Has your lovely Levina stayed away too long, then?'

'She's *not* my Levina and mind your own business. Lady Felice Marwelle is in my guardianship while she's down here, so just remember that. Deventer sent her to sort out the New House and gardens and he's left no instructions for her to be distracted by cuckolding limners and the like.'

'So you're her keeper, then. Is that it?'

'You'll not say as much to her, if you value your head, but that's the general way of things. She's my employer's daughter and I'm responsible for her.'

'Right,' said Marcus, rudely staring.

'And take that stupid grin off your face. Now listen; you can keep your ears and eyes open while you're here. There's something going on at night. Thieving, I expect. That's the usual problem on building-sites. Rival builders stealing stuff. But so far I've not discovered anything missing.'

'So how d'ye know there's something going on?'

'A boat on the river at night. The only one hereabouts belongs to the chap who works the mill forge, but I've not been able to track him. I spent hours over the last two nights waiting to see if he comes through the kitchen garden or the other way round.'

'But no one came?'

'No.' His fingertips pressed gently against the deep toothmarks at the base of his thumb that still bled from time to time. 'Perhaps you could take a watch?'

'Sure. Anything else?'

Sir Leon glanced at the box under the table piled with books and ledgers, measuring instruments and letters. 'Yes,' he said, 'there is. What d'ye know about a priest called Montefiore?'

'Father Timon. Mmm…' Marcus's voice wavered, fruitily.

'You knew him?'

'No, but I met him. He was chaplain to the Paynefleetes.'

Sir Leon frowned, suddenly rivetted. 'The Payne-fleetes here at Wheatley? Dame Celia's brother? I never knew that.'

'Well, that's not so surprising. The Paynefleetes of Wheatley Manor also have a house in London and they could have been there when you began work here. That's where I met him, but he left them soon afterwards.'

'You met him in London?'

'Yes. I painted the Paynefleetes' maid, Thomas Vyttery's daughter Frances. You didn't know that?'

'No, how do I know what you get up to in London? So Thomas's daughter was the Paynefleetes' maid, was she? He's never talked about her.'

'A dark-haired beauty, almost as lovely as—' He

caught his friend's glare and retreated. 'Her mother, Dame Audrey, asked me to paint her daughter's portrait while she was with the Paynefleetes in London. So I did.'

'And what does this have to do with Timon Montefiore?'

Marcus spoke irritatingly slowly, as if to a child. 'Well, they were lovers. The maid and the chaplain.'

'Whew! F for Frances! How d'ye know?'

Marcus quirked an eyebrow at his friend's odd response. 'How do I *know*? For pity's sake, lad, I'm trained to *see*.'

'She died though, didn't she?'

'Yes, after young Montefiore had been packed off in a flurry of silence ostensibly because he was a Roman Catholic priest who was not supposed to be performing anywhere, let alone with a dissenting family like the Paynefleetes. Word gets round quickly in London, so I believe they packed him off to a Berkshire family where he's now probably busying himself with another patron's daughter, or maid, or whatever. The family managed to keep it all remarkably quiet, but I get to hear the gossip, you see. I didn't take to the man, particularly.'

The hairs on Sir Leon's arms bristled uncomfortably as he pictured the scene, against his will, of a young priest ingratiating himself into Deventer's family, charming the mother, seducing the daughter. Is that what had happened? F for Frances *and* for Felice, one or both? The sacrament box, unused and forgotten. A hasty departure. Her grief and anger. 'How old would he have been, this priest?' he said.

'Late twenties, perhaps. Soft-spoken. A quiet character. Intelligent, but not to be trusted, from what I gathered.'

'Thieving, you mean?'

'Dismissed for theft even before he reached the Paynefleetes, but that's only hearsay.'

'Then who on earth recommended him?'

'Leon, my friend, the priesthood closes ranks tighter than clams when one of them needs help. He wouldn't have any trouble finding another priest to recommend him.'

'So how does Dame Audrey find the money to pay for a portrait? I thought you were expensive.'

'I am, but I don't make a habit of asking my clients where they get their money from. I just collect it, with thanks.'

'Plus the gratuities. You're disgusting, Donne.' Sir Leon laughed.

'Delightfully so, and you're green with envy because building houses for wealthy old men doesn't give you the same opportunities. Or does it?'

'Come on down to the hall. You look as if you could do with the company of stout men, for a change.'

'How so?'

'Your brain's going soft, lad.'

Despite his conspicuously carefree manner, Sir Leon's curiosity was far from satisfied by the discovery of the wayward priest's inclinations or by his connection to two women who bore the same initial. Ironically, the apparent solution to the enigma of the Lady Felice's confusion had lasted only a short time before suffering more complications too difficult to unravel, though the priest's reputation indicated that he was capable of multiple offences.

And as if this was not enough, the sudden appearance of Marcus would do little to aid the self-imposed task of taming the beautiful sharp-tongued wildcat. She would use Marcus as a tool, and Marcus would play the part to the hilt, willingly skimming the bounds of the warning like a master. Well, let them do their worst; he had always been a match for Marcus, both intellectually and physically, and the lady herself would soon learn just how far she could go before he took her in hand again.

Sir Leon's guardianship of Lady Felice provided Marcus with a delicious temptation he had no intention of resisting. There had always been an element of rivalry in their good-tempered friendship, the latest and most serious manifestation of which was Sir Leon's erratic friendship with Lord Deventer's dazzling niece, Levina Deventer, which had previously irked Marcus more than he cared to admit. Any opportunity to pay his rival back in the same coin was something for which he had waited patiently, so it was no concern of his what Lord Deventer had instructed his surveyor to do; *he* would take the maid from under their noses. Clearly she had little liking for her new guardian; one had only to look at her to see how she resented his authority. Women were so transparent, bless them.

For Felice, Marcus Donne's arrival could not have been better timed. With the chivalrous and amusing limner, she could now show Sir Leon how little she cared for his presence or needed his ungenerous warning about the man's manners. He may have been the first limner she had ever met, but he was certainly not the first flirt. She knew exactly how to handle such men.

If only the same could be said of Sir Leon, who had put himself outside her experience from the start. With her horses and waggons gone, she had now no option but to comply with his decision concerning her immediate future, but she would make him regret his overbearing interference before the end of the week. That much was certain.

These resolutions were comforting for being easily acted upon; other hurts lay deeper and would have to wait for some more impressive retribution to salve them.

The opportunity for Marcus to acquaint himself more closely with his willing target came later on in the day as delicious aromas wafted across the courtyard from the kitchens of the Abbot's House. The sun had lowered itself slowly until it rested upon the western edge of the cloister roof, flushing the derelict square with pink and accentuating the colour of Felice's gown. It was this vision that greeted Marcus

Donne as he emerged from the shadows of the far side.

At first, Felice thought the sound of the door opening might be Sir Leon and she had been prepared to make a very dignified but obvious exit. But then the honey-coloured velvet caught her eye and she waited, half-pleased, half-disappointed. She watched as he looked around him as if to get his bearings and felt herself respond to his genuine pleasure at the sight of her, thinking that it would not be difficult to enjoy his company, for his charms were not all superficial.

The eager boyish smile was now replaced by that of a self-assured man who knew how to regulate his absurdities to suit his audience. With only the object of his interest to hear him, he could allow his flattery to fall more accurately, drop by precious drop. 'A Felice-itous meeting,' he said, approaching her through the untidy grass. 'A rose-washed Felice bathing in the sun's last rays. Now there's a picture waiting to be painted, my lady.'

'And I'm waiting for a summons to supper, Mr Donne,' she replied, prosaically. 'You're welcome to join us.'

'And I, my lady, am lost. But my host expects my presence at supper on my first day here and I dare not disappoint him.' He came to stand before her, smiling gravely. 'Pink is your colour. I shall paint you wearing that gown.' His eyes swept over her, lingering on the soft mounds of peachy skin where the stiff bodice supported from below, then returning to hold the unsureness in her eyes with a slow and lazy smile. 'Another evening, perhaps?'

She regretted her too-hasty invitation at once, and there was too much here to answer, so she answered none of it. 'This is the cloister, sir, where the monks studied and took their exercise, or so I believe. I shall make a garden here again as soon as I can organise my workers and draw up a plan. Whichever comes first.' She turned, leading the way to the sunny wall where she and Sir Leon had sat only yesterday. 'I'll have the walkway roofs repaired and this mess cleared…' she pointed with a pink shoe '…and then I'll have paths and plots and a fountain in the centre. Just there.' She nodded towards a heap of rubble, knowing that his eyes had not moved from her face and neck.

Marcus sat beside her on the wall and angled himself to lean against a pillar, resting one foot on the stonework between them. 'Go on,' he said, clasping his knee.

She knew the game but found it disconcerting, even so, to be expected to talk of mundane matters while a man drank his fill with his eyes and thought his own private thoughts. But with perhaps a little more effort she could do the same, for he was an artist and knew how to pose, how to show off his shapely legs, his prominently embroidered codpiece, and how to hold her attention with his own. Inevitably, his lack of response brought her monologue to a dwindling halt. 'You're not listening to me,' she chided him gently.

His eyes were sensuously invasive. 'I was…
somewhere else,' he said, gesturing to prevent an impending withdrawal. 'No, don't go. It's a habit, I'm
afraid, to watch rather than listen. But you must surely
be used to having men look at you, my lady.' The
voice was seductive, designed to entice confessions.

'I don't notice, sir,' she said, holding back a smile.

'Tch! Untruths already. What chance do we have
of friendship then, would you say?' When she made
no reply, he leaned forward to rest his chin upon his
knee, refusing to release her from his intense scrutiny.
'You've not been here long, I understand, and I've
only been here once before. Do you think we might
explore the place together? My sense of direction is
remarkably good, as a rule.'

For a second, it occurred to her that he might have
been warned about her, but his expression was sincere
and she saw no reason to refuse him as long as it
fitted in with her duties. Better still, it would take her
well out of Sir Leon's way. 'You're staying a while
then, Mr Donne?'

'Long enough to paint your likeness, my lady. That
can take anything from three days to three months.'
Now his eyes were merry, reminding Felice of another teasing smile and gentle laugh, of one who let
her talk while he attended, unlike other men who believed only themselves to have anything worthwhile
to say.

'Then I shall be glad to have your company, sir.
With an escort, there'll be places I may visit that I'm

not allowed to alone. Believe it or not, I'd like to see the work the men are doing on the building-site, especially the sculptors and wood-carvers, but I've been told not to go near them.'

The knee went down as Marcus Donne leaned even closer. 'What…you were warned off? Whatever for?'

Drawn into the charade, she shrugged her shoulders, wondering how far to go for his pity. 'Well, I can only suppose that Sir Leon's masons will suddenly go berserk at the sight of a woman,' she said, innocently, 'even though they're mostly old enough to be my father. He must employ some very unpredictable workmen, I fear.'

'But that's ridiculous! They're all respectable men. That cannot be the reason. Leon's never been vindictive, whatever else he may be.'

'Really?'

His fair brows drew together at that. 'I'm mistaken?'

'You know him better than I, but I can find no explanation other than vindictiveness for sending my horses, waggons and carters back to Sonning without my knowledge. I don't even have a horse of my own to ride, so I'll not be able to go far.'

Marcus made no attempt either to excuse or condemn his friend, realising that there must be more to this than mere pique. The lady had a fire held tightly under control, and her dislike of Leon could be useful as long as it was handled carefully. 'I brought several horses with me,' he said. 'At least two of them are suitable mounts for a lady. We'll use mine.'

'They're in the guesthouse stable?'

'Yes. Plenty of room over there now—most of his are out to grass.'

Felice looked beyond the arch where the end of the stableblock was just visible and where only that morning she had seen Sir Leon's bay stallion being quartered at the expense of hers. 'Then why not bring them over here so that I won't have to traipse over to Sir Leon's stable? My own saddle's still here.'

Their exchanged smiles enclosed an almost child-like conspiracy and Felice saw herself escaping at last from the despotic surveyor's reach.

The call for supper broke the mood as Mistress Lydia stepped through the archway in her search for Felice, then she halted as the door at the far end of the cloister opened to admit the young Elizabeth, followed closely by Sir Leon.

Elizabeth Pemberton had been hired only a year ago mainly for her skills at needlework, which were indisputable. Sadly her skills in other directions were less remarkable for, no matter how repetitious her duties, she seemed unable to remember or anticipate what they were. She was sweet and gentle and well aware of the clerk of the kitchen's adoration, but his duties in that vital area were even less easy for her to accept, which was the prime cause of this latest drama. Both Felice and Lydia sometimes found the temptation to shake her almost irresistible, but this time it was unnecessary, for the lass was already well shaken.

Sir Leon led Elizabeth across the scruffy square

plot where, in the pinkish fading light, Felice could see her tear-stained face and red nose and the way her arm rested trustingly along Sir Leon's.

His expression was anything but kindly as he voiced a command to Mistress Lydia without the slightest reference to her mistress. 'Mistress Waterman, be so good as to take this young lady indoors before I have another riot on my hands.'

Elizabeth, her bottom lip trembling, was passed over to Lydia who looked to Felice for approval, recognising the discourtesy to her mistress. But Felice intercepted the move, furious at being disregarded. Though reluctant to have words before servants, her first need was to know what had happened to cause Elizabeth's distress.

'One moment, if you please, Sir Leon. You seem to have overlooked the fact that I am responsible for Mistress Pemberton and it is I who will decide where she goes. What happened? What is this riot you speak of?' She would have been grateful at this point to have had Marcus Donne at her elbow, but he remained discreetly on the wall, uninvolved, and she was left to face the surveyor's intimidating bulk on her own.

Sir Leon's eyes were like two dark slits of anger that bored accusingly into hers, but his voice was deceptively polite, 'Then if you are indeed responsible for her, my lady, may I suggest you take your obligations more seriously? Take her indoors, Mistress Waterman, if you please,' he snapped at Lydia.

Lydia prevaricated no longer, but took Elizabeth by

the arm and led her away. As Felice turned to confront Sir Leon once more, she caught his glare at Marcus and the inclination of his head towards the door;
a clear signal for him to leave.

Preparing for the storm, Felice toyed with the notion of imploring Marcus to stay but thought better
of it, especially as the limner showed no inclination
to dispute the command. The alternative was to follow her maids, but the prospect of venting her anger
upon Sir Leon was too great to relinquish and she
released it well before the cloister door had closed
behind her new ally.

'I have never known such rudeness, such…'

'Spare me the tirade and yourself the energy my
lady. If you've never known such rudeness, I've never
known such irresponsibility. Have you no idea what
your women are up to while you sit here lapping up
compliments? Have you no control over them?'

'Yes, I have, Sir Leon, but I can hardly tie them
both to my girdle-chain while I sit around lapping up
compliments, as you so churlishly put it. Nor can I
follow Mistress Elizabeth round like a shadow. If she
gets into a predicament now and then, she can usually
manage to get herself out of it. And tears follow as a
matter of course, sir.'

Without warning, he took hold of her upper arm so
tightly that she could feel his fingers through the padded sleeve, and marched her unceremoniously back
to the low wall where she had been sitting with Marcus. 'So much for the sharp tongue, lady,' he growled,
pressing her down on to the wall and sitting himself

beside her. 'Now you can listen to mine, for a change.' He pointed to the distant door. 'Out there, your silly maid wandered alone into a crowd of apprentices and seemed to think it would be a good Sunday sport to play one rival gang off against the other. No matter that they've been warned about fighting, especially on the site, your lass actually egged them on and then wondered why *she* got roughed up at the same time. If those tears are part of an act, as you appear to believe, what does she do when she's truly scared, I wonder? If I'd not stopped them, she'd have been flat on her back by now in the mortar-maker's yard with a crowd of—'

'No!' Felice yelped, coming to her feet. 'You've said enough, sir! She's young. She doesn't think.'

'Those lads are young too, but they *do* think. Only of three things, I warrant you, but she'd better be told fast what they are or she'll be in more trouble again than she can handle. And if you'd been about your duty, my lady, instead of…'

'Instead of what, sir? Talking? Sitting? Sharing a pleasantry or two before I forget what a pleasantry sounds like? Is that a crime, suddenly? Should I lock her up in case one of your thick-headed apprentices gets one of his three thoughts in the wrong order?'

He stood, resting one foot on the wall and leaning towards her with an elbow on one knee, and though he had no intention of displaying in the way that Marcus Donne did, Felice was well able to see how his muscular thighs were more powerful, his chest deeper, his shoulders broader. 'Do what you like with her,' he said, 'only don't come running to me when she finds herself out of her depth again. I warned you of what might happen and now I've got fifteen lads to discipline tomorrow, thanks to your co-operation.'

'Then give your stupid apprentices more to think about, Sir Leon, and they'll have less time to fight over a young female. And don't give any more orders to my servants. Don't tell my guests when to leave. And don't blame me when your workers adopt your manners. I bid you good day, sir.' Giving him notice of her intention to leave had not been a part of her plan, but she was livid with anger and her plan had been turned on its head.

He caught her around the waist and swung her against the stone column, holding her resisting arms in a vice-like grip. 'I bid you good day also, my lady, but you've left one thing off your list, haven't you?' His body pressed hard against hers to make an off-beat duet of hearts between them.

'I forget nothing, sir, except your gracelessness,' she snarled.

There was nowhere for her head to go, and the impulse to watch as his mouth took hers gave her no chance to evade him as she knew she should have done. Besides, this was something her heart had begged for, desired and entreated, despite the strident callings of common sense and outrage, despite knowing that the kiss was derisive, meant to chasten, to mock her weakness and to demand her capitulation.

Whatever he had meant it to do, it did, as once again his mastery drove every thought from her mind except the dazing seduction of her lips. There was no need for her to respond in either direction, for he was taking without her permission, holding on to her wrists and thus giving her no reason to chastise herself for another uncontrollable participation. And had it not been for the closing of her eyes, she might have been able to pretend to be unmoved, but it was now too late for that.

He watched them open and slowly flicker into wakefulness. 'I believe you do forget, lady, that I will have the last word. And as long as you insist on forgetting, I shall insist on reminding you. Understand?'

She looked away, unable to meet the dominance in his grey eyes. 'No, Sir Leon, I do not understand any of this except that you are as careless of a woman's honour as the apprentices you are about to punish. Explain the difference to me…if you can.'

'The difference, my lady, is that your maid was in no position to appreciate those lads' attentions whereas the same cannot be said for you, can it? Or do you close your eyes and melt in any man's arms, eh?'

'You are despicable! Let me go!'

'The last word? Was that it?' he mocked, touching her lips with his to hold her silent. 'Good. That's better.'

But if she had thought to be released by her infuriated shove against his chest she was to find that it had the opposite effect, for her wrists were still held and her involuntary gasp was stifled by his mouth. He took his time, drawing her easily with him into a kiss that swamped her with wave upon wave of sensation until his hands released hers and found a way across her back and shoulders, bending her into him.

She clung, helplessly adrift, her gasp now surfacing to emerge as a cry that brought them both to their senses. His arms supported her and lowered her to the wall where she sat, hearing the swish of tall weeds against his legs as he strode away, neither of them knowing who had had the last word, after all.

Chapter Four

She had not thought he would take advantage of her again, not like that, and not after she had made abundantly clear her intense dislike of him. Unfortunately, telling herself repeatedly of her dislike did not have the effect upon her heart that she intended, for it remained entirely unconvinced and determined to recall how it felt to be held by him.

'Contemptible! Brute! Oaf!' she muttered, climbing into her great bed. 'It was meant to humiliate me, no more than that. Forget it. It means nothing either to him or to me.'

But she could not forget it and, at her lowest ebb in the blackest hours of the night, she again entertained the idea of escape on one of Mr Donne's horses. However, the practicalities of such a move were still being worked out as she fell asleep.

By morning, some of her original rebelliousness had recovered. With it came the hate and a soupçon of fear that Sir Leon was taking his role as custodian far too seriously.

Now she was determined more than ever to get on with her appointed task, to impress her stepfather by her amazing efficiency and resourcefulness, and to stay from under the feet of his surveyor, as she had been instructed to do. She dressed in her plainest brown bodice and skirt with sleeves to match over a white linen partlet that gathered round her neck in a neat frill. She requested Lydia to coil her hair into a net at the back of her head.

'Wouldn't you be better wearing your linen coif?' said Lydia, dutifully twisting the thick ropes of hair. 'After what happened yesterday?'

'No,' Felice replied, tersely. 'After what happened yesterday, it's that high and mighty surveyor who'd better watch out, not me.'

First she set about recruiting the services of three women to begin a clean-up of the servants' down-stairs rooms at the New House. They were passing through the derelict cloister on their way to the building-site when she spied them through the archway, and in no time at all had re-directed them to collect brooms, buckets, mops and dusters from her own servants in the Abbot's House with orders to start in the scullery and work towards the big kitchen. She would come and inspect them in an hour.

The oldest of the three began a protest, saying that they were expected to carry lime for the plasterer who had not finished one of the ceilings but, having no

choice but to obey, they quickly opted for the pleas-
anter task.

Felice went back to the stableyard where two
young lads were carrying a heavy box between them
by its rope handles. 'You two,' she called, 'leave that
and come with me. I have a task for you.'

'Er…mistress…yer ladyship, we're not…'

'No excuses. Put that thing down and help. You
can do that later.' Anyone in her yard was, after all,
presumed to be one of her servants.

They lowered the box to the ground with a thud
and followed Felice across the cobbles to where two
more lads were sorting through a pile of rusty garden
tools ready to clean them. 'Clean this lot up,' she told
them, 'then take the best ones to the garden and start
clearing. I'll get some more men to come and help as
soon as I can find some.' The apprehensive looks exchanged by the two additions went entirely unnoticed.

She was prevented from returning to her indoor duties by the call of her own carpenter and his two lads.
'M'lady,' James said, pushing up his felt bonnet to
scratch at his head, 'the carpenter on the site won't
let us have any of his wood for the table and benches.
He says to get our own.'

'I thought that's what we were doing, James.
Surely it's all the same, isn't it?'

'Apparently not, m'lady. He says he has to account
for every—'

Well able to imagine what the site carpenter had
said, she cut off the explanation. 'Well, then, go and

find a suitable tree, James. You have axes, don't you?'

'A tree, m'lady?' James frowned, pulling back his bonnet. 'Nay, you can't just fell a tree like that. You need a saw-pit to make planks, you know.'

'Then dig a saw-pit. It's only a table and benches you're making for the servants' hall, man, not for the high chamber. It can't be difficult.'

James blinked. 'No, m'lady. Right, we'll go and find a tree. C'mon, lads.' He tipped his head to the two staring lads and lurched off, muttering, in the direction of the nearest group of ash trees.

Crossing the servants' hall, Felice was suddenly confronted by a red-faced whiskered man wearing a leather apron over his doublet and a battered felt cap jammed down on to a mat of sawdust-coloured hair. His expression left her in no doubt of his displeasure.

Aggressively, Fen and Flint lowered their heads, rumbling a threat.

'Good day to you, carpenter,' Felice said, anticipating the man's reason for being here. He had probably come to explain about the wood.

'John Life, m'lady. Joiner for thirty years and more.' He snatched his hat off and then replaced it on a rim of hair. 'And I've come to fetch my lads and my box.'

To her surprise, Mr Life walked past her to the outer door. 'Wait, Mr Life!' she called. 'Wait! What boys are you talking about?' But even as she spoke, the truth of the matter dawned on her. 'I stopped two

lads in the stableyard…they had a box…I thought it
was mine.'

With his hand on the latch, the joiner turned, ad-
dressing his remarks to the rushes on the floor rather
than to the lady of the house. 'Them tools, *m'lady*,
have been mine all my working life. Made each and
every one of 'em myself, I did, when I were…'

'Mr Life…' Felice attempted to interrupt the flow.

'…an apprentice. And them two lads are mine, too.
I'm paid to do a job for Sir Leon, *m'lady*, not to
provide you…'

'Mr Life!' she yelled at him. 'They were coming
out of my stable! Anyone who enters my stable without my permission will be put to my service and if
you keep your damn box there in future I'll confiscate
it, is that clear, as for your apprentices and tools I'll
have them returned to you in due course, now you
return the way you came sir.' Finally stopping to draw
breath, she pointed to the opposite door.

He walked stiffly past her, still grumbling. 'I shall
have to speak to Sir Leon about this…'

'You can speak to the devil himself, Mr Life, but
don't ever speak to me in that tone again. Is that
clear?'

Unperturbed, the clerk of the kitchen, who had
been waiting, seized the opportunity, list in hand.
'M'lady, would you?'

Felice sighed. 'Yes, Mr Dawson. Come, we'll sit
over here. But first things first; let me get those lads
and tools together again. Have the beehives started
producing yet?'

* * *

There were still several areas of production not yet in full swing, one of which was the brewery, and it was while Felice was with her steward, Henry Peale, inspecting one of the outhouses for this purpose that a shadow filled the doorway. Until the thud in her breast had settled, she ignored it, knowing that a confrontation with Sir Leon was to be the inevitable outcome of John Life's dissent.

'Three hogsheads a month should be enough, m'lady,' Henry was saying as he turned to look at the intruder.

'A word with your mistress, Mr Peale, if you will.'

Henry bowed to them both, leaving Felice in mid-sentence to his departing back view. 'Sir Leon,' she said, coldly polite. 'I have already said that I am capable of giving orders to my own servants without your aid, I thank you.'

He leaned against the door frame, intentionally blocking the light and her escape, his rolled-up shirt sleeves exposing muscular wrists and forearms that sent a new wave of goose-bumps into her hair. His own looked as if he had combed it through with his fingers, making deep furrows from brow to crown. 'The question is, my lady, whether you are capable of *recognising* your own servants without my aid. It appears not.' His tone was bitingly sarcastic.

'I have had a similar discussion with Mr Life, sir, and I don't intend to repeat it to you. The joiner, his lads and tools have been reunited and I've told him to keep his tools out of my stable, that's all.'

'It was not only the joiner I had in mind. He's a miserable old fool who finds something to moan about every Monday morning, but he's the best this side of London and I won't have him upset or I shall lose him. You've already antagonised my steward, now it's the joiner, the carpenter and the plasterer. Did you have anyone else in mind for today? Some advance warning would be helpful.'

'I don't know what you're talking about, sir. Let me pass; I'm busy.' She knew it was probably the last thing he would do when he came further into the new brewhouse to stand before her, hands on hips, and she saw how the icy sarcasm only thinly veiled his anger.

'Is that so, my lady? Well, then, let me explain. Those women you commandeered to…'

'I did *not* commandeer them, I simply redirected…'

'…to clean the ground floor were to have been carrying lime for the plasterer who still has a ceiling to finish.'

'I thought…'

'Which I told you when I showed you the rooms yesterday. And what's more, the workmen on the ground floor are still fixing the shelvings and fittings and they don't need women sweeping round their feet while they're doing it.'

She blushed, biting her tongue on the reply.

'So if you must indulge your passion for cleaning everything in sight, would you mind starting at the top of the house with your own servants, not mine? I can't afford to lose my best plasterer at this point. And the next thing…'

'I don't want to hear about the next thing,' she croaked, trying to push past him.

But he side-stepped, barring her way with one hand against the wall. 'The next thing is that the carpenter does not have an unlimited supply of wood to be carted off for your pleasure. He has to account for every plank, every nail, every…'

'Oh, for pity's sake, spare me!' Felice said. 'I don't need the carpenter's damn wood, or his nails. There are plenty of trees hereabouts. We'll manage well enough, I thank you.'

'Don't think it,' he said, dropping his hand. 'No one fells a tree here without my permission.'

'Except me, Sir Leon. I have Lord Deventer's permission to obtain whatever I need to prepare the house for summer, and if you refuse to supply me with what I need I'll get them elsewhere. My own carpenter knows how to…'

'*What?*'

She walked past him to the door. '…to fell a tree.'

Roughly, her arm was held, and she was swung against the wall to face him again, this time in the full blaze of his anger. 'You did what? You gave orders? What orders…where?'

'I…I don't know. Wherever.' Her eyes skimmed the door at the sound of shouting. The door was pushed back with a sharp crack on to the wall. Her arm was released.

Henry Peale reappeared, flushed and breathless. 'Sir Leon! My lady! There's a fight…a brawl…

they're trying to stop James and the lads from chopping the…'

He got no further, pushed aside as Sir Leon leapt through the doorway and across the courtyard, already running as he called, 'Where, man? Show me where they are.'

Picking up her skirts, Felice ran after them with Fen and Flint prancing alongside, yapping with excitement. Between the kitchen garden and the cemetery on the north side of the church, a line of ash trees had barely opened their leaves to make a delicate screen and it was here, much too close to the high wall and to the men who cleared the ground of rubble that the carpenter and his lads were in bloody conflict with each other. Both parties had axes and spades and both were using them to enforce their intentions, already resulting in cuts to foreheads, bleeding noses and lips, several broken teeth and tools. The fact that all six were Felice's own servants made the situation even more ludicrous: she would have preferred a display of amity amongst her own household, at least.

By the time she reached them they had been flung bodily aside by Sir Leon and Henry Peale, whose authority the men dared not challenge, and now they were scattered, dripping with blood and sweat.

Sir Leon was bawling at James as Felice approached. 'What in heaven's name d'ye think you're doing, man, felling a tree near a wall like that without ropes? What if it'd fallen into the garden, eh?'

'It would not, sir,' James said, holding a hand to

his bleeding ear. 'We'd have had it falling the other way.'

'And how many trees have you felled in your time? Can't you see that you'd have taken the top of the wall off? Go, take your lads and stick their heads under the pump, then wait for my man to come and tend you. You'll need a stitch or two if you're to keep your ear.'

'There's no need for your help, sir,' Felice said. 'My ladies and I can do all that's necessary.' It was not the best choice of words.

'I'm sure you can, lady. It'll take you all afternoon to do what's necessary here, by the look of things. Thank God they're your men, not mine.'

She took the chastened men into the servants' hall, remonstrating all the way, yet knowing that it had been her own failure, her own over-eagerness, which had been at the root of the problem. So keen had she been to appear efficient that she had not stopped to consider every implication, and now it was her incompetence that had impressed Sir Leon most. And she *had* wanted to impress him, indirectly.

'I'm ashamed of you, James,' she said, unfairly.

'I could have done it with no damage. Now what are we going to do about the furniture?'

'Never mind that. What are we going to do about your ear?'

As things turned out, she and the maids had just begun to make bandages and to bathe wounds when Adam Bystander brought two servants with salves, a basket of moss to pack the cuts, styptic made of egg-whites and aloes bound with hair to stop the bleeding, and a jar of theriac, which Felice had always known as treacle. According to Adam, it was good for anything from burns to bronchitis.

With the mess washed away, the actual damage was much less than at first appeared, and even James's ear was stuck back together again with every prospect of success.

Adam Bystander was a good-looking young man of solid build, with crinkly hair the colour of hazelnuts and amused brown eyes that searched with a bold confidence whenever he listened or spoke. It was this quiet self-possession that Lydia found particularly attractive, even though they had spoken little when they had walked side by side yesterday. His fingers were skilful with the men's wounds and soon the tasks were complete, the debris of surgery cleared away.

Adam placed a hand over Lydia's wrist in full view of the others. 'Tonight?' he said, softly. 'You'll be there?'

Lydia blushed, glancing at her mistress. Felice nodded. 'Yes,' Lydia said. 'I dare say.'

Felice thanked the young men and sent them back, barely able to conceal her wretchedness at the way her good intentions had fallen, one after the other, like a row of ninepins. Still smarting from Sir Leon's latest tongue-lashing, she went back to the brewery where she could cool off, alone. Her own workers would keep the affair to themselves and eventually dismiss it entirely; they would never lay any blame at her door. But that was small comfort when one person in particular whose good opinion she had hoped to gain now held her in the utmost contempt.

It was Marcus Donne who came to the rescue, news of the latest affray having travelled fast across the ruins of Wheatley. Marcus was always avid for news. He appeared as Felice emerged from the new brewhouse and walked by her side into the vast kitchen garden where clearance had resumed after the fracas. There would be no escape from his enquiries, she knew that. Bracing herself, she tried to make light of it but he was trained to notice every detail: he was also determined to make what capital he could out of his lovely companion's problems.

'You're upset, dear lady,' he purred. 'I can see it in your eyes. Don't allow him to affect you so. You did your best. No one could have done more. How were you to know what his plans were?' And so on.

'I could have asked, I suppose.'

'He'd not have told you. Anyone can see he's in no mood to co-operate. I suppose he was still angry about the apprentices.'

'He told you what happened…yesterday?'

'By the time I reached the guesthouse it was everywhere. Was he very severe? I know he can be.'

'He was angry. He had every right to be.'

'You're too fair, my lady. But then, he's your guardian and I suppose you feel an obligation to be loyal to him.'

'He's *what*? My guardian? God's truth, whatever next!' She stopped in her tracks and stared at the fair-

haired man with the disarming blue eyes. 'Where did
you get that notion, for pity's sake?'

'From him, my lady. Why, have I said something
to upset you?'

'No, Mr Donne, nothing at all, but I'd like you to
know that, whatever Sir Leon tells you about any relationship, guardianship, custody or understanding, it
has absolutely no foundation in fact. Lord Deventer
has not appointed him to any position except that of
surveyor. He is not my keeper and I am not his responsibility. I owe him no obedience or favours of
any kind except to keep out of his way. There, now,
does that explain things, or have I missed something
out?'

'Whew!' Marcus Donne stroked his chin, making
a mental note of the exact blue of the whites of her
eyes, and of the slightly swollen lids. Last night's, he
judged, being expert at such things. 'Yes, indeed it
does, my lady. In which case you will perhaps be free
to accept an invitation to accompany me to the May
Eve bonfire tonight. We're both strangers here so we
may as well stick together. Yes?'

'Yes,' she said, with rather more force than was
necessary.

'Good. Then I shall collect you at dusk. Now, will
you show me the new bit of wall? Ah, there it is with
a door to the river path. How convenient. The men
will soon have this place tidied up.'

Felice stared at the patch where flattened stems
looked as if someone had rolled on them, and her
hand automatically closed over the silk pouch hang-

ing from her waist. Inside it nestled a tiny gold object in the shape of a spear-head. 'Yes,' she said. 'I'm sure they will. The sooner the better.'

It did not usually take Felice so long to be dressed, nor would she have made quite so much effort for Marcus Donne if there had not also been another's interest to hold. Naturally, she would not admit it, but her heart knew why she was taking so much care and why her mind was already racing ahead to find a chink in the surveyor's implacable exterior that would allow the point of a dagger to penetrate. She smiled at her reflection in the silvered mirror, recalling how Sir Leon's apparent weakness was to have his orders contravened.

In the last light of day, the bedchamber of the Abbot's House came alive with softly glowing reflections on its patterned ceiling, tapestried walls and multi-paned windows that shone like jewels. Some had coloured glass at the top that cast pools of colour on to the rush-strewn floor, catching the toes of her soft red leather shoes with patches of amber and blue. There was now no sign of the previous mess: her flute and sheet-music lay tidily upon the chest, her writing table and prie-dieu stood to one side, her bed now hung with pretty but faded curtains and an oddly ill-matched but favourite coverlet. It was her own room, private and cherished.

She smoothed her hands down her bodice and tiny waist, turning sideways for a reflected view of the green-blue shot taffeta. 'Thank you, Lydie and Eliz-

abeth,' she said to the two admiring maids. 'Now go
and get ready, quickly.' She dabbed rosewater on to
her wrists and neck, well satisfied.

The two deerhounds rose to their feet as the maids
disappeared into the adjoining bedchamber that had
once been the abbot's small chapel. Their heads were
lowered, watching the door to the stairway with
pricked ears, their whip-like tails beginning a slow
swing that gained speed as the door opened.

'Mr D—' Felice began her greeting before her
smile faded. The tall powerful figure of Sir Leon took
her so much by surprise that he had time to close the
door before her heart could regain its natural rhythm.
The large chamber appeared to shrink. She turned
away to hide the sudden flush of confusion. 'My entrances and exits may be somewhat dramatic, Sir
Leon, but at least they give you some warning, which
is more than can be said for yours. Do you never
knock?'

He chuckled. 'No, not on my own doors, my lady.
Do you?' He looked around the chamber with approval, this time. 'You've made some progress in here
since my last visit. Pity the same can't be said of
everything else, but I believe you're beginning to see
who's in charge here, so we'll soon be working well
together.' His patronising tone raised her hackles immediately, as he had known it would, but he gave her
no time to defend herself. 'First thing tomorrow—'

'Sir Leon, if you will excuse me, I'm preparing to
go to the bonfire. It had occurred to me that you might
have come to apologise, but I'm obviously being far

too optimistic. May we discuss business some other time, do you think? Tomorrow morning, first thing?'

'Apology?' His laugh was deep and rich. And genuine. 'Ah, no, lady. Not after I saved so many of your men's lives. But certainly we can talk in the morning, if you prefer. My men will be waiting at cock-crow, but I shall instruct them to knock first, of course.' With that mysterious announcement he turned towards the door. 'Have a pleasant evening.'

'Er...wait! Please.'

His hand paused upon the latch. 'Yes?'

He held her eyes and, even from that distance, Felice understood that here was something significant thinly disguised as the ordinary discourse of colleagues. Yet nothing about this man had been ordinary, so far, especially not his exceptional charisma which was all the more potent for being totally natural, as unlike Marcus's posturing as it was possible to be. Or Timon's quiet charm, for that matter. 'Mr Donne will be calling for me,' she said, for want of something better to say.

'Yes, I know.'

'Well, yes, of course you would. I expect he told you that we spoke this afternoon.'

Sir Leon removed his hand from the latch and strolled across to the deep window-seat where he sat, filling it with his frame. With his back to the fading light, his dark head was surrounded by a pink glow that caught his chiselled features like a crag at sunset. He rested his hands on his thighs, his feet wide apart. 'He told me. Yes. Which is why I'm here. But it can wait. I didn't want to take your servants completely by surprise, that's all.' His tone was deceptively agreeable.

Completely at a loss, Felice shook her head. 'Please make yourself clear, Sir Leon. Is this some new chastisement you've devised because of what happened today?'

'Lady…' he sounded hurt, '…you malign me. Of course not. You're already aware of my plans to move out of the guesthouse. You knew that before you moved in here. Now I cannot begin any rebuilding over there until it's cleared, and the New House must be kept clear for your preparations, which leaves this place as the only shelter for me and my men. I came to tell you that my men will be here with my furnishings at dawn ready to bring them in. I hope it doesn't rain. There'll be room enough in here for me and my equipment, and our limner friend will not be staying long, whatever he chooses to believe. Plenty of room upstairs.' He looked around him as if to decide where to place his belongings, measuring the bed with deliberate interest.

'No!' said Felice, in a choked voice.

He looked at her in mild surprise, without comment.

'No,' she said again. 'This is preposterous, Sir Leon, and you know it.' She sat heavily upon a low stool with her skirt billowing around her, outwardly calm but trembling with fear beneath the embroidered bodice. Thankfully, no one could collapse inside a whalebone corset. 'You cannot do this. You agreed.'

'Ah…agreements. Easy to forget, eh?'

'Not *so* easy, sir, since it was made at our first meeting.'

'The day before yesterday. And you remember that because it was in your favour, no doubt; yet the one we made later in the day seems to have escaped your memory presumably because you didn't like the sound of it. Understandable, but bad practice. Perhaps we should have put it into writing.' He leaned back on to the window-panes and folded his arms across his wide chest, his eyes never once leaving her face.

Agreement? Felice struggled to understand what he meant, then her blood slowed in her veins and she felt a prickling along the nape of her neck as she remembered her vehement denial only that afternoon to the over-sympathetic Marcus. It came back to her, detail by detail, as if in a dream, knowing that it had erupted in a moment of fury.

'I shall tell him of our understanding,' he had said.

'And I shall deny it.'

'Deny it at your peril.'

And she had denied it. 'No, Sir Leon, I did not forget. I denied it as I told you I would because I cannot accept it. You must have known that.'

'Cannot, or will not?'

'Both.'

'Then the only way for me to enforce it, my lady, is to show that it exists. Two unrelated people of the opposite sex living closely under one roof are expected to have an understanding of some sort, are they not? And by the time I've spent a night or two in this room, that understanding will be more or less impossible to shake off, however hard you deny it. It should give the village women something to talk about.'

She thought of Marcus's horses, soon to be in her stable.

'No,' he said, reading her thoughts. 'You'll not get far.'

Fuming, and reeling from the cleverness of his scheme, she glared at his darkening silhouette as if he were the devil himself. 'I hate you,' she whispered. 'I *hate* you!'

For an answer, he swung his gaze slowly from her face to the wide curtained bed and back again. 'Easily remedied,' he whispered back.

'What is it you want from me, sir? Be truthful for once, if you please.'

'I think you know, lady. First, I'll have an acknowledgement of our relationship, a public one, and then I'll have the obedience that goes with it. And then I'll consider delaying my move into these rooms for the time being. That's not too much to demand, I think.'

'*You* may not think so, but I cannot for the life of me understand why, when you hold my honour in such contempt, you wish to publicise a relationship which must be as abhorrent to you as it is to me. Surely you could allow me to get on with my appointed task without wrapping it up in this ridiculous garb? My stepfather failed in his duty to my mother when he sent me here unannounced, but I cannot believe he'd have wanted my freedom curtailed so severely, my means of transport taken away, my every move watched and criticised, my servants ordered, my person manhandled by an unscrupulous stranger. It's intolerable!' She stood and turned aside, her voice trembling with fatigue and anger. 'Now you want everyone to believe you're…I'm…we're…'

'Lovers?' he said from across the room. 'No, but that's not quite as abhorrent as you seem to think it is, nor is the impression I've gained from our brief encounters, whatever you intended.'

'Don't shame me any further, sir, I beg you. Say no more on that.'

'Why? Because you can't explain it? Because it brings back memories still raw, does it?'

'Stop!' she yelled. '*Stop* it!' Tears welled into her eyes as a sea of confusion surged into her breast. 'You'd be the *last* person to understand.'

'Wrong. I might even understand before you do. However, one thing at a time. When word gets round that you're down here, as it will, there'll be few who believe Deventer had nothing in mind but a straightforward working relationship, even if he did.'

'Ah, I see! You have a reputation to uphold. Yes, I can see how that would matter to you,' she said, scornfully through her angry tears. 'Well, don't keep it bright at my expense, sir. I can forge my own relationships without my stepfather's help. Or yours.'

'Steady, lass. You're running ahead of yourself again. We're talking about a guardianship, remember, at the moment.'

'Do guardians make love to their wards then, these days?'

'It certainly wouldn't be the first time it's happened. But it will stop tongues clacking for a while, that's the main advantage.'

'This…this guardianship, Sir Leon. It would not involve further…intimacies? Do I have your assurance on that?'

He came slowly to his feet and approached her like a cat until he was close enough to read her face in the gloom. 'I do not think, my lady, that you are in a position to bargain, are you? Shall we get the first stage over with first, then we'll see about the rest?'

'Blackmail, Sir Leon. How many stages are there? Where do they lead? And what do I get out of it, exactly? I don't relish the idea of acquiring a colourful reputation like the men and women at court. Mine was white when I came down here to Wheatley and I'd like it to be the same kind of white when this fiasco comes to an end.'

'White, was it, lady?' he whispered. 'You're sure of that, are you?'

She swung her head away, mortified by his inference. 'I was speaking of my reputation, sir, nothing else. I do not want my name linked with yours merely for your convenience. Indeed, I don't want it linked with yours for any reason.'

'Then that must be one of the disadvantages of being a woman,' he said, pitilessly. 'Now, do we continue this discussion in front of Donne, or have we reached some kind of conclusion?'

'Guardianship, is it? Is that a notch up from custodian, or a notch down? Do remind me,' she said, scathingly.

'That's what Deventer would have had in mind, I believe. It will do to begin with.'

'Hypocrite!' she spat. 'As if you care a damn what Lord Deventer has in mind.'

'That's the wildcat. Now we begin to understand one another. You'll tell Donne this evening what the situation is, without the drama, if you please. Say your anger made you forget; anything you like, but make it clear. Now, come here.'

She remained rooted to the spot, glaring at the darkening windows.

'Come here, Felice.'

Trembling inside, she went to him, dreading what was to come and fearful that her inevitable response would mock at all she had been asserting. 'No,' she whispered. 'Please don't.'

His hand reached out and slipped round to the back of her neck, drawing her lips towards his. 'So it's not me you want, then? Someone still nagging you, is he? Then change your mind, lady, before I change it for you.' He released her with only the tenderest brush of his lips across hers like the touch of a moth's wing, leaving her to wonder not only what he meant by that but whether his strange demand would really be as uncomfortable as she was making it out to be.

Chapter Five

The discovery that Marcus Donne had not, after all, revealed the details of their afternoon's conversation to Sir Leon came as something of a relief to Felice, who had hoped for Marcus's confidence, at least. Nevertheless, she was extremely angry that her outburst that afternoon had somehow landed her deeper than ever into Sir Leon's power.

'Then how did he know?' she said, keeping her voice low so as not to be overheard along the busy pathway to the village. Torch-boys carried flaming brands before them, sending plumes of smoke over their heads and dancing shadows across the moving figures. 'If you didn't tell him what I'd said, how on earth could he have known?'

'Dear lady,' Marcus said, clamping her hand between his sleeve and doublet, 'if I spilled private conversations so easily I'd never be employed again, believe me. I am nothing if not discreet. I can only assume that when I'd told him how upset you were, his intuition told him that you may also have said something rash. Anyway, there's no harm done, is there? He scolded you yet again and made you promise to put the matter straight, which you have done, so nothing's changed, has it? He'd already told me that he was responsible for you as soon as I arrived. Yours was a natural reaction, my lady; think no more about it,' he said, not believing for one moment that she would take his advice any more than he himself would. This would not be a difficult conquest, with the lady already halfway there.

What nonsense, Felice thought. Everything's changed. If details of this guardianship are not all over Wheatley by now, they will be by the end of this night, for although Sir Leon's threat had been based on speculation, she would now have to accept his authority in everything or suffer the consequences. Lord Deventer's direct intervention in this matter was not something she could count on. Most disturbing of all was Sir Leon's refusal to promise no further intimacies and his cryptic message about changing her mind. It didn't need changing. She did want him, but not while her loyalty still belonged elsewhere and not while Sir Leon's only intention was to gain her obedience and to win her stepfather's approval. For her, it was a heartbreaking situation to be in; for him it would no doubt continue to be highly entertaining.

Until that evening, Felice had not realised how many people were employed at the abbey as builders, craftsmen, labourers and servants, kitchen and stablemen. Behind and before her they streamed into the village over the little bridge, past the thatched cottages and towards the village green where a mountain of wood, mostly from the building-site, was ready to be lit. May Eve was the beginning of summer and the start of festivities that not even the church was able to prevent.

It was only when she joined the group that included the Reverend John Aycombe and Dame Celia, Thomas and Audrey Vyttery and the complete Paynefleete family that Felice realised she and Marcus had been closely followed by Sir Leon Gascelin. She prayed he'd not overheard them.

On all sides of the wide green, cottages huddled together in the darkness; against the paler western sky rose the stone bulk of Wheatley Manor, where Dame Celia's brother and his family lived. These were the Paynefleetes, whose generations of wealth and nobility gave them extraordinary advantages in every sphere, property in several southern counties and, not least, the distinction of lighting the May Eve fires.

It was a crowded and merry occasion with laughter and shrieks of excitement as the flames licked and roared, sending sparks into the black sky and lighting rosy faces. Last year's chestnuts were thrown into the red-hot ashes to roast; there were gingerbreads to eat and dripping slices of roasted ox from the manor kitchens, hunks of new bread, honey-coated apples on sticks and barrels of perry, cider and ale.

Lydia stood with the protective Adam, who successfully warded off attempts to draw her into the chain-dance until she herself pulled him along. Elizabeth followed on with Mr Dawson of the kitchen and a clutch of other hopefuls, and Felice silently prayed that the lass would not take too much of the potent cider to which Marcus had taken a liking.

She had managed to evade any direct contact with Sir Leon, but he seemed never to be far away until the rowdiness intensified and even the vicar appeared to approve of the horseplay. Then, when her eyes searched for him for reassurance, he and the Vytterys had gone, and Marcus's impatient hand around her waist was anything but protective.

'C'mon,' he insisted. 'It's the dain-chance. Everybody's got to do the dain-chance on May-hic! Hey there! Wait for us! C'mon, Feleesh. Put your cider down.'

Hastily, Felice relinquished her drink to Dame Celia, who laughed her approval of Marcus's enthusiasm while the two were drawn into a thirty-strong chain of bodies and dragged along a sinuously snaking path around the fire, through groups of people, along the dark track and round to the fire again. Old and young, lively and infirm, all those in the chain-dance wreathed about, broke and reformed, gathered newcomers and whopped untuneful snatches of song to the sound of pipes and drums. The din was deafening.

In the dark, the chain of hands broke with a sudden tug, and Marcus fell heavily backwards, cannoning into Felice and knocking her into the man behind whose sweaty hand caught at her shoulder as she fell, pulling at her sleeve. Instantly, the pile-up of bodies collapsed into helpless cider-inflamed laughter, tangling arms and legs and, for the most part, rendering them unwilling and unable to recover. Two men were lying on her skirts, preventing her escape, while another was taking the opportunity to kiss her neck with wet and smelly lips and an unconcern for her identity that caused her to lash out in all directions. Which body was Marcus she had no idea, for the darkness was intense.

She yelled, screaming to be free of groping hands, and then there were grunts and yelps and spaces beyond her, a pair of arms encircling her, pulling her upwards. 'No…no!' she yelled. 'Get off! Get away!'

'Hush, lass. It's me. Come this way…come on. I've got you.'

She stepped on bodies and over them, supported by strong hands and an arm about her waist, unable to see but recognising the voice. His voice. 'My shoe!' she called out. 'I've lost a shoe!'

'No matter. Leave it. Are you hurt?'

'Er…no, I don't think so. Oh, no!'

'What?'

'My hair. My net has come undone and my sleeve's ripped off.'

They stood apart from the screeching mêlée but close to each other, Felice taking an unexpected comfort from the rock-firm stability of Sir Leon's embrace, and making no protest as he redeemed the silver mesh from the tangle of her hair and shook the rest of it out over her shoulders.

'There. Now take your other shoe off. You'll walk more easily. D'ye want me to carry you?'

'No.' She shook her head. 'Thank you, I can manage now.' She pushed herself away, but he enveloped her in his long cloak and kept an arm about her waist, holding her firmly to his side.

'Come,' he said, walking her towards the pink glow in the distance. 'There must be some advantages in having a guardian. Hold on to me.'

Obediently, she slipped her shoulder beneath his and walked barefoot over the cool grass towards the fire, thankful that the occasion itself provided an excuse for such familiarities. Half-expecting him to release her from his protection, she halted at the edge of the crowd and dropped her arm from his waist. 'I think…er…I should find Lydia,' she said.

'Adam's with her. She'll be safe with him.'

'Yes, but…'

'And Mistress Pemberton is over there, see. And you're staying with me.' As if to reinforce his words, he drew her on through the crowds towards those she had left, greeting them with laughs and accepting a juicy slice of beef with which he fed her.

She stood with her back to his chest, enclosed with him in the same woollen cloak and with one of his arms across her like a barrier. As her hair found its way into her mouth, he swept it aside with his thumb.

'What happened?' said Dame Celia. 'Trampled underfoot?'

With her mouth full, Felice nodded, blissfully unconcerned by the unkempt sight she now presented. The fire was warm on her face and feet and the cider had begun to release the cares of the day, taking them

away beyond recall, and as she turned her face upwards to watch a shower of sparks, she felt his chin
on her forehead and knew an intense longing she had
never experienced before with any other man.

'What happened to Marcus?' Dame Celia asked,
merrily.

Felice felt Sir Leon smile into her hair. 'With
Betty,' he laughed.

'Who's Betty?' she said.

Dame Celia's face was a picture of shocked amusement, her rolling eyes almost providing the answer.
'The village…er…'

Sir Leon's arm tightened. 'Betty is a very accom-
modating lady,' he said. 'Marcus will be all right with
Betty until about noon tomorrow.'

'Does she know him, then?'

'She certainly will by noon tomorrow, my lady.
Now, will you open your mouth for a piece of this
sticky apple? You can ask Marcus himself for more
details when he recovers.'

The noise and dancing continued as they took their
leave of their hosts and headed away from the fire's
glowing warmth, still clinging like lovers and calling
goodnight to the groups and couples and shadowy
forms. And despite the soreness of her feet, Felice
was scarcely aware of the rough ground on that dark
and silent walk back to the abbey. Almost silent.

'My head feels funny,' she whispered.

'I should have warned you. It's the cider. Take it
slowly.'

'There's something I was supposed to be saying to you. Something angry.'

'That goes without saying. It'll keep till tomorrow. And I know what it is, anyway.'

'How do you?'

'I just do. Wait!' he whispered. 'Stop! What's that?' They had reached the part of the path that ran parallel to the river across the front of the New House. A new moon caught a patch of shining water where V-shaped ripples dragged along behind a shadow that made a soft plash-plash in the quiet air. An owl hooted, and the moving shadow answered it.

'Do rowing boats hoot?' Felice whispered.

'They seem to at Wheatley,' he replied. 'Keep still. Let it pass.'

They waited until it had disappeared up-river towards the mill, then continued their slow amble towards the Abbot's House. When he passed her porch and continued along the river path towards the mill, she made no objection to the detour.

In sight of the mill's dark outline they waited, flattening themselves against the high wall of the kitchen garden as the boat returned on the river's flow, one oar steering expertly away from the bank. Then it was gone. Footsteps approached softly out of the darkness and, without any warning, Felice was pushed hard against the wall by the engulfing warmth of Sir Leon and held immobile as a shadowy figure passed them.

Her nose was against his neck and the faint but intoxicating aroma of his maleness overcame her senses, heightening the longing she had felt earlier and clouding all but the desire to be kissed, to submit, to accept and give without reserve. But the moments passed as he listened, twisting his head away to watch.

He took her arm in one hand and opened the new garden door with the other. 'Come this way,' he whispered, urgently. 'I want to see where he's going. If he's returning to the abbey buildings we can head him off quicker this way, and if he's going to the village we can watch from the kitchens.'

Baffled, uninterested and disappointed, she slipped with him through the door where there had recently been a mere gap in the wall. Vaguely, she recalled how she had walked the same route in bare feet, a brief moment of bliss and a sudden parting. Then, she had been glad to get away from him: now, she would have given anything to stay, to begin again and make a better conclusion.

Forgetting her bare feet, Sir Leon hurried her along the dark path that the workers had begun to restore. The cloak slipped and trailed over one shoulder, dragging her torn sleeve further down and jabbing her flesh with the pins that attached it to the bodice. Removable sleeves could be a boon, but not when one was being hauled through a midnight garden.

Exasperated by his haste and especially by the re-direction of his interest, she pulled her hand out of his to clutch at the spiteful pins at the top of her sleeve, yanking it away in anger. 'You go on,' she said. 'I'll catch you up.'

'Stay where you are. I'll come back for you.'

He dived away into the blackness towards the garden entrance, leaving her to wrestle with her bulky skirts, heavy cloak and drooping sleeve. Then, seething with indignation and frustration, she hitched it all up into her arms and stalked after him, ignoring his command to wait.

'Wait on yourself, Sir Leon,' she muttered, heatedly. 'And then wait some more. We'll see who can wait longest.' Purposely avoiding his route, she ran round to the back door of the Abbot's House and let herself into the pantry, up to the servants' hall on the first floor and up again to her bedchamber without being noticed. There, fumbling and tangling with an array of laces, hooks, pins and ties, her head swirling madly, she fell onto the bed. She was asleep before she touched the pillow, and this was how Elizabeth and Lydia found her only ten minutes later. It was another half-hour before Adam Bystander knocked on the door to ask Lydia if her mistress was in there, by any chance.

'Well, of course she is,' she replied, pertly. 'Where else would she be?'

As the pagan festival of May Day could not be allowed to exist in its own right, it was given a cloak of respectability by the feast days of Saints Peter and James, who drew a much-reduced congregation the morning after the bonfire. Admittedly, it was early, many of the worshippers holding their heads for reasons other than prayer, but Dames Celia and Audrey were predictably staid.

'You all right, my lady? You look rather pale,' said Dame Celia to Felice at the end of the service.

'Headache,' said Felice, thinking that the strong communion wine could not have helped matters. The sun pouring in through the large eastern window hurt her eyes, and she turned away with a frown.

The events of last night had drifted through the service in a concoction of memories, both irksome and pleasant, those concerning Sir Leon being particularly difficult to untangle. She recalled a sense of temporary compromise that had developed into an expectation on her part which, she now realised, was probably more to do with the cider than anything else. And after her earlier request for no more intimacies, she supposed it was only natural for him to grant a lady's request. All the same, she found it hard to suppress her indignation that he had so easily been able to overcome any urges he might have felt in favour of a cursed boat on the river. At least she now understood why he had been in the garden that night, thinking that she had been involved in these mysterious activities. She also remembered what she had meant to say to him about yesterday's conversation with Marcus, but that would now have to wait, for he had not taken his place by her side in church, and she assumed he must still be asleep.

She was wrong; he was waiting at the back of the church, though if she had expected him to say something she was to be disappointed; his bland greeting was general rather than particular. The man was so unpredictable.

He wore the new style of knee-length breeches known as Venetians, brown with vertical panes of silver-grey to match his doublet. He swept off his feathered velvet cap and bowed, smiling, apparently unaffected by the cider. Marcus was nowhere to be seen.

The light at the western door was even more intense. Unable to remove her frown at the pains in her head and feet, Felice's first words to Sir Leon came out with a sourness she had not intended. 'Good day to you, sir. It looks as if both you and the vicar will have to make do with anyone you can find today, doesn't it?'

'Oh,' he replied, 'there'll be no work done on the site today. Most of the young ones are still out there in the woods and the older ones find it hard to hold their ale, these days. Dame Audrey,' he remarked to the steward's hovering wife, 'you're looking particularly grand today. Will you be at the festivities later on?'

Dame Audrey had not spared any available space on her bright green silk bodice on which to hang a brooch or jewelled pin, and even her girdle-chain was weighted with clinking objects as she moved: scissors, a tiny watch, spectacle-case and a golden locket no larger than the palm of a lady's hand.

Her reply was predictable, in view of her early departure from last night's bonfire. 'No, Sir Leon. May hasband and aye have always trade to observe the calendar according to Her Majethy's decree, you know. Aye think our vicar should show his disapproval of these goings-on bay benning them. Heaven only knows what these silly lesses will hev on their hends in nane manths' tame.'

The silly lasses to whom she referred were at that moment filtering out of the woodland that surrounded the village and abbey, arm in arm with the lads and carrying boughs of May blossom with which to decorate the May Queen's bower. There would be maypole dancing, music and laughter, of which the Vytterys apparently disapproved.

Felice could find no suitable response to that, nor did she care to scan Sir Leon's face for signs of amusement, but there was no need, his eyes having caught a more interesting topic.

'Heaven knows, indeed, Dame Audrey. Is that a locket hanging from your girdle? A portrait?' He bent to look at it more closely, then at her. 'May I?'

For a moment, Dame Audrey hesitated, as if about to refuse, then she relented and hauled it up by its chain and lowered it carefully into Sir Leon's waiting hand. 'You may open it, if you wish,' she said.

The tiny domed lid sprang back to reveal a portrait of a young woman, her face no larger than Sir Leon's thumb-nail. She was dark and very lovely, her hair covered by a close-fitting black cap, her oval face enclosed in a small frilled collar, her eyes dark brown and red-rimmed as if she was prone to weeping.

Felice peered, equally enchanted. The young lady's hair was as dark as her own but Dame Audrey was fair-haired and blue-eyed, her husband grey-haired, his eyes pale. So who was the young lady? 'A relative, Dame Audrey?' she said. 'She's very good-looking.'

'My daughter Frances, my lady,' the dame said, quietly, taking the locket out of Sir Leon's hands and closing the lid. She held it lovingly like a new-hatched chick.

Completely taken by surprise, Felice realised that she should perhaps have waited longer for information instead of pressing for it, but her next question slipped out in the same uncontrolled fashion. 'Does she live hereabouts, dame?'

Dame Celia stepped in to save her friend. 'We lost her, my lady, just over a year ago. This is Mr Donne's portrait of her. We still miss her so.'

Felice's head thudded. On impulse, she took Dame Audrey's hands between her own and held them tenderly. 'I'm so sorry, dear lady. Truly I am. I would never have...oh, dear...that was clumsy of me. Do please forgive me.' She took a pretty lace handkerchief from her sleeve-band and handed it to Dame Audrey, and the situation was overtaken by the boisterous arrival of the Reverend Aycombe who appeared not to notice that group's momentary unease.

Felice, however, was troubled by the incident, particularly as she felt she could have been warned in advance about the Vytterys' personal tragedy, which did much to explain their obvious unhappiness. If only she had known.

There was no denying that the quality of the painting was excellent, perfect in every detail and as life-like as if the young Frances Vyttery had been sitting there inside the golden filigree case. Upon the bright blue background, Felice had noticed the date, *Anno Domini* 1559, painted in a delicate scrolling hand, and she wondered again how Dame Audrey was able to afford such a valuable object, or whether Marcus Donne had presented it to her as a gift. And how well had he known his subject? A miniature portrait was a personal object usually commissioned by a husband, wife or lover.

Partly to escape the May Day rituals, Felice slipped away to the kitchen garden to discover what had once grown there and to make a rough plan for the men to use the next day. Lydia was the first to understand: her mistress's feet were still sore, she still had a sick headache, and she didn't want the effort of making herself affable to Sir Leon. Or to Marcus, for that matter.

'Here, love,' Lydia said with genuine sympathy. 'Take your pad of paper with you, and your charcoal. Make your plan on that, and don't bother about young Elizabeth; we'll keep an eye on her. Here, take an apple with you.'

Felice was sitting in the shade of a drooping ash tree when Sir Leon found her, her head leaning back against the flaking whitewashed wall, the pad of paper discarded by her side.

He took her noisily discouraging sigh in good part. 'I know, I know,' he said, reassuringly. 'You wanted to be alone, you've got a sore head and, most of all, you wanted to avoid me. And now your plans won't work.' He came to sit on the old bench beside her.

'How d'ye know they won't?' she said, without moving.

He picked up the pad of paper and looked at the mess of lines, scribbles and rubbings-out, turned it round several times and smiled. 'Well, I suppose it depends on what you have in mind,' he said, turning it again.

Lethargically, she took it from him. 'It makes sense to me,' she said, looking at her plan and then at the acreage before them. 'That's the northern side.' She tapped the top edge of the paper.

Delicately, he gave the paper a quarter turn. 'Yes?' he said.

'Go away. I know what I'm doing. And why could you not have told me about the Vytterys' daughter? You must have known.'

'There didn't seem to be an appropriate time to suddenly start talking of the Vytterys' daughter. Not even then. It's the first time I've seen the portrait; perhaps she wears it because Marcus is here.'

'You've not seen it before?'

'Never.'

'But you knew she'd died,' she accused. 'What happened?'

'I've no idea. Thomas has never mentioned it and I've not asked. I didn't even know Marcus had painted her until he told me on Sunday. Now, lady, am I absolved?'

'No. How did you know the details of my conversation with Mr Donne?'

'I didn't know.'

She opened her eyes and turned to stare at him in disbelief. 'Then how did you know I'd denied anything?'

'Denied our understanding? I guessed you would at the first opportunity. And I was right, wasn't I?'

'What if you'd been wrong?'

'You'd soon have let me know. It was worth a chance. I got what I wanted.'

'It was dishonest, sir.'

'No. All's fair in love and war, they say.'

'Thank you for the warning. So you won't object if I do the same.'

'Try it, by all means, my lady. I shall soon let you know if I do.'

'I'm sure you will, sir, but I doubt I shall know the difference, your objections coming so thick and fast.'

'Whew! Sharp! Now, would you like me to help you to plan the gardens? I could draw you a rough diagram and you can tell me how you want it set out.'

'No, thank you. You've disapproved of everything I've done, so far. It would be a complete waste of time to tell you how I want anything.'

His chest gave a deep chuckle like a rumble of thunder. 'Oh, dear. That cider has a lot to answer for, doesn't it? I didn't want you tamed *that* fast, lass, not when I was beginning to enjoy myself. Here,' he said, taking the paper from her, 'let me make a start and then you can heartily disapprove of everything I do, just to get even. Yes?'

She could not resist a smile as she watched him stroll away with the pad and charcoal, drawing without looking. 'And if you see a red shoe anywhere,' she called, 'it's mine,' and closed her eyes again.

'You lost them both? Serves you right for walking off.'

Two encounters so close together without a fight began to look like the beginnings of a truce, at last. Even more so when, for the next two hours, they plotted the kitchen garden in something approaching harmony, if one discounted the occasional disagreement about the points of the compass.

'Look,' he said in exasperation. 'Over there you can see the apse of the church. Which way does the apse always point?'

'East.'

He took her shoulders and faced her in the same direction. 'East,' he said. 'Now, point to the north.'

She stuck out her right arm but he pushed it down and pulled up the other, holding her wrist out. 'North. So *that* is the south-facing wall where the apricots and medlars will grow. Right?'

'But you just said….'

'No, the other side of it faces north. This side faces south.'

'Did you find my shoe?'

'Look over there.'

She discovered it perched on the handle of the old broken-down wheelbarrow that she had bumped into

during their first confrontation but, as he had suspected, she would not go to collect it. Finally he re-
trieved it himself, making her blush angrily at his unashamedly teasing laughter.

Sir Leon had not asked why she had left him last
night without an explanation, so she assumed it did
not matter to him, nor would she raise the subject of
the mysterious man and his boat in case he asked her
for reasons she would have found uncomfortable to
provide. Even so, she would like to have known why
he had decided to spend the afternoon with her instead of at the May Day games.

From the kitchen garden they went to the cloister
for more planning, by which time Felice was bound
to assume that he enjoyed her company almost as
much as she enjoyed his, in spite of the air of controlled antagonism that held the delicious promise of
a fight. If he was intent on taming her, there was no
reason why she should make it easy for him.

By comparison, the company of Marcus Donne that
same evening held none of the same undercurrents.
He was unfailingly charming and amusing. He told
her as much as he could remember about the accom-
modating Betty and, with almost no persuasion, went
on to talk about people he had met and painted. He
remembered very little about his time with her at the
bonfire last night but begged her to forgive his lapse;
the cider was liquid gunpowder, he said.

He hoped her guardian had not been too tedious.

'Tolerable,' she said. 'Have you known him long, Mr Donne?'

'Since we were lads. He's a mite older than me, but we've always been friends. We meet when we're both in London.'

'Sir Leon has a house in London?'

'Yes, on the Strand, but his other house is in Winchester. He does most of his entertaining in London, though.'

'Entertaining who?'

With some difficulty, Marcus contained the smile that threatened the seriousness of her barely concealed interest. Leon had berated him for his less-than-chivalrous conduct last night, particularly for failing to care for Lady Felice as he should have done. Added to this, the buxom Betty had made demands upon him that no country-bred lass ought to know about. His pocket had suffered, too.

'Who?' he said, guilelessly. 'Oh, Leon's always been popular in court circles. He's well sought after, especially by the ladies.'

'Ah, of course.'

Marcus had no intention of letting the subject rest there. 'He's been linked with so many of the court beauties: Lady Arabella Yarwood, the Countess of Minster's twin daughters, Marie St. George, Levina Deventer, Dorothea…'

'Who? Levina? My stepfather's niece? He knows *her*?'

'Why, yes. Of course, I almost forgot. You're related, are you not?'

'Only by marriage, thank heaven, and then only distantly. So Sir Leon and Levina have been friends, have they?'

'Still are, my lady. That affair's been on and off the boil for the last three years. They're mad about each other, but her money's tied up till her father dies. Pity, really. They make a fine pair.'

'But Sir Leon cannot be short of money, surely. And he'd not allow that to stand in his way, would he?'

'Hah!' Marcus barked with genuine regret, but appreciating the sudden pain in her eyes. 'Houses and servants cost money to keep up, dear lady, as you well know. There's not a man alive who can afford to ignore the wealth that comes with his chosen one, or the lack of it. She'll need considerable funds to keep her happy. Court beauties come expensive, my lady, and none more so than the lovely Levina. That one demands the best of everything.'

Heavy ice-crystals formed around Felice's heart, chilling the blood in her veins. Lord Deventer's notorious niece was the one he would have liked Felice to emulate more closely. She was about four years older than Felice, handsome rather than beautiful, overflowing with vitality, extravagance and style, demanding and holding the attention of everyone within her circle. The two of them had met only last year at the height of Felice's grief over Father Timon, and her dislike of the dashing niece was then transparently mutual.

Felice was no prude, but news of Levina's persistent scandals which Lord Deventer found so diverting sounded to her more desperate than amusing, and the thought of Sir Leon being the favourite of her many lovers made Felice feel sick with disgust that he could show such little discrimination in his choice of women when he could have had the best.

'What is it, my lady?' Marcus asked, tenderly. 'You are unwell?'

'No,' she whispered. 'I saw the portrait you painted for Dame Audrey today. It's beautiful. She's very proud of it.'

'Thank you. She should be; it's one of my best.'

'Did you know that Frances Vyttery had died?'

'Oh, I heard. Summer sickness, I suppose.'

'Yes, I suppose so. It must have cost Dame Audrey a great deal of money, Mr Donne. The portrait, I mean.'

'I would paint your likeness for nothing, my lady.'

'Well, thank you, but doesn't one need a loved one to give it to?'

'I have an idea. We will share it. I shall allow you to keep it for six months and then I have it for the next six. Then it would belong to both of us.'

At last she smiled, liking the sound of his offer, but that night she wept bitter tears at the relentless inconstancy of her mind and the uncontrollable jealousy that twisted her innards. Now, it seemed that she must accept her heart's involvement with a different existence in which her love for Timon bore no part. She had been used to calling it love, but the overwhelming emotion that now held her in its terrible

grasp was something she could never have imagined.
It was a sickness; a madness. Men died of it, she'd
heard, and women, too. She could well believe it. It
would have been more bearable if she had thought
that his heart was similarly obsessed, but she knew
that it could not be, and the notion that she might
have to suffer this pain for the rest of her life was the
blackest thought of all.

Being a stranger to the real thing, Felice could
hardly be expected to know the other side-effects of
love—like anger, for instance, anger that she had not
discovered more about the object of her desire before
falling beneath his spell. It was unfair. Illogical. She
was sure she would not have succumbed to this dreadful affliction if she had known he could love someone
like Levina Deventer.

Just as disturbing was Marcus Donne's cynical implication that it was only Levina's lack of a substan-
tial inheritance that was keeping Sir Leon from marriage with her. After three years, what other reason
could there be? Levina was the fourth child of Lord
Deventer's youngest brother and had therefore never
been in the running for anything more than a modest
allowance and the promise of a limited dowry. Her
extravagances in London were largely financed by
friends, lovers and sundry indulgent relatives, including her uncle, none of whom could be relied on to
subscribe to a marriage-fund to line the purse of a
prospective husband. Her father, with other offspring
to finance, would never be as wealthy as his eldest
brother whereas the Lady Felice Marwelle, as the el-

dest daughter of the late Sir Paul, was potentially wealthier by far than Levina could ever hope to be, for all her show.

As dark hour after hour crawled by, these implications grew out of all proportion, finally convincing Felice that Sir Leon Gascelin's real reason for taking her in hand was most likely to ingratiate himself into Lord Deventer's favour, to obtain his permission to marry her and then to avail himself of her considerable marriage-portion which would allow him to set the abominable Levina up as his mistress in his London home. He would be able to squander it to his heart's content while she, Felice, would be kept contentedly manicuring the gardens here at Wheatley near her mother and their growing family. Her mother would naturally be happy with the latter arrangement, and Lord Deventer with all of it.

If love could turn to hate in an instant, the discovery of this ghastly plan would have turned the tables completely and for all time. Unfortunately, one of the other side-effects was that the two were often inexplicably entwined, and Felice found that she was unable to untangle them, being so new to love.

Having sown the seeds, Marcus Donne sat back to watch with interest as the situation developed over the next few days, assuming that Felice's increased interest in him was due to his escalating interest in her. Confident that his plan was working well, he saw nothing particularly significant in the tension that always surrounded the meetings between the lady and her guardian, not even when the sound of their voices could be heard above the hammering and sawing.

He heard Felice's fierce reprimand as he rounded the corner of the great staircase in the New House. 'You're impossible!' she yelled. 'And anyway, it's my mother I'm trying to please, sir. If her tastes happen to disagree with yours, that's unfortunate, but she's the one who'll be living here.'

'I don't care who's going to live here,' Sir Leon was heard to reply, 'you'll not cover those walls with painted cloths. It's tapestries or nothing. You may have an old-fashioned mother, but I have a reputation.'

It sounded to Marcus as if the lady was walking away, but then a door slammed and the argument continued. 'If you must bawl at me, do it when we don't have an audience of workmen. I've not brought enough tapestries with me from Sonning for all these walls. If you'd built them to fit the hangings, as other builders do—'

'Other builders can do what they like. And if you'd spend more time preparing some lists instead of posing for our limner friend, you'd know more about what was needed up here.'

Marcus heard a rattle of paper and saw a flash of white. 'What d'ye think this is? Whilst you've been fiddling about out there, I've been in here since early morning making lists as long as my arm. And what good will that do when I've no way of getting to the merchants? Shall I *walk* to Winchester?'

'Give them to me. I'll see they get there.'

'Not on your life, sir. You'd change everything on them. And what I do with Mr Donne is not your concern.'

'It's very much my concern, my lady. Don't get too friendly,' Sir Leon snapped.

'Why ever not?'

Marcus strained to catch the reply but the door nearest him was the next to close, and all their words were cut off.

'Because,' Sir Leon said, speaking more quietly, 'our friend's interest tends to gravitate from a lady's face with alarming speed. Don't say I've not warned you.'

Contemptuously, Felice turned to go. 'Then you two have more in common than I thought, sir. I bid you good day. I must not keep him waiting any longer. Thank you for another warning, but I find his attentions more appealing than yours.'

His stride reached her before she reached the door. 'His attentions? What are you saying? Has he touched you?' His eyes were suddenly like cold steel, demanding the truth of the matter.

But Felice was determined to press the point, even if it hurt her most. 'Yes,' she said, refusing to lower her eyes modestly. 'Yes, he has. He took my chin and moved my head into the correct position. He has such gentle hands, Sir Leon.'

He placed a hand on the wall to prevent her escape. 'Is that so, lady? Well, then, allow me to remind you yet again that if ever his hands stray into your guard-

ian's territory, he'll be on the road to London faster
than you can blink. Do I make myself clear?'

'No, sir. You are being your usual obscure self, I
fear. A guardian may not claim any part of his ward
as his *territory*, especially without her permission.'

'I can easily prove you wrong on that point also.
Do you wish for a demonstration? I can oblige,' he
said, lowering his head to hers.

'Your concern for my safety is touching, Sir Leon,
but it sits rather at odds with your offer. Am I to
believe that you want for yourself what you would
deny your friend?'

'Believe what you wish, but as soon as your mind
has decided to accept what your body is telling you,
we can have a more serious discussion on the matter.
Until then, lady, stop playing games and get on with
what you're supposed to be doing, for all our sakes.
Is that any clearer?'

'But for one small point. By "games" I suppose
you mean having my likeness painted?'

'Now who's being obscure?' He opened the door
to let her pass.

It was not the outcome to the argument she had
wanted, having left her with no score to speak of in
her favour. And having felt at one point as if she
might win, she was now left with a far-from-winning
smile to greet Mr Donne on the stairway.

'Yes,' she answered his call, rather too loudly. 'I'm
coming down. There's little more I can do up here
until I get more co-operation.'

It was made no easier for her to accept Sir Leon's

warnings by knowing that they were to some extent justified, if a little exaggerated. While finding it impossible not to like Mr Donne, and not to be impressed by his painting ability, she was well aware that his interest was not confined to her face alone.

If anything, his attitude towards her was intensifying from the friendly to the lover-like, and Felice's jibe about his gentle hands was not entirely a device to rouse her guardian's anger. The painter's hand had strayed only yesterday to the nape of her neck where a tendril of hair had been caught by her starched collar, and she knew that the caress that followed was not part of the rescue. It had interested rather than aroused her, for though Marcus Donne's fair good looks had a certain attraction, his manner was too similar to Timon's to be comfortable, which she now understood to be a diluted version of the real thing.

Nevertheless, despite Sir Leon's obvious concern, Felice was quite sure she could manage the situation and emerge unscathed with a portrait, for what she had purposely failed to tell Sir Leon was that Mistress Lydia had been with them at every sitting, so far. Marcus had made use of the excellent light in the large chamber above Felice's, the windows on both sides giving superb views of the conventual buildings on one side and the river and woodland on the other.

After a two-hour session, Marcus took advantage of Lydia's departure down the stairs to approach Felice as she looked through the window to the courtyard below. He slipped an arm about her waist and held her, gently, speaking just below her ear. 'Perhaps you could find a task for Mistress Lydia to do at our next sitting, do you think? There are one or two areas I'd like to examine in more detail. In private.'

The temptation to defy Sir Leon, even for the wrong reasons, was strong, but so was the memory of his hands on her, his potent kisses. Voices from the stairway interrupted them and, taking Marcus's hand, she peeled it away and slid it to one side, giving him no answer.

Dame Celia Aycombe, the vicar's homely wife, appeared in the doorway, her face glowing with the exertion of two flights of stairs. 'My dears,' she said, 'how are things progressing?'

'Coming along nicely,' said Marcus. 'Another day or two, perhaps.'

Chapter Six

With Dame Celia, Felice found some respite from Sir Leon's seemingly constant differences of opinion on everything ranging from the decoration on the walls to the size of the candlesticks. But as they walked together through the spacious rooms of the New House, the dame's sympathy was not quite of the same order as Marcus Donne's.

'He does have such very good taste though, my dear,' Dame Celia said. 'He knows all the latest trends; indeed, I believe his *is* the latest trend.'

'Tapestries on walls are nothing new, Dame Celia. That's what he's insisting on in the best bedchamber.'

'Jan van der Straet's are,' she said. 'Sir Leon was one of the first to use his designs here in England before he was snapped up by the Medici in Florence. There's no one here who can compete with the Flemings, you know. I'd follow Sir Leon's advice every time.'

Felice's resistance to the surveyor's ideas had not

been based on any sense of her own superiority but
on her mother's strong preferences that had collected
the showiest items from the homes of three husbands
and crammed them all together. To Lady Deventer, if
you had it, you showed it, discrimination being an
excuse for not having it. This placed Felice in some
difficulty since she could easily predict how her
mother would react to Sir Leon's restrained elegance.

They entered the best bedchamber through a nest
of smaller rooms with cupboards as big as closets.
Even without furnishings, everything was proportion-
ate and pleasing to the eye.

Dame Celia had not missed the ups and downs of
Felice's relationships. 'I'm glad you and Marcus are
such good friends. When will the portrait be finished?
Are you pleased so far?'

Felice swept a hand across a sawdust-covered window-seat and sat sideways to the view beyond. 'I
hope it will be as attractive as Dame Audrey's,' she
said. 'Was Frances an only child?'

'The only one,' Dame Celia said, opening a door
on the far side of the room. 'Where does this lead?'

'Nowhere. It's a maid's room, I think. What did
she die of?'

'Your mother will be needing a new nursery
nearby. Does she breast-feed or use a wet-nurse?
What did she die of?' she repeated, closing the door.
'Childbirth, my dear. They lost the baby, too. Very
sad business.'

Felice knew how common such deaths were but

this was something she had not expected to hear. 'But…she wasn't married, was she?'

'Frances? No, dear, she wasn't. That makes it even sadder.'

'What happened, Dame Celia?'

The lady was preoccupied with the pattern of gilded knot-work on the ceiling. 'Lovely…lovely,' she whispered. 'Well, she was sent off to have her child in Winchester with one of Audrey's friends who lives at the Sisterne House—you know, the home for sisters who'd been at the nunneries in the area. Of course she'd have been allowed back to live with my brother's family here in Wheatley if she'd lived—not as a lady's maid, but they'd have found some kind of work for her, if only so that she could leave the child with her parents. Such a silly girl, getting herself caught like that.'

The sun sparkled on the river, sending shimmering diamonds across its surface, and Felice wondered for a fleeting moment what she was doing there in that strangely echoing room, hearing about the tragic death of an unknown woman whom this kindly woman was calling silly. 'Who was the father?' she asked. 'Do you know?'

Dame Celia's short laugh held no humour. 'Oh, it could have been one of several men, I believe. She never lacked for admirers in London, and my brother and his wife entertained almost constantly. It was hushed up in case my brother was held responsible for the girl's safety, but if a lass is determined to court danger, she will, no matter what her employers do to prevent it. I feel sorry for the Vytterys. They'd have loved a grandchild.'

'And did they hold your brother responsible, dame?'

'No, I don't think so. They've been very philosophical about it, though I doubt not that they're still grieved.'

'She was a lovely woman.'

'Yes, a lot like you in some respects, dark-eyed and the same independent spirit. Everyone loved her.' She wandered off into the next room, calling back to Felice, 'Now this could be the nursery, my lady. Come and see what you think.'

'Marcus Donne!' Felice said emphatically to Lydia at supper that evening. 'There can't be any doubt about it.'

Lydia disagreed. 'I don't know how you can be so sure when Dame Celia believes it could have been one of several. Besides, he wouldn't…'

'He would, Lydie! And he painted her portrait in London and that means he had plenty of time to get to know her. Look how fast he tried to impose himself on me. Nobody's safe with him, even Sir Leon told me that. I saw the weeping in her eyes on that portrait.'

'I still think you're being too hasty. He's a flirt, and maybe he goes a bit too far when he thinks he can get away with it, but he'd not last long as an artist if he sired a brat every time he paints a woman's portrait.'

'That's as may be, but I believe Sir Leon knows more about Marcus's reasons for being here instead of in London. Keeping out of someone's way, I suspect. Well, I'm not going to sit for him again, Lydie. A man who can carry on as if nothing had happened in those circumstances is an unprincipled wretch, and I want nothing more to do with him or his portrait.'

For the next few days, Felice made herself unavailable to the fervent, if puzzled, Mr Donne until he came to realise that something other than the pressure of work was causing a hiatus. Careful to make no particular mention of the problem to Sir Leon in case it should be misconstrued, it was none the less only a matter of time before the observant surveyor noticed what was happening. Or rather, what was not happening.

'Four days?' he said to the limner. 'Of course she's available. She's been keeping out of my way too, but at least I know why. Which is more than you seem to, my friend. What happened at the last sitting?'

'I painted. She sat,' Marcus snapped. 'What else can I tell you?'

'You were alone?'

Marcus sighed. 'No. Mistress Waterman's always been there.'

'Oh, really? She didn't tell me that.'

'No. She doesn't tell you much, does she? You should try listening.'

So it was with that in mind that he sought Felice out in one of the small downstairs offices in the New

House where she and Mr Peale, the house steward, sat before a pile of lists, ledgers and accounts.

'Ah…' Felice looked up from her list '…here's Sir Leon come to tell us that we cannot have this room because he wants it. Good day to you, sir. We were just moving out. Come, Henry.'

Still smarting from Marcus's rebuke, Sir Leon bit back his retort and spoke to the steward first. 'Henry, the men have just brought up the eel traps from the dam. If Mr Dawson wants a basket or two, get him to send his lads over to my kitchen and say I sent them. But be quick.'

'Yes, sir. Indeed I will. Thank you. Please excuse me, my lady.'

'Certainly, Henry. And where may I send one of your men, Sir Leon?'

'Felice,' he said, closing the door.

'Oh, dear, now what have I done?'

'It's not that which brings me here.'

'All right, what haven't I done? I can't wait to hear.' She gathered her papers as she spoke, convinced that she was being moved on.

'No, don't go. I shall be using the offices on the other side. Stay here, if you wish.'

'I probably won't, but thank you. Now, my sins of omission. What are they this time?'

He leaned against the door and folded his arms, conscious of her bristling hostility and not knowing how to dispel it. She was wild, like a fearful creature, mistrustful, vulnerable and full of resentments. And too beautiful for words. 'No sins,' he said. 'I wondered what Marcus has been up to, that's all.'

Her eyes searched his for some meaning. 'How should I know? He lives in the guesthouse with you, doesn't he?'

'You've not been sitting for him for four days. He believes you're avoiding him.'

'Then you should be well satisfied. It was you who repeatedly told me not to get too friendly. You've been careful not to offer me a sensible alternative but, as you see, I'm taking your advice until something mutually acceptable appears.'

'Felice,' he said, again.

'Yes?'

She was not making it easy. Why should she? 'Felice, has Marcus been misbehaving?'

'With me? No. Is that all?'

'Not with you, then with whom?'

She looked away. 'Ask him. It's none of my business.'

'With Lydia? Elizabeth?'

'Oh, for heaven's sake! Of course not. Don't let's go through all the possibilities, *please*. The dairymaid and the laundrymaid haven't complained, either.'

'There's something wrong and I need to know what it is.'

'Why?' she flared. 'You've spent plenty of time telling me how not to do this and that, who not to make a friend of, who not to think of, who I should forget. Now you think there's something amiss when I stop doing what you've been telling me not to do in the first place. Make lists, you said…' she waved an arm at the pile of papers '…I'm making them. Look…look! Are they wrong, too?' By now her voice had become raw with anger, and tears had begun to flood her eyes. 'Tell me,' she croaked. 'Put me in my place again. I can take it.'

He wanted to take her in his arms, but knew that she would fight him off. 'No, it's nothing to do with any of that. You've done well. But if there's something happened between you and Marcus…'

'All right!' she spat. 'If it will make you go away any faster I'll tell you why I'm not sitting for him. It's because he's an unscrupulous lecher who carries on seducing women even after the mother of his child has died in childbirth. A man who can do that is too ungodly even for my company. There now, does that satisfy your needs?'

Sir Leon's arms slowly unfolded. 'What?' he said, frowning. '*Marcus*? Nay, you cannot mean… Marcus?' He swept a hand round his jaw, holding it together. 'How do you know all this?'

'I *know* it!'

'Yes, but how? You can't make that kind of accusation without evidence. Proof. Do you have proof?'

'Well, of course I do, sir. You've seen his portrait of the Vytterys' daughter that he painted in London at the Paynefleetes. Well, it was after that that she was sent off to Winchester to have a child, and it was there she died last year while he went on painting and trying it on with every available female. You said it yourself, plain or pretty, it makes no difference. He's responsible for two deaths, Sir Leon, and he has the gall to behave as if nothing has happened. It's indecent. What more proof do you need than that?'

'But Felice, none of that is proof. It's not even evidence, it's more like supposition. Because a woman has her portrait painted a few months before she has a child, you can't pin the blame on the painter, just like that. Think of all...'

'How do you know it was only a few months? Did he tell you that?'

'Well, no, but I know when he was at the Paynefleetes' London home and I happen to know when the Vytterys' daughter died because Dame Celia told us, didn't she? I admit that the dates are close, but that doesn't mean he must be responsible. He's not the only man in London to know the Paynefleetes' household.'

'You're protecting him. After all you've said to warn me, and now suddenly when your warnings take shape you'll not believe it. I might have known.'

'Felice, will you stop to think. Think!' he said, firmly but gently, instantly reminding her of that same instruction delivered under such different circumstances.

She covered her face, unable to look at him or be seen.

'I'm sorry. Listen a while. Are you listening?'

She nodded into her hands.

'Do you really think that Marcus would have the effrontery, and the insensitivity, to return to Wheatley

if he'd been guilty of what you say? Do you really
think the Vytterys and the Aycombes would remain
his friends if they believed that he could have been
the one involved with Frances Vyttery? And the
Paynefleetes: do you think they'd allow him anywhere near if he'd betrayed their trust in that way?
Of course they'd not. Marcus may be a womaniser,
but he's not stupid enough to put his profession in
jeopardy to *that* extent. You've no doubt deduced that
he's here to lie low for a while, but not for anything
like the Frances Vyttery tragedy. That's not Marcus's
way of doing things.'

Felice sat on her stool and stared woodenly out of
the window where men had begun to clear the cloister
of debris and weeds. 'I'd better apologise to him,' she
whispered.

'Have you accused him, then?'

'No, not personally.'

'Then there's nothing to apologise for, is there?
Leave it to me.'

'No…no! You cannot tell him.' She turned to him
in alarm. 'You must not.'

'I won't. I'll say you've been busy trying to please
me. Isn't that what you were doing these last four
days?'

'No, sir. He knows I'm not stupid enough to attempt the impossible.'

'Has it been as bad as that, lass?'

She declined to answer that. 'So, if it was not Marcus, who was it?'

He trod the ground carefully, picking his way

through the facts he knew and those he was not able to reveal, aware that she sat like a hawk ready to pounce on any mistake. 'Well, that's not something that need concern us, is it? I don't know how much the Vytterys and the Paynefleetes know, but I believe it's best if we put it to the back of our minds. She was obviously a foolish woman, wasn't she?'

Despite all his care, his painstaking route led him straight into the trap, and now she reacted to his heedless censure with all the instincts of a she-wolf with her litter. Her eyes blazed angrily. 'Oh, yes, indeed, sir, she was, wasn't she? But I believe she might have been as confused as I am about who to trust and who not to. It's an affliction we foolish women are prone to, didn't you know that? We're sent here and there to do this and that, and we're forced to obey and accept anyone who sets himself up as a protector without knowing whether they're wolves in sheep's clothing or sheep disguised as wolves. It's all very confusing. And then, to cap it all, we have bairns and die. Now that's *really* foolish!'

She turned her back on him, attempting to hide her pain as well as her fury. But he had seen both. He had been told to listen, and now he heard a mixture of anguish and confusion, insecurity and bitterness, and a personal experience that she had so far done all she could to hide. And while he suspected what form this had taken, there was still no way of telling how deeply she had been involved, whether the priest's real passion had been for the mother of his child or

for the lovely young woman who came after. Perhaps
he would never know.

He broke the heavy uncomfortable silence of the
little room as gently as he was able. 'No, not foolish,
my lady. Forgive me. It was the wrong word to use.
Men can be so clumsy with words. She paid a heavy
price. Too heavy. But men become confused every
bit as readily as women, remember, when they read
women's signals they're not meant to see. That's what
I warned you about with Marcus; the more experienced the man the more signals he picks up, and then
the woman had better not send any she prefers to keep
to herself.'

'Sometimes she cannot help it, sir,' she said, in a
small voice.

'As you say, sometimes she cannot help it.'

'And then what's she supposed to do? What else
can she do but pretend that these private longings
don't exist?'

'Why so? Would it not be better for her to talk
about them?'

'No, sir, I think not. She would have to be very
sure of her confidante before she could trust him to
share her thoughts. Men in particular are so clumsy,
as you've just pointed out.' She kept her back to him,
her fingers toying abstractedly with the ivory needle-
case at the end of her girdle-chain, impressing her
fingertips with its sharply carved roses.

Sir Leon could see that she was shaking. 'Felice,'
he said.

'Please…leave me. Go, sir.'

'I'll speak to Marcus.'

'Yes, thank you,' she whispered.

It was some time before she stopped shaking and before the words between them had settled, still tangled with double meanings that both of them had recognised and understood. But not until now had she known that he could be lost for words.

As the brilliance of the sun slanted through the windows, Felice stood motionless in the upper room of the Abbot's House contemplating the tiny half-finished portrait of herself on Marcus's miniature easel. It fitted into the lid of his travelling paintbox and had been covered over by a fine silk cloth to keep any dust off its surface, as was also the array of paints and brushes, oyster-shell palettes and packets of dried pigments. The limner even wore silk shirts so that no fibres escaped on to the ultra-smooth vellum surface of the painting. His hair was always newly washed, his nails immaculate.

The portrait already showed a miniature Felice, a steady gaze into the distance and the fine outline of the three-quarter view that limners favoured, the shadowless and peach-toned skin. But Felice could not see the likeness to the Vytterys' daughter that Dame Celia had mentioned, perhaps for politeness' sake, except in the dark hair and eyes. Yet in how many other ways had they been alike?

'Like it?' A voice spoke from the doorway.

'Marcus! Oh, I didn't hear you come up. Er...yes,

it's looking good. It'll soon be finished now, I suppose?'

He strolled forward and replaced its silken shroud. 'Not for a while, I fear. Another time, perhaps.' His long delicate fingers roamed deftly over his tools, collecting them and placing them one by one in the box. 'I must pack them, my lady.' He smiled at her, gravely.

'Marcus, stop! What d'ye mean? You're not going, are you?'

He stopped, still holding a squirrel-hair brush. He took her chin in one hand to hold her face still, dragging the brush's sensuous furriness around her oval face from ear to ear and smiling at her startled blink. 'Going? Yes, my lady, I must go. Say you'll miss me. Say you'll die of a broken heart.' He touched her lips with the tip of the brush. 'Say it, even if you don't mean it.' His smile was of pure blue-eyed mischief.

'I shall miss you, Marcus. Truly. I cannot promise the broken heart, nor do I understand why you're going. Has Sir Leon told you you must?'

'Not exactly.' Marcus's squirrel brush was now following the line of each fine dark eyebrow. 'Keep still.'

'Then what?'

'Let's say it was a mutual decision. We both think it best if I were not here. He believes I may be a distraction, I think. No, don't open your mouth, I'm painting it.'

Impatiently, she held the brush aside. 'Marcus, that's ridiculous. I need someone to distract me from these endless lists. You can have a bed up here if he wants you out of the guesthouse.'

'He's about to move out of there himself tomorrow into some of the ground-floor rooms at the back of the New House but, no. That's not the real reason I'm going. I must get another commission, you see. I cannot afford to be without work for too long.'

'Yes, I see. But I wish you were not leaving me here.'

He touched the tip of her nose impertinently. 'Then come with me, lady.'

'To London?'

'Why not? My horses are in your stables. Let's use them.'

It would not do, nor did she believe him to be too serious about the idea. She could not live with Marcus, nor did she have contacts in London, but the idea was too good to dismiss without some further thought. 'Must it be London?' she said.

He shrugged. 'Personally, I'd rather not, but it's where I live and where I know the work to be.'

'Then why not go to Sonning instead and paint my mother?'

'Sonning? Isn't that in wildest Berkshire, somewhere?'

She went to take his arm, threading hers through a crust of pale grey-embroidered satin and surprising him by her sudden affection. 'Wildest? Hardly. It's near Reading, and that's nearer to London than Wheatley is.'

Catching the drift of her mind, he looked down at

her in amusement. 'I see. And the road to Sonning passes through Winchester. Is that it?'

'And I need to reach Winchester with my lists.'

'And you need an escort.'

'I need an escort and a horse or two, sir.'

'How convenient. And where do you stay in Winchester?'

'With my mother's friend, Lady Mary West. We stayed there overnight on our way down here: she'll be pleased to see me again so soon.'

'And what about permission to leave Wheatley, my lady? Am I correct in thinking that you intend to forgo that?'

'You are correct. All I need is for a certain person to be too occupied by a house-move to notice what I'm doing. It shouldn't be difficult.'

'And what of your mother? Will Lady Deventer want to have her portrait painted?'

'She will if I send her a letter for you to carry. At the same time you'll be able to tell Lord Deventer how things progress here at the abbey and what a fine job I'm making of things.'

'And how well you get on with your guardian?'

'Er...no, Marcus. It's best if you say nothing of that. It's not his concern, but you may tell him I'll be ordering goods for the New House in his name from merchants in Winchester. He'd better know of that.'

'Right. So I'll go and make myself agreeable to your lady mother. Is she as lovely as her daughter, by any chance?'

'She's very pretty. She's also seven months' pregnant.'

Not for a moment did Felice think that her mother's pregnancy would make any difference to Marcus's interest in her as a sitter, not with a hefty fee to be had. After all, he had painted the Vytterys' daughter in the same, though probably less advanced condition, though Sir Leon had been right to suggest that they should now put that subject out of mind, especially since she had mistaken Marcus so unjustly.

However, this was not the only subject she must try to forget during the day-long ride to Winchester over rough tracks bordered with white hawthorn and alive with cheeky hedge-sparrows. Spontaneous plans, Marcus had told her, were often the best, this one being perfectly timed to remove herself from the one who nowadays dominated her thoughts. It also gave her the chance to be truly independent of him.

She must, she told herself, get to the merchants to order more beds and linen, mattresses and pillows, more tableware and silver, kitchenware and food supplies. The lists were extensive, yet the prospect of all this in the days ahead could barely compensate for the ache in her breast and the knowledge that any annoyance she had inflicted upon Sir Leon by her escape was nothing to the gnawing emptiness she had inflicted upon herself. It did little good to compare it with that which she had felt over Timon, for now she had to contend with the whereabouts of Sir Leon's affections as well as her own.

She had no doubt that he would wait until her return, berate her soundly, then carry on from where they'd left off, but this diversion would help to show that, if Marcus was a distraction, that was exactly what she needed.

They had left Elizabeth behind because, Felice had told the weeping girl, Mr Donne had only enough spare horses for herself, for Lydia to ride pillion behind Mr Peale whose help she must have, and for a packhorse. Even this had taken some rearranging, their so-called furtive escape eventually becoming so difficult to conceal that it was a wonder the whole of Wheatley had not heard what was going on, even through the clamour of cock-crow and church-bells.

But the drizzling rain that followed them towards Winchester soon cleared, drying their cloaks with a gusting wind and scattering them with a confetti of white petals. It was late afternoon when they passed through the great West Gate into the High Street still seething with traders and last-minute buyers, porters and journeymen, tinkers, pedlars, beggars and drunks who reeled tipsily out of noisy inns.

'Keep going,' Felice called to Marcus's men who led the way. 'On past the cathedral and then turn right.' South, she said to herself, if the apse is still in the same place. 'It's called Colebrook Street, Marcus.'

Here in the eastern corner it was quieter, leafed with pale new trees and lined with houses enclosing the area that had once been Saint Mary's Abbey. Just beyond the little church of Saint Peter stood a large timbered house within a spacious corner plot made by the high city wall, the home of one of Winchester's best-known citizens, Lady Mary West.

The outward ambience of serenity was deceptive, for the Winchester widow was larger than life in every respect, booming her welcome to the unexpected guests as if she had known of their imminent arrival. She sailed down the wide panelled passageway to meet them from the garden that bathed brilliantly in the evening sun, the sides of her wide bell-farthingale knocking against everything, sending a silver tray crashing to the floor and her pet spaniel yelping for cover. 'Hah! Back already, m'dear?' she called merrily. 'Brought a beau with you this time? Well, if it's my approval you're after you'd better bring him out here where I can see him. What's his name?'

This unnerving habit of talking about those in her presence had been known to alienate people, especially men. But Felice succumbed to the mighty embrace of the padded figure whose magnificence would have made even the queen's ladies blink, and told her who and what Marcus was. As she had expected, Lady West took to his extravagant chivalry like a duck to water, linking her arm through his and noisily accepting his flattery without a single contradiction. Felice's worries fell away; it was as if she had come home.

For all Lady West's bluff heartiness, she was perceptive and exceptionally wise, kindly, and alarmingly undaunted by men; her reputation as a Roman

Catholic recusant was well known to the citizens of Winchester, many of whom sheltered beneath her authority. She had regularly been fined for non-attendance at the parish church, but not even the threat of gaol would make her change her mode of worship to this new-fangled Church of England. She had survived the changes of the last twenty years, and now the Winchester authorities were beginning to admit defeat.

She had been a friend of Felice's mother for many years; she knew Lord Deventer and, although she was aware that his surveyor was a neighbour of hers, she had never met the elusive man. However, it took her very little time to read between the lines of Felice's apparent disenchantment and Marcus Donne's somewhat premature departure from Wheatley. As the mother of a large grown-up family, she was still close enough to their doubts and disputes to understand love's cheating ways.

As she waved farewell to Marcus early next morning, she was sure that Felice would not have seen the last of him, having about him a keenness that in Felice was only skin-deep. He was pleasant, but nowhere near strong enough for this young lady who was of her father's mould rather than her mother's.

'There now,' she said to Felice as soon as Marcus's cavalcade was out of sight. 'No more men for a while. How does that suit you?'

'Well enough, I thank you,' said Felice with some

feeling, but smiling to sugar the impulsive reply. 'I like him, though.'

'Who wouldn't, my dear? I imagine your mother will, too. Now, shall we take a look at your lists and decide where to begin? I know all the best merchants in Winchester. And perhaps it's time to take a look through your wardrobe, while you're here, and bring it up to date. My tailor is very good; how about a trip to him, for a start?'

Felice and Lydia eyed each other's dresses critically, not for the first time. Lady Honoria Deventer's energies of late had not been directed towards her daughter's appearance, nor had Felice shown much interest in the styles she knew to be changing, little by little, the paddings and slashings, stiffenings and quiltings, the furs, puffs and braids. A farthingale was something she had never found to be practical enough for her purposes, and the one she had taken with her to Wheatley had been impossible to transport on the packhorse to Winchester during her escape. Now she was being offered a chance to remedy all that, and it was no coincidence that an image of the glamourous Levina Deventer passed before her mind as she said, 'I think it's about time too, my lady. I cannot tell you when I last had a new gown, and poor Lydie's been wearing my cast-offs for these two years or more.'

Lady West's high-class tailor, William Symonds, had a shop below his house in The Pentice, just off the High Street where, as a former mayor, he lived amongst Winchester's wealthiest citizens. One look at the well-stocked shelves told Felice that she was

not going to finish her business here without paying
heavily for it, yet, once amongst the bolts of velvet,
taffeta, tiffany and silk damask, she succumbed to the
excitement of having the exotic fabrics draped over
her. All around the shop were rows of farthingales
and ready-made corsets, half-made bodices and drawings of sleeve-details, kirtles, embroidered chemises
and partlets, rolls of gold braid and fine linen for collars, lace, feathers and patterned bands. She stopped
thinking about the cost, nor did she balk for long at
Lady West's inducement to be more daring.

'With your looks and colouring, you can get away
with anything,' Lady West said loudly from the other
side of the colourful shop. 'Here's some lustie-
gallant,' she called. 'And what about this incarnate?'

'Not red,' Felice said, wincing at the ruby brilliance. 'I've never been comfortable in red.'

'Nonsense, love. Tell her, Mistress Lydia, if you
please. Red suits her.'

Persuaded, Felice chose an orange-red called Cath-
erine pear, a bluish-white known as milk-and-water,
and a colourful silk called medley which they told her
was the height of fashion, though she would have
preferred willow. Naturally, it took them all morning,
though the servants carried back to Colebrook Street
only the farthingale and two exquisitely made corsets,
enough fine lawn for several cool smocks for summer
and, from the hosier, three pairs of real silk stockings.

'Shoes this afternoon,' said Lady West, energeti-
cally.

The change of environment, the indulgence of

pleasing oneself and the stimulating company of her hostess, not to mention that sudden relaxation of tensions, was an intoxicating mixture that Felice could not recall ever having tasted before. Still laughing at some silliness of Lydia's, she tripped happily down the wide staircase of Cool Brook House, resting on the lower landing where the balustrade balanced a massive pineapple on its angle. Lady West's voice mingled with a man's, flowing across the panelled hallway from the garden and causing Felice to hesitate rather than intrude upon their conversation.

Her heart somersaulted inside her new whalebone corset, her hand stiffening upon the smooth wood as the tone of the man's voice reached her softly through Lady West's loud chatter, and she knew then that all her hopes and fears had converged like tributaries into one fast-flowing river. He had come to find her.

It was immediately obvious that he had not come from Wheatley that day; his deep gold and sage-green doublet and matching trunk-hose that showed no sign of dust was set off by spotless white at the neck and wrists. He greeted her with a courtly bow, sweeping off his green velvet hat around which curled a peacock feather and, having replaced it, treated her to a lazy smile that took in every detail of her unwelcoming expression. 'My lady,' he said.

'Sir Leon. You are here on business?'

'Part business, part pleasure,' he said. 'We could have travelled together if you'd told me of your intentions.'

Lady West looked at Felice in surprise, but said nothing.

'Yes, sir. I realise that. Do you stay long?'

'Long enough to help you with the purchases and to escort you back to Wheatley.'

'I may be here some time, sir. Perhaps you'd better…'

'Good. These things are best not rushed. Lady West tells me you've not fixed a date for your return.'

'I've made no decisions of any kind except what new gowns to wear. On that I was given some encouragement; quite an unusual experience for me these days. That alone tempts me to outstay my welcome.'

Lady West was not slow to sense the hostile undercurrents on Felice's part. 'Impossible,' she said. 'Your welcome extends indefinitely, my dear. For ever, if you wish. My home is yours. Now, please excuse me if I leave you for a moment or two; I shall return presently.' She touched Felice's arm in passing.

Sir Leon bowed and waited for Felice to speak. When she did not, he held out a hand, hoping for hers. 'Come now,' he said, softly. 'Our parting was not on such bad terms, was it? Did you think I'd be angry?'

'At taking matters into my own hands? Certainly it had crossed my mind, since it takes only that much to anger you.'

'Well, then,' he said, smiling at her waspishness, 'now that we're both here, shall we begin anew, since we left our disagreements at Wheatley?'

'But we didn't, did we, Sir Leon? I brought my lists with me and I intend to order everything on them. Mr Donne went on to Sonning.'

'Yes, I know.'

'Elizabeth told you, I suppose,' she said, with resignation.

'She had no choice. I asked her.'

'Of course. So you followed, just to make sure I didn't go with Marcus.'

'I was scarce a half-hour behind you, lass,' he said, quietly. 'I knew exactly where you were going and I followed because you are my responsibility. I want no changes of mind while you're in Winchester. I take it that Lady West hasn't been made aware of our relationship?'

Alarm flared in her eyes, giving an edge to her tone. 'No, naturally I've told her nothing of that. If it makes no sense to me, I can hardly expect Lady West to understand it.'

'I think you misjudge the lady's abilities, Felice. She'll understand if I tell her. And why should she be kept in the dark when all Wheatley and your parents know?'

'My *what*? You've been in contact with them?'

'Well, of course I have. I'm in contact with Deventer constantly for one reason or another.' He drew her towards a wooden bench, the back of which rested against a high yew hedge that sheltered them from the house. 'Come, sit awhile. It's what friends do, you know.' He felt the resistance in her hand and smiled at her vacillation.

Finally, she sat, eyeing him warily. 'So they know of this clever arrangement, and they agree with you, of course.'

'Of course.'

'And Lord Deventer must be wondering why he hadn't thought of the idea himself. It never ceases to amaze me, Sir Leon, how men can know so much more about what women need than the women themselves. I don't suppose you could give me some warning of the next stage in your plans, sir, or would that be asking for the moon, d'ye think?'

'Probably. But perhaps when you begin to trust me, when you begin to take me into your confidence, then I'll start to tell you of my plans for you.'

'I already know of your plans for me, sir,' she retorted. 'I would have had to be alarmingly stupid not to have seen through them by now. It was the timing of them to which I referred.'

'Yes, that was also what I referred to. Perhaps we could work on that together, eh?' His fingers lifted a dark tendril of hair from her neck and replaced it on top of her head, scorching her with his touch and drying her next words before they could emerge. He waited, patiently. 'Well?'

'I came here for two reasons, Sir Leon,' she whispered, eventually. 'One was to continue the task my stepfather set for me, and...'

'And?'

'And the other...' She looked sideways at his hands and found herself unable to speak with any real conviction.

'Was to evade me. Yes, I knew that, too. I shall help you with one but not the other. We did it once before, remember? We can do it again.'

He referred to the planning of the garden, she knew, but things had changed since then. The painted face of Levina Deventer laughed silently over his shoulder and disappeared. 'I doubt it, sir,' she whispered, 'as long as others come between us.'

'Then tell him to go,' he said.

Chapter Seven

Lady West mopped a dribble of onion sauce from her mouth and laid her linen damask napkin upon the white tablecloth. 'It's been done before, my dear,' she said, philosophically, reaching for the lamb pie. She took the edge of the crust in her fingers and made a cut to each side, lifting the wedge on to her trencher. 'A young lady tries to escape her guardian's custody. Well, so what's new? The only thing that *does* surprise me is that he came after you so fast. Few guardians of my experience have taken their responsibilities as seriously as that.'

To be truthful, it was not only that which had surprised her, though it would have been unhelpful to say so. Astonishment would have been closer to describing how she felt when the man portrayed as the overbearing, interfering, arrogant and thoroughly unpleasant surveyor turned out to be a courteous, charming, and extremely handsome man of some considerable style, all of which spoke volumes to explain

Felice's hostility. Hardly surprising was her convenient memory-lapse concerning the roles of guardianship and ward, which she obviously resented as
much as he intended to enforce.

'Not too surprising, if you think about it, my lady,'
Felice replied, dipping a piece of her manchet-bread
into the sauce and watching it soak upwards. 'He's
doing his best to please my stepfather, of course. He'll
find my inheritance more than useful when he comes
to make an offer for my hand. *That's* what it's all
about.' She eyed the bowl of saffron-yellow frumenty
but decided against it. 'The insulting part is that I'm
not supposed to be able to see through it.'

'Felice, my dear…' Lady West looked hard at the
piece of lamb on its way to her mouth '…you cannot
seriously believe it.' She popped it in and chewed
happily while she explained, defying table manners
in her enthusiasm. 'I'd not met Sir Leon until today,
but I've seen his house, I know his men, and I know
what he's worth. I know,' she said, licking her fingers,
'what *everybody*'s worth in Winchester. He's a man
of substance known to the council as a subsidy-man,
one of the top ten taxpayers. And I don't for a moment believe that he needs to find himself a wealthy
wife or he'd have found one by now.' She waved a
little finger to a waiting servant. 'Help the ladies to
the salad,' she said. 'Lettuce and cucumbers picked
today. And apart from that,' she went on, picking out
a leaf of red cabbage as the bowl passed in front of
her, 'it's hardly likely that Deventer will have dis-

cussed any details of your inheritance with Gascelin, even though he is your guardian.'

'I doubt my stepfather knows the details himself.'

'There you are, then. It's not the money, my dear. You can take it from me.'

Fitting so neatly into Felice's theory, it was hard to let go of the idea so, as if to help her, Lady West took her two guests in her carriage on a tour of the town during which the coachman had orders to go via the Staple Garden and Northgate. Being an extravagant lady in every respect, Lady West's claim to know everyone's worth was bound to be exaggerated, but Felice and Lydia soon found out that this was not so as snippets of information about owners, occupations, families, religion, misdemeanours and aspirations, wealth and social standing came leaking out, much of them keeping them in stitches of laughter.

'Diverted all his sewage into next-door's cellar,' she went on, waving to an acquaintance. 'They couldn't make out where the smell was coming from for three months. Now he's the town clerk, so it obviously didn't hamper *his* movements.'

Up in the north-west corner of the city wall, most of the ground was taken up by gardens and orchards where once the wool-merchants had held their wool market, known as the staple. There were few houses here, but the largest one stood alone within tree-lined walls, allowing them only a glimpse through wrought-iron gates at the pink brickwork and silvered pepperpot domes capping hexagonal towers, and acres of shining glass that caught the sun.

South-facing, no doubt, Felice thought.

The coach slowed to a walking pace. 'Built only a few years ago on the site of four houses,' Lady West told them. 'He owns several shops in the town, including the best goldsmith.'

'And a tapestry merchant, by any chance?'

'Yes. Jonn Skinner, last year's mayor. How did you know that?'

'I daresay he'll be well represented at Wheatley Abbey,' Felice replied, with a sigh. But by the time they had returned home via the great Norman castle, the Kingsgate, the boys' college and the bishop's palace, Felice was utterly convinced that no other house in Winchester compared for sheer beauty and size to the one owned and built by Sir Leon Gascelin.

Well satisfied with the impressions she had been able to change with such relative ease, Lady West began to understand something of her lovely young guest's animosity towards her stepfather's surveyor. Having set his own highly individual ideas so firmly around a new project, he would have had to be a saint not to be exasperated by a nineteen-year-old maid's insistence on her mother's preferences. Honoria's conception of good taste had not improved during three marriages and a large brood of children. Heaven only knew how much of it her daughter had absorbed.

Accordingly, Lady West's private predictions materialised when Sir Leon paid an unfashionably early visit to Cool Brook House the next morning as she was speaking to her chaplain after mass in her tiny chapel. The man hurried off at Sir Leon's appearance, anxious not to be identified.

'A difficult life,' she whispered, loudly. 'They have to be so courageous, these days, never being sure of their friends. Come on, Sir Leon. I've had wine and wafers sent into the garden. The wasps are already showing an interest.'

'You were expecting guests, my lady?'

She raised her eyebrows and darted a look at him, sideways. 'You, Sir Leon. Just yourself. I may be old, but I know a thing or two.'

He smiled and held out his arm for support down the stone steps. 'I'm sure you do, my lady. That's partly why I've come, to find you alone.'

'Ask away,' she said, allowing herself to be seated in a basket chair. She handed him a tall Venetian glass of elderflower cordial that glistened like honey between his fingers. 'You'll want to know more about Lady Felice, I expect; this guardianship was a rather hurried business, I take it.'

'An emergency device,' he said. 'She'd have abandoned the task if I'd not thought of something drastic. Deventer approves.'

Lady West nodded. 'And she doesn't.'

Sir Leon seated himself opposite her, facing the early sun. His legs were shapely and well muscled, clad tightly in dark green hose as far as his thighs, his glinting grey eyes well aware of his hostess's admiring scrutiny. He waited for her to continue.

'Well, you've come for some information, though I may not give it, for all that.'

The grey eyes laughed back at her warning. 'I'd not expect you to betray any confidences, my lady, but I'd like to know something about Lord Deventer's chaplain.'

'Then why don't you ask him yourself?'

'Because he'd want to know of my interest, and I prefer him not to.'

'You're not one of the queen's spies, are you?'

He knew she was not too serious: this woman knew everyone's persuasions without asking. 'Did you know the Deventer's chaplain before the present one?' he said.

'Before Bart Sedburgh? Yes, Father Timon. He came from the Paynefleetes of Wheatley. You'll know them, of course.'

'Yes, I know them well enough. Have you any idea who recommended him to Lady Honoria when he left Wheatley?'

'Yes. I did.'

'You?'

'Why so surprised? Roman Catholics have to stick together in these precarious times, sir. We have to help each other. Hakon Paynefleete knows I have contacts of the same faith, and when he asked me if could find a position for Father Timon, I put him in touch with Honoria. She wanted someone suitable to tutor hers and Deventer's combined broods. They have a clutch of young lads, you know.'

'I see. Did Hakon Paynefleete give any reason why Father Timon was leaving him?'

'Said he'd been told that if he didn't get rid of the chaplain he'd be clapped in gaol. Paynefleete, that is, not the chaplain. *He*'d be hanged, most like. You know what it's like in London where the Paynefleetes have a house. If you ask me, it was a bit foolish taking him with them; I'd not last long if I lived there; I'm fortunate to be tolerated here.'

'So Hakon told you *he* was in danger?'

'Correct. But the chaplain wasn't with Deventer long before he died, you know. Did you know that?'

'I had heard. Sad business. He was well liked, I believe.'

Sir Leon was staggered by Hakon Paynefleete's deceit. In spite of the chaplain's dishonourable conduct with their maid, the Vytterys' daughter, he was nevertheless allowed to move on to another family. 'Lady West,' he said, 'does Lady Felice know that it was you who recommended Father Timon to her mother?'

'I doubt it. It was not her concern, after all, and we all have to be so careful about giving information on the whereabouts of priests. Why, has she spoken of him?'

'No, not a word. Nor would I like her to know that we've been speaking of him, my lady. As you say, it's not her concern.' Anticipating her next question, he went on, quickly. 'I'd like to assist Lady Felice with her purchases for the abbey while I'm here. Would you allow me to call, to take her into town…shopping? I have one or two workshops I'd like her to see.'

'On foot?'

His smile was audible. 'I have horses for her and Mistress Waterman. She and my valet have taken a fancy to each other, you see. May I bring them round?'

'If they're as comely as yourself, sir, Felice and Lydia will not be able to resist them, will they? But don't head directly for John Skinner's tapestry workshop, I beg you. That would be exceedingly undiplomatic.'

If Sir Leon had expected to find the same compliance in this ward as in her hostess, he was to be disappointed. She protested, in private to begin with, at some feeling of betrayal. 'My lady' she said, 'I've come all this way expressly to shop *without* him. I'll not go through all those arguments again, and one cannot dispute before merchants, can one? He'll get his own way, no matter what I've decided, and I may as well not have any say at all.'

'I think you'll find, my dear, that away from Wheatley Sir Leon will be quite prepared to accept your choices on most things.' Lady West had good reason to believe this, having advised him to begin with the household goods with which his tastes counted for little. 'Begin at the linen-hall on Ceap Street and don't let them charge you more than three shillings for tablecloths, ten for quilts and four for a pair of sheets.'

'I had hoped to go with you, my lady,' said Felice.

'You shall, my dear, you shall. For the important purchases, we'll go together. Plenty of time.'

'This is quite ridiculous,' she snapped to Lydia later on. 'It's bad enough having him here in Winchester without having to be watched over when I'm buying. Can't we give him the slip, Lydie?'

She said something very similar to Sir Leon himself as he came into the large terraced garden wearing high riding-boots and looking very sure of himself. 'No, sir,' she said, watching two butterflies chase each other around the spikes of lavender. 'I'm sorry, but today I've made other arrangements.' She had no wish to sound petulant, but this was getting uncomfortably close to the manoeuvring tactics she had striven so hard to avoid, his impeccable courtesy here at Cool Brook House melting no ice with her. It might have impressed Lady West, but she herself knew the cutting edge of his tongue, and his inflexibility.

'Oh, dear,' Sir Leon said, 'Mistress Waterman was so looking…'

'Oh, don't give me *that*!' she snarled, suddenly angry. 'Yes, I know Lydia wanted to ride with your Mr Bystander, but we are talking of more important issues than that, Sir Leon, we are talking of making me do something I am determined not to do. Now, I suggest that, to settle the argument, *you* take the lists and shop on your own. That way at least one of us will be pleased. Here you are.' She held them out, catching Lydia's eye as she did so. 'What's funny?' she said, crossly.

'Come,' said Lydia, laying a gentle hand on her arm. 'Just come and look at this.'

'Oh, no! If it's a carriage, forget it.'

'It's not. Come on.'

Reluctantly, she was led by the hand through the door in the garden wall and into the cobbled stable-yard where grooms talked, holding horses. They spread out as the group approached, bringing one horse forward to meet Felice, a pure white mare with a long mane and tail like unspun silk, dark eyes and muzzle, ears pricked delicately towards her. Its legs were fine, tail held high, coat shining like satin.

'Oh,' Felice said. 'Oh, you…you *beautiful* thing.' She halted, looking with reproach at Sir Leon's amusement. 'This is most unfair,' she whispered. '*Most* unfair!'

'No. As I said, all's fair in love and war. Sheer bribery,' he whispered back. 'Think you can ride her?'

The saddle was new pale Spanish leather embossed with a scrolling pattern, the stirrups of chased silver, the bridle studded and patchworked with coloured leathers and silver; the effect was exquisitely delicate.

Neither of them had seen Sir Leon ride before on his powerful dark bay stallion whose eyes rolled continually towards the two mares, Lydia's being a pretty light chestnut with a blonde mane and tail. With Adam, they made an impressive quartet but, with

three servants bringing up the rear, they turned every
head on the streets of Winchester.

As Sir Leon had said, it was sheer bribery, but it
worked, and the next days were unbelievably different
from the contentious times at Wheatley when good
relations had been a mere oasis in a desert of conflicts
from which Felice had not been able to find an escape
except by the easiest route of giving in.

After the linen-hall they had visited the carpenter
on Middle Brook Street to look at designs for bul-
bous-legged tables, chairs with wider-than-usual seats
for ladies' skirts, massive court cupboards and tester
beds with richly carved surfaces, wide enough for a
small family.

'When my own carpenter is allowed access to some
good wood,' Felice said archly to Sir Leon as he lifted
her up into the saddle yet again, 'I'll be able to set
him to making some pallets and joined stools. At the
moment, he's using whatever he can scrounge.'

Sir Leon arranged her skirts over her legs, hardly
rising to the bait. 'At the moment, my lady,' he said,
'your carpenter has already made extra pallets and
joined stools and is now using my best oak to make
a set of shutters for your bedchamber windows.' He
held her eyes, boldly.

'Oh,' she said. 'You gave orders to my carpenter?'

'Certainly I did. We both felt it was the safer
course.'

Only a few days ago, she would have made a fuss,
on principle, but now she was content to let it pass,
there being no point to make.

'Where next, my lady? The mercer, is it?'

'No, silverware, if you please.'

'Jewry Street,' he said to Adam. 'Isaac Goldsmith's shop, then home.'

Felice was tempted to argue, almost to test him. 'No, not home. To the apothecary, I think, and then the brewer.'

'They'll be putting up their shutters in another ten minutes,' Sir Leon said, swinging himself up into the saddle. 'How long d'ye need with the goldsmith, five minutes?'

'An hour, at least.'

'Well, then, which is it to be?'

There was something quite delicious in losing an argument one didn't need to win anyway, a far cry from the unseemly Wheatley squabbles.

She had thanked him for the beautiful white mare, warmly and sincerely, though each night she wondered what lay behind this amazing change from severity to kindliness. She called the mare Pavane because her movements were graceful, like the dance, and she was allowed to stable both mares in Lady West's stables which, they said, was another mark of his new trust in her.

Sir Leon's new easy manner was the cause of some sleepy discussion at night when the two women lay side by side, tired after the day's exertions followed by a sociable evening.

'I'd no idea he had a singing voice,' Felice whispered. 'It's rather good.'

'Beautiful,' Lydia said. 'It almost made me cry when he sang about summer turning to cold December. He was looking at you, you know.'

'Yes, and thinking about someone else, no doubt. But he plays the lute well, too. I loved his duet with Adam. Do you think he's intentionally showing us his other side, Lydie, or is it just coincidence? He wants us to go and see his house tomorrow; Lady West's dying to have a look inside.'

'So am I, love. Tomorrow's Sunday. No shopping.'

'Early church; the little one across the road.'

'She doesn't attend the cathedral?'

'Once a month to avoid being fined and to see who she can see.'

They rolled over, back to warm back, and fell into the silent darkness. A muffled question found its way out, before sleep. 'Hasn't he kissed you since we came?'

'No. Not once.'

'Not even tried?'

'No.'

'Are you relieved?'

'Relieved. Puzzled. I don't know, Lydie. Perhaps this is just his new friendly phase. At least I can deal with this. I think.'

In the dark, Lydia did not see her mistress's eyes fill with tears, but she felt the sudden spasm, and laid a gentle hand upon her thigh until it ceased.

In the little church of St Peter Colebrook, which had formerly belonged to the nunnery of St Mary, the changes from Roman Catholic to Protestant were less obvious than in most other Winchester churches. The altar was still where it had always been, the statues and crucifixes, officially banned by the queen, were here tolerated by the town council because of Lady West's formidable influence, her large donations being responsible for the upkeep of the church and the priest's stipend.

The congregation still had a sprinkling of former nuns from both St Mary's and from Romsey Abbey, most of them living either at St John's Hospital near the Eastgate or at the Sisterne House in the southern suburbs outside the city wall.

Lady West introduced Felice to some of them, noisily as usual, promising to find Sister Winifred and Mistress Godden, both of whom had been at Romsey and would be sure to know Dame Celia and Dame Audrey of Wheatley. Sister Winifred was not hard to find after the service, not daring to ignore Lady West's bellow outside the western door. The elderly black-clad sister turned with an expression of patient exasperation and waited for Lady West's magnificent black amplitude to bear down upon her like a gigantic magpie.

'Most of them are deaf,' Lady West yelled at Felice. 'You have to shout at them, poor things. Winifred, dear, where've you been?'

Good-natured or not, the question came as an extra discomfort to Sister Winifred. The former Romsey nun, unlike the two Wheatley dames, preferred to retain her habit, her name, and her nun-like demeanour,

keeping her eyes downcast until the proper introduction had been made. Then she looked up, showing
Felice the world-weariness and disillusionment in the
drooping eyelids and mouth that she had seen in
Dame Audrey's once-pretty face.

Contrary to Lady West's announcement, Sister
Winifred was not deaf and so, while the noisy benev-
olent magpie was discussing the finer points of the
sermon with the priest, Felice, Lydia and the former
nun strolled towards the little wicket gate that enclosed the cemetery.

'Lady West believes you may remember two ladies
I've recently met who now live at Wheatley. Former
nuns of Romsey like yourself, I believe.'

'I was Mistress of the Novices there until it closed,'
said Sister Winifred in a small disciplined voice. 'You
must be referring to Celia Paynefleete and Audrey
Wintershulle, I suppose, though Celia was never a
novice.' There was no joy in her admission, and Felice saw instantly that there had been neither friendship nor close connection between them. She was,
after all, a good ten years their senior, and there
would be little by way of gossip to be had from this
dame's tight-lipped mouth. 'Good families, both of
them, but that doesn't count for much nowadays, does
it?' she said.

In the context of her reduced circumstances at the
hospital for poor but well-bred ladies, Sister Winifred's dour remark was understandable, but Felice
suspected another meaning. 'The Paynefleetes are
Dame Celia's brother and sister-in-law,' she said, 'but

the name of Wintershulle is not a familiar one. Are they a local family?'

'Well, for all they helped their daughter, they may as well have lived on the moon. Families usually stick together in times of trouble, but not the Wintershulles. They didn't want to know.'

Felice's arms crawled with prickling hairs. She had been mistaken, the tight-lipped mouth was not so much reluctant as bursting from want of a hearing. Discretion told Felice not to encourage her, but the words slipped out so easily. 'Know what, sister?'

Sister Winifred gripped the wicket gate with swollen knuckles, also fighting with the habit of discipline but, as she pushed the gate open, the inner defences were breached, breaking through into an outburst that carried more weight than mere gossip. 'They didn't want her back when Romsey closed down,' she said. 'Celia was all right. She hadn't taken her vows and she'd kept her nose clean. Not like young Audrey; she should never have been allowed to train as a novice. It was against my advice, though I blame those young priests at Wheatley. It's always as much the man's fault, isn't it?'

Felice glanced at Lydia, seeing a mirror there of her own horror. 'Yes,' she whispered, mechanically. 'They get away lightly, sister.'

Three abreast, they trod the pathway through long mounds, gravestones and bundles of flowers, not far distant from the chatter of church-goers. *Go on, woman. Go on.*

'That was the trouble,' Sister Winifred said, bitterly. 'The nunneries always needed priests to take our services, to instruct our novices, see to our accounts, hear confessions, administer…ah, heaven only knows what they administered. For most of them it didn't much matter; they knew their days were numbered and many of them were too young, anyway. *Far* too young. It was not good for those young lasses.'

'There was trouble?' said Lydia.

'Tch! Trouble!' Sister Winifred shook her head, hardly looking up. 'By the time we closed down in the spring of thirty-nine, the young Wintershulle lass was three or four months gone with child and not a soul wanted to know about it. Not even the father.'

'The Wheatley sacristan? Thomas Vyttery?'

'Aye. They had the devil's own job to get him to admit it and marry the lass. Celia's father took her in till they were married. He even gave them a cottage to live in and Father Thomas a job in the church.'

'Chantry priest, I believe.'

'Aye, but chantries were closed down soon after—you'll not remember that—so his job went, too. Life seemed to go sour on them, while young Celia and her family had it easy by comparison. Like mother, like daughter.' She sighed, shaking her head. 'I've said enough, my lady, she being a friend of yours, and all.'

'Well…er, not exactly. Wait, please.' Felice touched Sister Winifred's arm, pleading for her to stay, to tell her the rest which she half-knew already.

'Like daughter, you said? That would be Frances, would it?'

Lady West's voice called lustily from the church end of the path, putting an end to further enquiries, though Felice felt that Sister Winifred would have answered, given the chance.

'I'm not the one to be telling you this,' the sister said. 'It's Ellen Godden you ought to be talking to. She and that Wintershulle lass were friends. She's usually here at church on Sunday mornings, but not today.'

'Where does she live, sister?'

'The Sisterne House. Quite a few Romsey women there. I bid you good day, my lady. My way lies yonder.' She left them so hurriedly that it was obvious she regretted what she'd said and wished to avoid Lady West's inevitable questioning.

'Well, dears. What have you been chattering about, eh? Come, you can tell me as we walk, but hurry, it's starting to rain.'

In their hurry, the conversation mercifully turned to the general instead of the particular yet, in the shelter of Cool Brook House, Lydia could see her mistress's determination to investigate further.

'Don't,' she said. 'Let it lie, love. It's nothing to do with us, is it?'

'Not directly, no. But I must know, Lydie.'

'Why? Why must you?'

'You know why. Because whoever was responsible got off scot-free, didn't he? And I want to know who it was could do that to a maid and walk away smiling. She was pregnant, Lydie. She was my age. It broke her mother's heart. You saw Dame Audrey, wretched and bitter. They've all clammed up to protect her, but they're protecting the monster who did it, too.'

'I'll come with you.'

'No. Stay here, Lydie. I'll only be half an hour or so. Lady West's having a nap, so I'll be back before she wakes.'

'It's raining. You'll get soaked. Do let me come.'

Felice was adamant about her need to meet Ellen Godden and to go alone. It was Sunday afternoon, she reminded her maid, and few people would be about, especially on a damp day. She dressed in loose comfortable clothes, sensible shoes, dark hooded cloak and a purse of coins to pay the porter of the Sisterne House, once known as the Sustren Spital, the small hospital for former nuns. Her white mare would be an obvious target for thieves and, anyway, it was not far on foot, she said, giving Lydia a last hug and slipping out through the garden door.

The pathway led on to a track through a field bordered by dripping may-blossom and now slippery with wet grass, the fine rain whipping uncomfortably across her, wrapping her skirt around her legs. The town wall was locked at Kingsgate, but the small postern door was opened for her, allowing her access into the southern suburbs where well-built houses were surrounded by plots and orchards. The deeply rutted track was already filling with brown water and the grey sky was low over the town, cutting out the light and obscuring the great tower of the cathedral behind her. But the Sisterne House was further than she thought, and soon she was obliged to stop and look back at the now straggling cottages, sure she must have passed it.

A young lad passed furtively by, carrying two dead rabbits and calling his lurchers to heel, making Felice wish that she had not left Flint and Fen behind at Wheatley. At her enquiry, he pointed away from the town into the distant field where a cluster of white-washed thatched cottages huddled together in a sweeping cloud of rain.

'Over there,' he said, looking her up and down. 'You in trouble then, lady?'

She was tempted to box his ears, but gave him a groat from her purse instead and thanked him. By the time she reached the muddy courtyard and ram-shackle stables the rain had soaked through to her shoulders and legs, numbing her hands and face. The porter at the lodge was unwelcoming but came alive at the sight of a half-crown which Felice had the wit to hold on to until she had his full co-operation. 'This is to let me in *and* out,' she said. 'Understand? I am Lady Felice Marwelle, staying at Lady West's residence.'

It had the desired effect; he led her towards a dark passageway and a series of battered wooden doors, one of which had studs and bars across it.

'Mistress Godden,' the porter said, pointing. 'She'll be able to help you, my lady.'

Felice frowned. 'It's not...' but stopped at the

man's pale stare, realising how it must seem to him.
This was, after all, where Audrey Vyttery's daughter
had come to have her child.

Mistress Godden answered the door herself, but
cautiously, as if to resent any disturbance, her eyes
already sympathetic. 'Yes?' she whispered.

'Lady Felice Marwelle. An acquaintance of Dame
Audrey Vyttery. May I speak with you, briefly?'

Instantly, the woman held the door against her visitor, her eyes widening in alarm. 'Nay, look…m'lady,
I'm simply a goodwife. I had nothing to do with…'

'No, wait, Mistress Godden! I've not been *sent* by
her. In fact, she knows nothing of my visit. I have no
axe to grind, I assure you. Please, may we not speak?
I'll not take much of your time.'

'I've got a lass here. Well, she'll be a while yet,
and you're soaked. Come on in.' She opened the door
just wide enough for Felice to squeeze through, shoot-
ing heavy bolts into position with a cracking sound.
'You in trouble yourself, then?' she said, searching
Felice's trim figure.

Mistress Ellen Godden was probably of Dame Audrey's age, and her years at the nunnery in Romsey
were now, like hers, only a distant memory. Apart
from being clothed entirely in black, except for a
grubby brown-stained apron, there was nothing to reveal her former vocation, not even her manner, which
was confident and openly curious. Wisps of grey hair
lay across her forehead, and these she continually
pushed away, showing nails caked with grime.

Quickly, she untied her apron and threw it into a corner.

The room was small and would have been ill lit even without the day's heavy cloud, and it took a moment or two for Felice to see that one wall was a woollen curtain where the end of a pallet and a pair of bare feet could be seen. A groan came from behind the curtain.

Mistress Godden turned towards the sound. 'Pant!' she called, motioning Felice to sit. She gave a wry smile. 'First one,' she said. 'Always takes longest.'

Felice took a stool, horrified by the squalid place where spiders' webs hung like lace across the steamed-up window, and a table was piled high with grey towels, linen bundles and soiled clothes, bowls and a pair of rusting shears, a wooden bucket and a large tabby cat eating the remains of a mouse.

'No,' she said, holding back a sudden urge to be sick. 'No, I'm not in any trouble, mistress. Sister Winifred told me where I might find you.'

'Then it must be urgent, m'lady, for you to come on a day like this. And if it's information you want about Audrey's lass, I can't help you. I'm not supposed to be doing this, you know. It's a man's job, according to them, that is. They'll have me for a witch if word gets round.'

'From what I've heard already, mistress, it doesn't appear to be much of a secret, but I can understand your need for caution. Perhaps a small contribution will make things easier?' She brought her purse forward and delved, showing the midwife two gold coins.

'What is it you wish to know, lady? About Audrey's lass, is it?'

'If you please.'

'Tch!' Mistress Godden turned irritably towards the curtain again. 'Pant!' she called. 'Go on, keep panting. You've got hours to go yet, lass! Well,' she said to Felice, 'I suppose if she'd wanted to go on living, she would have. But she didn't see? The babe was dead inside her. Had a terrible time getting it out, and she didn't help much.'

Felice had begun to shiver. 'Wasn't her mother here to help?'

'Heavens, no. I managed alone, as I always do.'

'I knew that Frances Vyttery died, mistress, but what I need to know is the identity of the father. Can you help me there?'

The woman looked away, clearly uncomfortable with the turn of the interrogation. 'Ah…now…look. I'm just involved with the mother and child, not the father. If they wanted *him* to be known, they'd not be coming to me, would they? None of my business, that end of things, m'lady. Why not ask Dame Audrey herself, eh?' She stood up, disturbing another cat as she did so. It sniffed at the apron on the floor and began to lick it.

The gorge rose in Felice's throat, tempting her to give up and go. The two gold crowns pressed into her hand, and she delved for yet another one, holding them out to Mistress Godden. 'Please,' she whispered. 'I believe you can tell me. Am I correct?'

The midwife studied them and sighed. 'You'll not be revenged,' she said, indulgently. 'Whatever your reason for wanting to know, you'll never be glad for knowing. They'll never change, m'lady. No amount of knowing will ever make a difference to them and they'll never pay for it like women do. Ask her,' she said, tipping her head towards the curtain.

'All the same, I need to know. Was it her employer, Hakon Paynefleete? Is that why no one will say anything?' She believed she had hit the mark when Mistress Godden sat down again rather quickly, making both cats look up in alarm, but the woman shook her head, searching Felice's eyes for an alternative way round the truth.

'Nay,' she said. 'She and her mother both got caught in the same net, didn't they? Audrey with her priest and Frances with hers.'

'What? Her *priest*?'

'Aye. Paynefleetes had a young chaplain at that time. They got rid of him, quietly, of course. No fuss. Sent him packing, but it was too late, even for herbs. Frances was well gone. I reckon he should have married her but they wouldn't have that, the Paynefleetes. They weren't supposed to be having a chaplain, let alone a married one, and by the time the young lass came here she'd tried several times to get rid of it. I reckon that's why she was in such a state.'

Shivering and nauseous, and heartily wishing she

had taken Lydia's advice, she stood up to go, holding the coins towards the woman.

'That's a lot of money,' the woman said, suddenly reticent.

'Yes, it is. Who was this cowardly chaplain? Where did he go?'

'Ah, as to that, m'lady, I can only tell you half. He had an Italian sounding name. Monte-something?'

Felice swayed and clutched at the filthy cluttered court-cupboard. 'Montefiore?' she whispered.

'That's it!' the midwife's face lit up in recognition. 'Father Timon, the lass called him. Been lovers for the best part of a year, from what I could gather.' She held out a hand and took the coins. 'You know him, then? My, but you've gone white as a sheet, m'lady. Here, sit down and—'

'Unbolt the door! Let me out of here!'

But the howl from behind the curtain rose to a scream and Felice had just enough time to wrestle with the bolts, wrench the door open and slam it shut again before lurching blindly down the darkened passageway and out into the pouring rain. Gasping with shock and seeing nothing she recognised, she blundered across a yard and through a flock of preening geese, splashing through deep puddles and into marshy ground that ripped off her shoes, one after the other, throwing her like an unshod horse on to her hands and knees.

Time and again she fell, sobbing dry rasping moans, whipped by the rain and lashed by a new unrelenting wind. A clap of thunder cracked above her, and she ran through sheets of lightning that showed her only mile upon mile of water-meadow and, far off in the distance, a solid square tower that some reasoning told her must be the cathedral. The point that the cathedral was not situated within water-meadows entirely escaped her.

Headlong she stumbled, blind and uncaring, towards a wooden thatched building that in the semi-darkness she took to be a house. Then, almost screaming with frustration, she found that it had only one door. She lifted the wooden bar that held it shut, pushed at the heavy panels and fell face-downwards on to a dry floor scattered with clover-hay and there, as the storm in her heart matched the one outside, she gave in to torrents of blackest despair.

Less concerned by Sir Leon's obvious anger than for her mistress's safety, Lydia squared up to him with commendable courage. 'She wouldn't *let* me go with her, sir. I pleaded, but she insisted on going alone.'

'Two hours, you say?'

'More than that, sir. It was just after the mid-day meal, and she said it was not far, but I fear she must be soaked, if not lost.'

Sir Leon was very wet, his hair stuck down like black leather, his face as grim as anything Lydia had seen at Wheatley. With his valet, he had arrived at Cool Brook House to escort Felice to his home, only to find that he was too late to prevent her from doing what he had prayed she would not do. It had been the main reason for his vigilance, and now he had only himself to blame. 'Little fool,' he muttered. 'Come, Adam. I know where this place is. We'll find her, mistress.'

Lady West collided with them at the door. 'Ah, Sir Leon. What a pleasant…oh! You're not staying?' she called after them.

The Sisterne House was no place for men, so it was hardly surprising when their imperious demands met with a disappointing response. Mistress Godden was in the middle of a difficult 'illness' and could not be disturbed, not even by money, which said something for her commitment. Sir Leon and Adam rode on, picking their way through deep mud and belting rain to the roar of thunder, their way lit by blue-white flashes that made the horses dance in alarm. It was during one such illumination that Adam spotted Felice's shoes.

'Right. That's it!' said Sir Leon. 'She's gone ahead. You go back, Adam, and tell Lady West I've found her. Tell them she's safe.'

'But, sir…' Adam yelled above the din.

'Tell them, Adam. There's only one place she can shelter round here and that's either at St Cross or in one of the barns. I'll soon find out. Go!'

The wooden bar of the door was still swinging loosely in the wind as he pushed and led the big bay stallion inside, almost tripping over a woman's wet cloak covered with hay. The air was warm and sweet-smelling, and even in the darkness Sir Leon had no difficulty unsaddling the horse and leading him over to a pile of loose hay.

'There you are, my lad,' he said, softly. 'Try some of that while I have a look round. And don't let anybody in. Or out.'

Chapter Eight

Through swollen eyelids, Felice saw the door open and, from her hiding place at the back of an empty byre, knew that it was a man and horse who, like herself, probably sought shelter from the rain. She had piled hay into a dense mound and, in the safety of the darkness, had stripped off most of her wet outer clothing and laid it over the wooden partitions to dry. Now, she began to wish she had not.

Silently, she wormed herself even further down into the prickling warmth, willing herself to be invisible as flashes of lightning lit up the intricate network of rafters above her. The man waited, watching, and then began a leisurely removal of his wet clothes and boots, laying them as she had done over the nearest partition. By this time his identity was clear and her outrage was doubled. Her teeth chattered with fury at his intrusion.

The thunder drowned out all other sounds, but she knew his search had begun as he moved from stall to stall, stopping as he came across her wet clothes, waiting again for the next terrifying flash to show him her whereabouts. Suddenly, the tension was too much. Like a hare, she leapt aside and over the partition into the next stall, then the next, crashing into the black shadowy form of his horse and away to the other side of the great barn where empty sacks were piled high like a wall. She snatched one and threw it in his direction, not waiting to see him catch it but dodging his closeness in a mad, irrational, frenzied panic, fleeing his outstretched hand and feeling his warm laugh on her back.

Her chemise was still damp, hampering her legs, so she pulled it between them and ran blindly across the stone floor, feeling the hay thicken underfoot and hold her like heavy water. She fell, rolled away, and was stopped by the bulk of him landing on top of her, pushing her deep down and giving her no leverage. As in a recurring dream, she knew that something similar had happened before, that she had fought and escaped, and that she and her attacker were unknown to each other. Yet this time, knowing seemed to make no difference, for she refused to acknowledge him, plead with him, or remind him of that time when neither of them had claimed a victory. This time, her anger was greater than her fear, and the damage she had every intention of inflicting upon him would be little to the damage her pride had suffered within the last hour.

Unable to budge him, she used tooth and claw savagely and without a shred of mercy, biting hard into

his arm and raking his bare chest with her nails, knee-
ing him when he rolled away in surprise and hearing
with satisfaction the grunt of pain. But he was tough,
and quick, and she was not allowed to get away as
she had believed she might in the face of such unmitigated aggression.

Again, he threw her backwards and found her
wrists, holding them in a cruel grip above her head
that left her no means of retaliation. As if she had
been in water, she felt herself drowning, awash with
hair, hay and the restricting weight of his body. Mercifully, she felt him rise and drag her upwards, lift
her out of the suffocating deepness into his arms,
holding her close against his body, still powerless to
move but free of the stifling, seething bog of hay. She
sat across him, unable to do more than pant, gasping
at the air in raucous mouthfuls, already aware that her
intentions were now even more confused against the
enclosing safety of his arms.

'No…no!' she sobbed. 'Not you.'

'Shh!' he whispered, rocking her. 'This is no time
for talking.'

'Let me go!'

'No. Not this time.' As if wading through foam, he
carried her easily to where the stallion stood quietly
munching in one of the stalls, and there she was de-
posited, in front of the horse's nose, on the hay. He
spoke to the stallion, not to her. 'Keep her there, lad.'
He patted his neck and disappeared, leaving Felice to
wait with only the horse's massive head before her,
lit by the occasional flash of lightning. The dull roar

of rain came to her like the sound of a waterfall, and the crack of thunder muffled his return.

She felt his wet hair against her cheek and forehead as he carried her to the byre where she had first hid and where he had now spread a layer of empty sacks over the hay to make a smooth deep-filled bed. Enclosed by partitions on three sides and by the floor of the hay-loft above, the new imposition of his caring and the closeness of his body emphasised her own change of direction.

'This is not what I...' she began, defensively.

'I know. You want to fight me...hurt me... anybody. But I believe I have a better idea.'

'You always believe you have a better idea,' she snarled.

He smiled, laying her down. 'Yes, but just this once you might agree with me. I think it's quite possible.' He lay half across her, resting upon his elbows and lifting the strands of damp hair away from her face, unsticking them from her neck.

'What are you doing?' she whispered.

'Starting where we left off last time.'

'You told me to *think*,' she protested. 'You said...'

'That was then, and you did well to think in the circumstances. But now he's out of the way, and you need think no more.'

She writhed, pushing at him in anger. 'Just like that! Stop thinking! You believe it's that easy, don't you? What do *you* know...or care?' Out of control, her fists beat at him but were caught again and held away, and although she did her best to evade him, his mouth silenced her angry protests and showed her how easy it was to stop thinking.

'I do know, and I do care,' he said, releasing her wrists, 'and we'll talk about it later.' He would have liked to have asked her if she was still a virgin, not knowing how far the priest had progressed with his instruction, but he knew she would resent such an enquiry and anyway, he would soon discover the answer for himself. But she was full of bitterness and hate, needing to take out her aggression on him, for want of a better adversary, and a fight was not going to be the pleasantest initiation for a virgin into the delights of love-making. It would require all his skills as a lover to turn her understandable antagonism into rapture.

He did not start where they had left off in the garden that night; he began at the beginning with sweet searching kisses that caught her attention and held it completely. And slowly, for they had all the time in the world, his kisses deepened and moved away from her lips downwards, covering her throat, and when he thought she might revert to angry words again, he found that her eyes were closed with tears filling the corners and falling into her hair.

Without comment, he eased her damp chemise over her head, folded it up and placed it beneath her hips, freeing her beautiful firm breasts to his mouth and hands and, still with the spectre of the deceiving priest between them, made her gasp at his softly biting caresses. Her arms came up at last and held his head, taking part in the rite, enfolding him, fondling his ears and damp hair, searching the wide expanse of his shoulders.

She caught at his hand as it slid over her stomach to begin its quest towards the secretive quivering place and, although her legs parted of their own accord, the grip on his hand told him all he needed to know about her body's ownership. She had given it to no one; of that he was sure.

He rested his hand, letting it lie beneath hers. 'It's all right,' he said. 'I know. I'm the first, and I shall be the only one. You're mine, woman. You've been mine from the beginning, and you'll be mine to the end.'

'The guardianship…?'

'Was to hold you. This is to hold you even faster.'

Almost imperceptibly, his hand was allowed to continue on its way, exploring, persuasive and then insistent on an entry that was followed immediately by the gentle assault of his body, reaching even further into her, making her cry out in an excitement that instantly craved for more.

Expertly, he dipped and stroked, heightening the exquisite tension and stretching it almost to breaking point as she abandoned herself utterly to his mastery, moaning with the yielding pleasure of it.

The thunder rolled away and the rain continued to lash the deep thatch above them, sending the wind to whine and moan around the corners to harmonise with the cries of the enraptured woman within, and time lengthened as the light faded completely. He had not known her need was so great, nor had she recognised it for what it was, an emptiness to be filled, a hunger to be satisfied. So when the time came that she believed her needs had been met, a wave of feverish excitement surged through her body, taking her completely by surprise and making her swing away sideways to escape its force.

But Sir Leon had anticipated its arrival after his lengthy preparation, and he brought her back under him, twisting his hand into her long hair to keep her there. Relentlessly, but with supreme control, he guided her through the climax and heard her cries of ecstasy, felt her heave beneath him and then the fierce clasp of her fingers on his arms gradually relax. Understanding her bewilderment, he pulled her tenderly into his arms to lay in a close embrace and they stayed there, without speaking. They heard someone enter and leave again almost immediately, and they knew that the worst of the storm had passed.

Aware of a slight tremor in her body, he pulled her even closer and swept his hand down her back, pulling her hair away from the new tears. 'Do you want to tell me?' he whispered.

'I cannot,' she said. 'It hurts.' There was a silence, then came her remembrance that his questions were no longer ambiguous concerning her previous relationship but now quite specific. 'You knew?' she gulped.

'A fair idea,' he replied. 'Conjecture, mostly.'

'About the Sisterne House, too?'

'That was a guess. It would not have been St Cross Hospital; that's for men. And Mistress Godden has something of a reputation. I take it you found out what you wanted to know. Is that why it hurts?'

'Yes.'

'Your first love?'

She nodded.

'And now?' His arm tightened again as he kissed her forehead. 'Will he go, d'ye think? Will he leave us alone?'

It was an impossible question to answer at that moment, her wounds being so fresh and the new experience of his loving being so persuasively close. She could have promised to forget, but the events of the afternoon were etched clearly in her mind, though jumbled and far too poignant, and a promise would be meaningless after that. Just as terrible was the confluence of this most recent commitment and her concern about the placing of his heart, for now she was reminded that men's hearts were not necessarily where their loving was. It was what she had wanted, but did she know any more about *him* than she had about Father Timon? A woman's shriek pierced her thoughts.

'Eventually,' she said. 'Being a man, I'm sure he will.'

The bitterness was not lost upon him. He swung himself over her, leaning upon one elbow to look at her in the dimness, every soft word now clear in the hay-scented stillness. 'Is that what you think, my lady? That I'll leave you, after this?' His fingers slipped into her hair.

Again she felt the incredible surging of desire

where each part of his body touched hers, and the black fears about his attachment to Levina Deventer were whisked away into the depths like bats into a cave. Without answering him, she held his beautiful head between her hands and drew it close to her mouth. 'Love me again,' she breathed into him. 'Show me.'

'I *will* show you,' he said. 'I have that much in my favour.'

Thomas Vyttery, Sir Leon's perpetually unsmiling steward, stood in his employer's office in the upper storey of the guesthouse, waiting for some response to his request. Unconsciously, the hand by his side clenched and unclenched, its fingers seeking each other's reassurance. His other hand held a sheet of papers that hovered over Sir Leon's desk as if about to be dropped in some impatience. Or despair.

The Reverend John Aycombe, seated on the stool at the desk, tidied a pile of notes with exaggerated slowness and lay them carefully to one side. Then he tipped his black cap forward on to his forehead, scratched at the base of his hairline and righted it, tying the strings beneath his chin.

'We've had our orders, Thomas,' he said with maddening calmness. 'That's all there is to it, I'm afraid. You'll have to take it up with Sir Leon when he returns.' His immobility suggested that he knew this answer was not going to satisfy the former sacristan of Wheatley Abbey.

Thomas's paper stopped hovering and landed with

a smack on the desk, though the effect on the former
abbot was minimal.

'And you know as well as I,' Thomas Vyttery said,
testily, 'that that's *not* all there is to it. It's bad enough
having that…that *woman* down here messing up our
plans…'

'Your plans, Thomas. *Your* plans.'

'…without this to make matters worse. You told
me you'd dissuade him from moving the sacristy to
the north-west end and from digging up the chapter-
house floor, and now I see they've been given the go-
ahead. They're about to start on it. Today. Look!' His
bony finger jabbed at the pile of papers. 'And I'm
expected to feed them while they do it.'

Almost tenderly, John Aycombe, Master of Works,
pushed the guilty papers out of Thomas's reach. 'I
said I'd try, Thomas, and I did. But Lady Felice wants
to start work on the garden that will cover the old
cloister and the foundations of the chapter-house, and
Sir Leon's decided that we need the sacristy space for
our expanding congregation.'

'*You* decided that, Father Abbot. You decided that
yourself, didn't you?'

John Aycombe sighed and looked away. They had
rarely seen eye to eye though they'd known each
other as novices, professed monks, priests, and as
contenders for the abbacy, then as abbot and sacristan,
though he himself had scraped in by a whisker with
the casting vote of the Bishop of Salisbury. Since
when he and Thomas and half the inmates had shared
a bone of contention, their promises of loyalty made

in the knowledge that the last abbot would be hand-
somely pensioned off, whereas the rest of them would
not. John had done what he could to sweeten the pill
by appointing Father Thomas as sacristan. Except that
Father Thomas had expected to be appointed prior,
no less. John had not wanted Thomas Vyttery to be
prior any more than he'd wanted him to be sacristan,
and now he often wondered which of the offices, if
any, would have satisfied him.

'No, Thomas,' he protested mildly. 'Of course I
didn't. But if the congregation is swelling year by
year, it stands to reason that we have to make more
space available for them. You saw what a squash it
was on Sunday, and soon we'll have the whole of
Lord Deventer's household with us, so what better
time to do it than while we have the builders here, on
site? Anyway, all churches nowadays have vestries at
the other end of the church.'

Such irrelevancies were like a red rag to a bull.

'Have you forgot?' Thomas poked at John Aycombe's shoulder to bring him down to earth. 'Look
at me, John Aycombe! Have you forgot who's buried
in the chapter-house? Have you forgot how I get a
living, the living you promised me would outlast me
and Audrey? Well, *have* you?'

John Aycombe's bottom lip was sucked in and released. Of course he'd not forgotten. How could he?
But Thomas should have let go of these old affairs
by now and got on with the present: there were others
who had suffered as much, if not more, one way and
another.

'No, I've not forgotten who's buried there, Thomas, any more than I've forgotten your relationship with him. That kind of thing was very much disapproved of, you know, and maybe the time has come for you to let him rest in peace.' Too late he realised the absurdity of the chastisement when the grave was about to be well pounded by the feet of builders and more rubble before Lady Felice's garden was constructed over it, in which state not even Thomas would be able to visit it as he had done in supposed secret these last twenty years and more. As abbot, he should not have allowed the friendship to continue, but the end was in sight by then, and what did it matter? 'And as for the living you speak of,' he went on rapidly before Thomas could pick him up, 'you and Audrey have done very well out of it, man. You can hardly complain that the deal was ungenerous, not after all this time. I suggest that you remove what you can before the men begin and leave the rest where it is. As I said, there's nothing I can do until Sir Leon's return.'

Thomas Vyttery's usual pallor had changed to an unhealthy green, his hands now clenched into tight fists. He took a noisy rasping breath. 'Take it *now*?' he almost screeched. 'In broad daylight just as they're about to start knocking the wall out? Have you taken leave of your senses? How can I do that, John Aycombe? Tell me. And while you're about it, think back to the time when you needed *my* help, if you will. You've always had the best of the bargain, haven't you? Always landed on your feet, in spite of—'

'That's enough, Thomas!' John Aycombe rose to his feet, as sure of his authority as he'd always been, even as Wheatley's youngest abbot. He would not listen to his catalogue of accusations. He had tried to put matters right; no man could have done more, and Thomas Vyttery had done a good deal better than the rest of them for a decent living.

His shoe caught the corner of a beechwood box that stood on the floor beneath Sir Leon's desk. 'Listen, Thomas,' he said. 'I have a lot of catching up to do. Some of the men got drunk over May Eve and now I find that one's been thieving and gone missing. We'll talk about this later, eh? Do what you can for the time being. Nay, cheer up, man. All good things have to come to an end some time, don't they? You must have known that, so it's no great surprise. I'll catch up with you later.'

He smiled behind the closing door. What a fuss about nothing. Yet he stood for a few moments as his smile faded, wondering what other good things would come to an end, and had he made as much effort to forget things as he was advising Thomas Vyttery to do? The bottom lip ventured inwards again.

From the stool, he bent forward and lifted the beechwood box on to the desk, recognising it immediately as a Catholic priest's portable mass set. Why had he not noticed this before? And what was it doing here in Sir Leon's room? Carefully, he lifted the lid, exposing the red leather lining, the silver chalice and plate, the rosary, crucifix and candlestick, the small box of wafers. A small well-thumbed bible held a bookmark of parchment.

Fumbling, and in sudden haste, he opened the book and found the owner's signature, Timon Montefiore, then the symbols that required no explanation and the initial *F*. Now his chest tightened painfully as he glanced at the verses, knowing them by heart, and from there to the end-page where the lock of hair still lay in a soft curl. His hands shook and tears trickled down his face, falling on to his chest like glass beads.

'The sins of the fathers,' he whispered. 'The sins of the fathers.'

After a long time, he gathered himself together, replaced the items in the box and closed the lid. He would leave it until dark, and then he would collect it when the men had finished work on the site. It would not be difficult to explain its absence to Sir Leon: thieves were an ever-present menace.

Shaking with anger, Thomas Vyttery marched down the nave of the church and entered the sacristy, closing the door with a slam and at once shutting out the chatter and clatter of workmen who already gathered like vultures. He looked around him at the shelves where the daily vestments of the clergy were folded in neat piles, candles laid in order of size, boxes and casks, bibles, prayer-books and chests of tools for repairing and cleaning the organ, the clock and the two remaining bells. Years ago, these same shelves had gleamed with polished plate; vestments had lit the small room with their glowing colours,

purple, red and green, sparkling with gold thread and
jewels. Now all was black and white, plain and func-
tional.

All good things come to an end, indeed. Trust John
Aycombe to think of that glib comment when everything he touched turned to gold. A knock on the door
made him turn in fury. 'I told you to…'

The intruder did not hesitate politely, but stepped
inside and closed the door behind him—a thick-set
man wearing a filthy leather apron over his tunic, tied
round the middle with twine, his grimy shirt-sleeves
rolled up to his biceps. His head was enclosed in a
flap-eared cap that framed his ruddy face like a pig
in a bonnet.

Thomas turned back to his study of the cope-chest.
'What do *you* want?' he said.

'You'll be wanting some help with that lot then,
eh?' said the smith. 'So, considering that I'm the only
one around here that you can trust, here I am. How's
that for Christian charity, Father Thomas?'

'I've told you not to call me that, Smith. It's not
appropriate. And why have you come here in the daytime, for pity's sake? What d'ye think that lot out
there will make of it?' He tipped his head towards
the door. 'Well, since you're here you might as well
stay and help. It's in both our interests.'

'Ah, well. That's what we have to discuss, isn't it,
Mr Vyttery? Just like you'll have to discuss with the
gardeners how to avoid trampling all over that friend
of yours outside where the chapter-house used to be.

Now that's going to be a tricky one, isn't it, Mr Vyttery?'

Thomas stared at the smith, whose brawny arms were now folded implacably across his leather apron in as uncompromising a pose as one could devise. Thomas would not ask what the objectionable man meant, for it was plain that his extra help would require extra money. 'Forget it!' he snapped. 'I'll manage alone.'

'Ah, but you see, Mr Vyttery, it's not quite as simple as that, is it? I can't forget, can I? As you said, it's now in both our interests, and I don't think you're in a position to refuse my offer of help right now.' His face crumpled into a bland smile at the blatant animosity in the steward's eyes. 'You see, I might just have a word with Sir Leon, when he returns. Or I might even have a word with the gardener and tell him he needn't be too careful when…ah! No, you don't, old man. You'll have to put a bit o' weight on before you can tackle Ben Smith.'

Thomas's thin patience had broken. Without his usual caution, his assault upon the smith had reached only chest-height before his wrist was caught and held away in a painful sideways twist. 'Toad!' he yelped. 'Don't you *dare* speak of that to *anyone*, do you hear? No one!'

His wrist was released in a push that unbalanced him further. 'No one? Well then, you'd better co-operate, Mr Vyttery, or that superior you were so friendly with might get a little disturbed, and so might Sir Leon and Lord Deventer. Now you'd not like that, would you? Don't forget, old man, that I was digging these graves as a lad when you were Father Thomas, and I've seen what you and he used to get up to.'

'Money,' said Thomas, panting and holding his arm. 'I suppose you think your help's worth more now than it was at the beginning? You've changed your tune, Smith. You were glad at one time to accept whatever I could spare.'

'Ah, but things have hotted up, you see, with that flighty young filly having plans for this and that. Got Sir Leon round her little finger already. Things've changed, Mr Vyttery. I'll need twice as much now, sir.'

'For one damned boat trip a week? God in heaven, man!'

Smith was at Thomas's throat like a bull-mastiff, holding his black tunic in one great fist beneath Thomas's tangled white beard. 'Yes, Mr Bloody Vyttery! And just *you* try taking a boat up-river in the pitch dark and see how far you get. If I'd got caught you'd have denied anything to do with it, wouldn't you?' He shook the fistful of fabric. 'Eh? I'd have been on my own, yes? Yet I only have to tell Sir Leon where to look, don't I, and that would put you back to square one. Now, let's talk about a real reward.' On the penultimate word, he threw Thomas backward on to the cope-chest like a rag doll.

Righting himself, Thomas wiped away a trickle of blood from his bitten lip, his fright and anger allowing him barely enough breath to speak. 'Lock the door,'

he wheezed. 'I don't want that lot in here. Now, if
you'll just pass me that tool chest up there…?'

The smith obeyed, willingly.

The incident of Felice's visit to the Sisterne House
brought her nearer to a quarrel with her maid than she
had ever been before. It was not only that Lydia was
expected to know where her mistress was, but that
Felice had gone knowing that the outcome would not
be to her liking, that she had refused Lydia's company
and therefore her comfort and, worst of all, she had
then taken an irrevocable step that defied any attempts
at reason.

'Reason has nothing to do with it,' Felice said, de-
fiantly. 'I couldn't have held him off, even if I'd
wanted to.'

'And you didn't want to. Well, obviously what you
saw in Mistress Godden's room didn't shock you
enough to stop you having a go yourself, did it? Let's
just hope nothing comes of it, that's all.'

'Oh, Lydie, don't spoil it for me. It was the only
good thing that came out of the whole afternoon. He
knew it was what I needed.'

'What *he* needed,' Lydia muttered, tying the cord
at the end of Felice's plait with a vicious tug. 'It remains to be seen what his intentions are.'

There was nothing to be said to that, for it was a
subject Felice had not broached, fearing the same lack
of devotion Timon had demonstrated, and although
he had said that she would be his to the end, he had

not been too precise about the time span or her role within it.

'We were to have seen his house today,' Lydia said, shaking Felice's skirt with a loud crack. 'Adam came back like a drowned rat, and I was left not knowing how much to tell Lady West.'

'I'm sorry, Lydie. I should have shared it with you. I'm still confused.' Her voice tailed off into a whisper, heralding another weeping.

'Nay…love!'' Lydia relented, taking her mistress into her arms. 'Don't weep any more. We're back to Wheatley on Tuesday and we'll soon see how things turn out after that, eh? And you've seen more of him than you expected to, haven't you, one way or another?'

The tears turned to laughter at Lydia's forthright views, especially when she admitted to a slight case of sour grapes at the non-appearance of a convenient hay-filled barn and a thunderstorm.

But the following day, their last in Winchester, brought with it not only more torrential rain but an exhausted messenger from Wheatley who almost fell from his horse on to the cobbled courtyard of Sir Leon Gascelin's stables.

It was late afternoon, and Sir Leon had just returned from Cool Brook House. 'Will! What on earth do you do here, lad? Why…what is it?'

'Bad news, sir,' Will gasped, clutching at his lathered horse for support. 'Fire, sir. Last night at the guesthouse. Whole place went up.'

'Merciful saints, no! Fire? Anyone hurt?'

Will shook his head, searching for a way to begin. Suddenly, his face crumpled. 'Mr Aycombe, sir. Nobody can find him. They think…oh, God!'

'John Aycombe, *lost*? In the guesthouse at night?'

'Aye, sir. Mr Vyttery's fair demented, he is. Place is still smouldering. Most of the men were in the village, so they couldn't stop it spreading. Sparks flew across, sir, and caught the stable thatches and then the stables went up, and…'

'The horses? Any horses inside?'

'No, sir. They'd all been moved across to the Abbot's House stables, like you said. But some of the mason's lodges went up. It's a mess, sir. I came as fast as I could.' His face was still grimy and wet with sweat.

'We'll be away at first light in the morning. Take Will inside, you lads, and tend him.' He turned to his steward. 'Samuel, get a message to Cool Brook House, will you? Tell the ladies we must be away fast at dawn.' He shook his head in disbelief. 'John Aycombe. I can scarce take it in. But what was he doing there, for pity's sake? Most of my stuff was being moved out as I left.'

The first light on the following day revealed dark lakes of water in the lowest fields, the roadways more like rivers, the tracks deep with mud. Some of the wooden bridges had collapsed in the floodwaters and the fords were treacherous, but the group of riders had gone on ahead, leaving the packhorses and extra waggons to make their own pace, and although they cursed the appalling conditions, Felice and Lydia were determined not to lag behind.

Their leave-taking from Cool Brook House was genuinely affectionate, the ebullient Lady West being completely unruffled by her guest's short lapse of common sense which, she said kindly, was by no means a unique affliction. Furthermore, her observations concerning a certain relationship had proved to be as close to the truth as one could get, whatever differences the two had once had now being apparently resolved. She was glad to have been instrumental in their new accord, at which rather pompous announcement she and Lydia had winked at each other, knowingly.

Squalling rain dogged them on their uncomfortable journey, stinging their faces, soaking their legs and chilling their hands into numbness. Waggon-teams approaching from the opposite direction were not inclined to deviate, the riders being forced to make detours and new routes wherever the ground was easiest. But there was a certain joy in the discomfort, none the less, whenever Sir Leon's grey eyes caught hers, reminding her that she was now his more than ever she had been Timon's.

The damp clothes chafed on her new Spanish leather saddle, but predictably her comment was misinterpreted. 'Sore?' he said, his eyes twinkling mischievously. 'We should be able to find a cure for that, m'lady.'

It was late in the day when they reached Wheatley

and the wooded approach to the abbey where the rain had done just as much damage as it had to the rest of Hampshire. The wooden bridge beneath the chestnuts was now awash, and the horses had to be led, resisting and nervous, across the slippery planks towards a building-site blackened, wrecked, steaming and chaotic. Soaking men still wrestled with masonry, their faces resolute and unemotional, fire being a common enough hazard to every householder these days.

Grooms came running to lead the horses and to be first with the news. 'Haven't found the vicar yet, sir. They're still looking,' said one.

Another had more recent news. 'Smith's missing too, sir.'

'What?' said Sir Leon, dismounting. 'Ben Smith? What the devil was *he* doing in the guesthouse? What's been going on while I've been away?'

'No, sir. Not in the guesthouse. Drowned, they think. Boat's missing, too.'

'Since when?'

'His woman hasn't seen him since last night, but the river's too swollen for a search. We'll have to wait a day or two for it to go down, sir.'

'Where's Thomas?' Sir Leon snapped.

'At home, sir. He wanted to help search, but it's too dangerous for an old man like him, and he was taking too many risks. Too upset to know what he was doing, they said.'

'And Dame Celia?'

'With her brother at the manor, sir. All your things

were moved into the offices at the back of the New House...well, most of them, anyway. I think there was your table and a few odd bits still to go, but nothing important. Shall you and Mr Bystander be sleeping over there now, sir?' The lad glanced up at the rain-soaked ladies and their mud-spattered mounts.

'Mr Bystander and me'll not be sleeping at all until we've made a few arrangements, lad. Go and make some space in the stables and tell the head groom to come and see me. We shall have Lord Deventer down here in a day or two, if he responds to my message.'

'Yes, sir.' The lad took another appreciative glance at the two new horses, determined to be the one to care for them and wondering at the same time what the gifts betokened, considering her ladyship's hasty departure with Sir Leon's artist friend a week ago.

Chapter Nine

That evening left no time for reflections on relationships or understandings or even on the future, the needs of the men on the site taking paramount importance over everything else. The servants and workers were both numerous and capable, but relieved to have their surveyor once more in charge, more than filling the gap left by the missing clerk of works, John Aycombe. Felice had time only for a quick change into dry clothes and an even quicker bite to eat before she was over in the kitchens of the New House to see what was needed to produce enough food for them all, the kitchens at the guesthouse having been demolished. The place had been due for reconstruction, but not as drastically as this. No one seemed to know how it had happened.

As well as having dozens of exhausted men to feed and accommodate in every nook and cranny, there were wounds to dress, burned hands, black eyes, cuts and bruises and a broken collar-bone, mountains of

wet clothes to dry and clean ones to regenerate from
every available source. Most of the guesthouse's last
inmates had been slow to move out and had therefore
lost many of their possessions, but goodnaturedly settled into the outhouses and stable-lofts, granaries,
storerooms and even in the newly built kennels await-
ing Lord Deventer's hounds.

The kitchens of the Abbot's House worked over-
time that night, preparing food that the guesthouse
could not. Kitchen lads carried sacks, boxes and baskets over to the new kitchens that were being put into
service for the first time. Animal carcasses had to be
re-hung, extra bread to be made.

At one point, Sir Leon found Felice coming away
from the great larder where the meat waited to be
cooked, the ubiquitous list in one hand. 'You should
not be in here, lass,' he said to her, softly, steering
her away into the passageway. 'This is no place for
a lady. Besides, it's time you'd finished.'

'Yes, I know,' she said, wearily. 'This is the last
check. Where've you been?'

'Searching the ruins. We found him.' He brushed
a grimy hand across his forehead and leaned against
the whitewashed wall where a blazing torch lit his
tired face.

'You found him...oh!' Felice's hand went to her
mouth. 'Badly burned?'

'No, not at all. He'd fallen into one of the emptied
cavities beneath the stone stairs where we'd been
keeping some stoneware bottles. It's one of the few
places the fire didn't reach because there's nothing to

burn. There was rubble and collapsed beams all around him, but it looks rather as if he'd got lost in the smoke and hit his head on the lintel as he fell. He's got a massive bruise on his forehead, but I'm beginning to wonder if he didn't simply have a seizure and collapse. He'd been complaining of chest pains for some time.'

'Oh, poor man! But why was he there at that time of night? Was he working late?'

'That's how it looks, sweetheart. I can think of no other reason.'

. 'Finish now,' she pleaded. 'You can do no more tonight.'

He looked at her without smiling, passing a hand quickly over her breasts. 'Can I not, woman? Then you don't know me so well.' He pulled her to him, crushing her inside one arm and kissing her hungrily, almost desperately. 'Go to bed,' he said. 'I'll come to you as soon as I can.'

Resuming their vigilance of their mistress, the two hounds followed her lazily back to the Abbot's House and to the familiar bedchamber where Lydia and Elizabeth waited and repaired men's torn and singed clothing. The rain had stopped at last, but the night air was full of woodsmoke and the stench of burnt bedding and, in her own room, the many windows were steamed with warm damp garments that hung before the blazing fire. But her bed was warmed, and sleep came instantly.

Several hours later, she propped herself up against the pillows to watch Leon undress before the glowing fire. He stretched, gracefully, like a beautiful night creature whose skin bulged tautly over muscles, whose chest was deep, his limbs lithe and strong. And as he gradually became aware of her attention, he turned and stood to watch her, full-face and un-ashamed, showing himself for the first time. He came to her and sat on the bed, slowly peeling away the covers that she held up to her chin.

She was well used to nakedness and to her maids' reactions to it, but the scrutiny of such a man made her aware of every tingling surface even more than in the darkness; being able to see where his eyes ex-amined as well as his hands seemed to double the thrill of each impending caress.

His fingers drew her long plait to one side, indi-cating where his next interest would fall but not the breathtaking excitement of it and, as she watched his eyes, the sensation of his fingertips plotting the ripe fullness of each breast, drawing slowly towards the hardening peaks, tipped her head back as if by a magic thread. Her eyes closed as she reached out for him and smoothed her hands over his magnificent shoulders, allowing herself to be taken into his mouth, melting her body for his delight.

She moaned, half-drowning in desire, and was swung round sideways across the bed, craving for the nakedness of him along her length. She heard his soft laugh. 'So soon set aflame, my wildcat, as I knew you could be. I could keep your burning all night, couldn't I? Eh? Shall I tame you now?'

'Brute! I hate you!' she whispered. It was all she could say to sting him and to manage her fear of his unconcealed arrogance. Lydia's warning floated aimlessly through her mind, mildly chastising her for knowing his body before she knew his mind, but she gave it no foothold. Still suffering quietly from the blow to her pride, she knew that this was the only way to salve it, to put Timon in the shade and make him totally redundant. Yet using one lover as an antidote for another was a dangerous drug, especially when she now knew that she had herself been used as a remedy for another.

The time for teasing passed, and his loving took her into realms she could never have dreamed of where she truly believed that, at times, he was as moved by her performance as she was by his. She had no means of knowing whether his hunger was always great enough to take him on in a seemingly endless union that changed in pace but never flagged, or whether she was an exception for him. But in all other things, he had never seemed like the kind of man who would use superlatives so freely, just for the sake of kindness; on the contrary, she had discovered to her cost that his praises were usually so stinting as to be almost non-existent. Now, however, it was as if he was the one who would burn all night.

'Sleep, brute,' she whispered at last.

'Tired, sweetheart? Have I tired you out?' He reached across her for the ale cup and held it to her lips, cradling her head.

'I'm still new to it, despite what you seem to believe.'

He finished what was left in the beaker and replaced it, lying on top of her, lightly. 'And exactly what do I seem to believe?'

'Well, that I've had some experience, for a start.'

'Which you have.' He kissed her nose. 'But let me tell you something, woman. Your newness, as you call it, feels more like a natural aptitude to me. You have a freshness, it's true, a delicious wonderment that takes the art of making love to a different level, but you also have a fire that feeds a man's passion as quickly as he burns it. I knew it when I held you in the garden that night. I've known it ever since. It's there in the daytime and it flares almost out of control here in the night, and that's priceless, my beauty. You know how to take a man's soul, but you also know how to give. You're an amazingly gifted virgin, my sweet.' He smiled, touching her lips with his. 'New, experienced; demanding, giving; sweet and fierce. A rare mixture and I intend to keep it. I'd not have you tamed too far. Have I been too brutal with you?'

'Very,' she said, enjoying the chance to disturb him. 'Is it any wonder I tried to leave? I believe you're impossible to please.'

'Difficult, but not impossible.' He rolled off her and held her close to his side. 'But I don't throw praise about indiscriminately, otherwise it becomes worthless. When I give it, I mean it.' He yawned.

'You're making me sound like a permanent fixture, Sir Leon.' She caught his yawn and snuggled closer

to him. 'Is that what you intend? Do I become one
of your mistresses, the one kept at Wheatley, or is
there some other role for me? Perhaps you should tell
me before Lord Deventer himself asks me about it.
He is coming down here, didn't you say?'

But it was too late. The rhythmic sound of his
breathing told her that these were questions that
should have been asked earlier.

With so many questions of her own left unasked,
the prospect of having to supply Lord Deventer with
some answers was not something to which Felice
looked forward. It was far easier to prepare for his
physical comforts than to face an inquisition regarding her new and deepening relationship with his surveyor which, so far, had been the cause of nothing
but confusion. Fortunately the chance to put these
problems to one side came early the next day when
the waggons from Winchester arrived piled high with
the purchases for the New House, and as this was the
moment for which she had been waiting, she felt
obliged to be in at least four places at once as the
pieces were carried, assembled and manhandled. Then
at last the best bedchamber, several of the guest
chambers, the great hall, withdrawing room and par-
lour began to shrink with the addition of beds, chests,
tables and stools, hangings and all the paraphernalia
of living. There were the inevitable hitches, misunderstandings and arguments, but Sir Leon's previously critical manner was noticeably tempered by a
need to set the place to rights as soon as possible.

To Felice's question about when they should expect Lord Deventer, Sir Leon was bound to admit, 'I really don't know. He's sent no word ahead, but I've no doubt he'll be anxious to see the damage. Is his room ready now?'

'Yes, everything. Beds made up and fires lit.'

'Kitchens?'

'Yes, ovens and spits working, larders stocked.'

'You've worked miracles. And I've got a load of trout from the Paynefleetes' fishpond, so with two kitchens working and all the supplies from Winchester, we should be able to manage. Have you heard anything from Dame Audrey?'

'Yes. I went to call on her.'

She and Lydia had called early upon both Dame Audrey and Dame Celia, the newly widowed vicar's wife. At her brother's house, the widow was in the comforting arms of her family, shocked but calm. She had known of her husband's chest pains but could not think what he was doing at the guesthouse when she had believed him to be at the church.

The brief visit to Thomas Vyttery's small but well-appointed house was not half so reassuring. Dame Audrey had hurriedly bundled away the embroidery she had been working on a sizeable frame which she was strangely anxious Felice should not see, and all questions to Mr Vyttery had been fielded by her as if she was afraid he would say something of interest. Which Felice didn't think was very likely. It had been a tense but revealing visit.

There had been one moment, as Dame Audrey was

showing them out, when Felice detected a softening
in the anxious woman's attitude as if she would like
to have confided in her, but it passed with the usual
acid smile and an evasion of eye contact, and any
thought that Felice had had about speaking of their
daughter's tragic death was abandoned. Waste of
time, Lydia had said on their way back.

It was a time for abandoned discussions, apparently. The one Felice had been preparing to ask Sir
Leon about how much of their new relationship to
reveal to her stepfather was cut short by a cry from
the outer door. A servant, breathless and damp, could
hardly wait to reach his master. 'The boat, sir!
They've found the boat!' he yelled.

'How many times have you been told not to yell
across the hall, lad?' Sir Leon frowned. 'Whose boat?
Smith's? But no body?'

The man's excited voice dropped obediently. 'No
body yet, sir, just the boat. It was on the bottom,
weighted down with…'

'Shh! Not here, lad.' Sir Leon led the way outside
into the heavy overcast greyness of the late afternoon
where a crowd of men carried a dark boat across from
the river towards the ruined guesthouse. 'On the bottom, you say?'

'Yes, sir. Come and look. Two heavy sacks
smashed straight through the hull. That's what filled
it with water and took it down just below the mill
bridge.'

The two sacks had already been cut open by inquisitive fingers, their contents marvelled at and hur-

riedly replaced. Gold plate, jewel-studded chalices, censors, chains and rings, beakers of silver, salt-cellars as big as buckets, clasps, buckles and bowls, priceless gems from the monastic church that were supposed by now to have been in the London coffers of the Royal Treasury.

'Riddle solved,' he told Felice later. 'The boatman was Smith stealing treasure from the church vaults that somebody had taken good care to hide from the king's receivers when the abbey closed twenty years ago.'

'But someone was helping him,' she said. 'The man who passed us on the river-path on the night of the bonfire.'

He took her elbow and turned her to face him in the darkly panelled entrance to the Abbot's House, enfolding her waist with his arms. 'I'm rather surprised, my lady, that you can remember anything of what happened that evening. Personally I'm more inclined to remember what didn't happen because a certain person took it into her head to stalk off in a huff.'

'Did she so, sir? I wonder why. Perhaps it was because she felt herself to be playing second fiddle to a shadow. If so, who could blame her?'

'Second fiddle, lady? Is that what needled her, then?'

She could have told him, before his mouth stopped her, that any woman so unsure of a man would be unnerved by his slightest lack of attention, especially when every other condition was tailor-made to suit his purpose. But as his embrace bent her into the strong curve of his body, the searchingly tender warmth of his kisses banished those lingering doubts, reminding her only of the hunger she had felt then, of the decision to give herself without reserve, if he had asked it. Fiercely, avidly, and trembling with a sudden surge of love for him, she slid a hand around his bare neck and into his hair that felt damp and warm, seeking even more sensations to add to her store whilst being aware that this was not to be hers for long. Like Timon, he would go. Like Timon, he had never been hers from the start.

'Tonight,' he whispered. 'I'll come to you tonight. Wait for me, this time. No more playing second fiddle to shadows, eh?'

Even without Lord Deventer's imminent arrival, there would still have been much to do to restore order to the chaos that followed the fire, for now her carefully laid plans for the rooms, particularly those on the ground floor, had had to be revised, and the New House, which had once appeared vast and spacious, had suddenly become cramped with men and their belongings. She had worked tirelessly all day, but was still finding shortcomings which Lord Deventer would surely mention, if she did not. Reluctantly, she had to admit that, but for him, she would probably not have been so fastidious. Then she allowed herself to be lulled into a sense of false security by the lateness of the hour and, instead of going to change out of her housewifely grimy clothes, she loosed her hair and took a last stroll into the orchard to check that the beehives had been closed for the night.

It was here, beneath the low leafy boughs of the apple and damson trees, that she was found by young Elizabeth who, overcome by her excitement, quite forgot to tell her why she was being sought. 'Suppertime, I think,' said the scatty girl, giggling. 'Oh, no…wait, it's not that, is it? Oh, yes,' she giggled again, reminded by someone's warm knuckle recently caressing her cheek, 'My lord says he's hungry and to hurry.'

'My *lord*?' said Felice. 'Are you telling me… oh…good grief!'

With loose hair flying and a new tear in her gown from the old wicket gate, Felice sped out of the orchard, across the stable yard and round the front of the Abbot's House where she was instantly caught up in the tail-end of Lord Deventer's retinue of men, packhorses, waggons and, rising above it all, the leather-covered roof of a coach.

'My mother?' she said to Elizabeth. 'You didn't say my mother was here. Now what on earth possessed him to bring her all this way?' The words dried on her lips as the carriage moved away, leaving its occupant to walk with Sir Leon arm-in-arm up the front steps of the New House. Even from this distance, Felice noticed the woman's swaying voluptuousness inside the long pointed bodice and extravagantly wide farthingale that almost swamped Sir Leon's legs with shimmering folds of silk.

'What a ridiculous gown for travelling in,' Felice snapped.

'I thought it was rather…' Elizabeth began but, seeing her mistress's face, thought better of it. 'Who is she?'

'Lord Deventer's niece,' came the terse reply. 'Levina.'

'What a pretty name.' Fortunately for Elizabeth, her eyes were too fully occupied with the woman's glamorous and totally impractical costume to notice Felice's murderous look.

It was not something Felice had feared because she had never for one moment expected it. Not here, of all places. He would have disappeared to London, eventually. That woman would have reappeared at Sonning, but not here at Wheatley, to claim her property so soon.

In a haze of anger and jealousy, she heard her name being called and, turning to search the crowd, came face to face with Marcus Donne who, in spite of being usually so observant, failed to recognise any of the signs that a woman would know as uncompromising dïslike of a rival.

'My lady,' he called, holding out two hands to take hers. 'You could not do without me, could you? Tell me you need me, or I'll die.' His laughing face begged for some witty reply and forced her to relent.

'Marcus Donne,' she said, smiling. 'There is no one in the world I would rather see at this time. Truly. But why have you come? Not merely to see the damage, I hope?'

The truth, had he been able to part with it, was that after only three days of Levina's visit to her uncle's house at Sonning, he was not willing to be left behind while she chased off to Wheatley to see Leon at the first opportunity. If she and Leon saw fit to resume their inconstant friendship, then he would resume his with the ward. Not to *see* the damage, but to do some.

'To see you, my lady,' he said, making her blush with his bold eyes that made no secret study of her loosened hair and dishevelled appearance. 'You should have sat for me like that. 'Twould have been my best ever.'

'I must go in, Marcus. Loose my hands, if you please. Will you come with me? It should be interesting finding rooms for everybody.'

It proved to be more impossible than interesting, it having escaped Lord Deventer's comprehension that a disaster and an unready house was hardly the place to bring an extended retinue of guests and their servants, especially a guest as elaborate as his niece.

Her strident voice had already reached the highnotes of demand by the time Felice and Marcus entered the great hall, her silver-grey spangled silk gown almost eclipsing Lord Deventer's orange-red legs and puffed breeches. 'Lord, how cold it is in here! Bring my bags, man! And find a chamber for me at the front of the house overlooking the lake.'

'It's a river, Levina,' Sir Leon told her. 'And we've put Lord Deventer at the front of the house, I believe.'

'Then change it, Leon dear. He won't mind, will you, dearest uncle?'

Dearest uncle spied Felice, and though he held her glance with little obvious approval, he preferred to reply to his niece before greeting his stepdaughter. 'Of course I don't mind. Give her what she needs… ah, here's the one we need to show us to our rooms. Do we have hot water, Felice?'

If that was to be her only greeting, Felice was willing to accept it, but Sir Leon was not. 'My lady,' he said, drawing her forward, 'will you act as hostess to our guests? You ladies know each other, I believe?'

Regardless of protocol, it was Levina's extra four years that motivated her to assume an instant superiority over a titled lady. 'Yes, we met once, didn't we, though I cannot remember much about you.' Her open stare was conspicuously cold. 'Have we caught you in the middle of your toilette?' she asked with undisguised sarcasm, glancing sideways at her uncle for approval of the jibe.

'Good day to you, Mistress Deventer.' Felice inclined her head and then, turning to her uncle, curtsied dutifully with a natural grace that put her distant relative's sneers to shame. 'You are welcome, my lord. And, yes, we have hot water and fires ready for you upstairs.' As she spoke, she reached up to gather her long dark hair into her hands, twist it quickly and hold the heavy coil up onto the crown of her head from where silken wisps drifted downwards into the curve of her long neck.

She heard Marcus suck in his breath behind her and felt the stares of everyone nearby, including her stepfather, but it was to Levina she spoke again. 'There now. Toilette completed. I'll get my maid to find you a chamber, mistress, while I show my stepfather to his.' Keeping her hair up with one hand, she brushed past the hugely puffed shoulder of her ill-mannered guest, called her two deerhounds to heel and led the way up the wide staircase to the accompaniment of silent admiration.

It was an ordeal she could never have repeated. Even so, it had an effect upon her stepfather she could not have foreseen, softening his abrupt manner and, she suspected, causing him to see her in a somewhat different light.

'Change rooms by all means, if you wish, my lord,' she said, dropping her hair. 'As you know, some are large, some not so large, but this is the one you and my mother will eventually occupy. Do you have a message from her to me?'

'Ahem! Er…yes, indeed.' He spoke too loudly, still astounded by the stranger he thought he knew. 'Yes, she's well. Sends her…er…love. Right, this'll do nicely, I thank thee. Looks better now with a few bits of…oh, where's *that* bed come from?'

'Winchester, my lord. It cost you twenty pounds. Curtains and bed linen and extra…'

'Yes, right! It'll do well enough. Do we get any supper?'

His boorishness never ceased to make her wonder. 'Supper has been waiting this last half-hour, my lord. We shall have it served as soon as you are ready for it.' She glanced at his state of unreadiness and judged it might take another two minutes, by his standards.

He would once have been handsome, she thought, in a heavily flamboyant way, but was now even more coarsened by an over-indulgence of every appetite, from what she knew of him. His hair was thick and almost white, making him appear taller than his impressive six feet, his eyes heavy-lidded and wrinkled and cleverly concealed from view. With a large family to tend, it was obvious why her mother found him attractive.

'Good,' he said. 'And where's young Donne going to lay his head?'

Having given the matter no thought, she opened the doors that led off the great bedchamber, showing Lord Deventer's servants where they could sleep and keep their master's belongings, noting with some relief how her two hounds kept close to her heels and refused any offers of friendship. The matter of Marcus Donne's head would easily be resolved, one way or another.

Recovering her equanimity was no new thing for Mistress Deventer and soon her voice was heard carrying across the first floor. Failing the room at the front, she would have one near Sir Leon's. Obligingly, Felice replied, 'Certainly, mistress, if that's what you prefer. He's downstairs near all the men. The rooms are minute, but you'll have constant company, and you'll be able to check each of them in at night and out again at dawn. This way,' she called, merrily, knowing that the yapping woman would not be following.

She had brought an army of servants, three maids

(one for her hair alone) and enough baggage for a
year. Felice's main concern was where to accommodate them all, even in such a large house, for until
the extra beds came from Sonning there would be less
than enough. For a moment or two, she and Lydia
watched the hysterics, unable to decide whether it was
put on for their benefit or whether the woman was
truly overwrought. They were fascinated by her costly
furs and jewels, her neck ruffs, shoes, paddings and
wirings.

'Probably collapse when all that's removed,' whispered Lydia rudely, closing the door on the scene.
'Did you see the bum-roll? Fancy having to wear that
thing tied round her waist like a monstrous sausage.'

They had been fascinated also by Mistress Deventer's striking attractiveness and her obvious skill with
cosmetics that reddened her cheeks and lips and ac-
centuated her arched brows with an unnatural black
that looked odd, they thought, with her fair hair. In
what they presumed was the latest fashion, Levina's
blonde tresses were drawn back off her face and
rolled over a heart-shaped pad, its point on her forehead, the rest of it covered by a jewelled cap which
included several waving feathers. But it was the dress
itself that had made them stare, being a bell-shaped
contraption of Lady West's dimensions and sump-
tuous combination of bright reds and golds enriched
with embroidery, braids, jewels and frills at neck and
wrist, balloons of padding on each shoulder and a
tightness as far as the elbow.

'Just as well Sir Leon designed wide doors,' Lydia

muttered, following her mistress down the stairs. 'She'd never get into the Abbot's House.'

'It seems to keep the men on their toes,' Felice remarked drily, thinking of Sir Leon's undisguised pleasure at her appearance, 'but he'll not find me competing on those terms. Popinjay!' she growled.

Lydia smiled. She had seen the men's looks at Felice's artlessness just now and, in her experience, the competition was already won.

After that disconcerting introduction, it was not to be expected that the two Deventers would even notice what was being presented at supper or the impeccable service at the table by newly liveried servants, the new linen napery, the silver plate and matching spoons and knives, all unpacked that day. The new kitchen yielded a feast which the superb Levina picked at distastefully and her ravenous uncle wolfed down without even tasting: trout and pike with oranges in their mouths, loins of beef, mutton and veal, capons and conies, new-baked bread, young lettuces and radishes, apple fritters, clotted cream and six different sauces.

'I'd have liked a marchpane,' Levina said, loudly, as the last dishes were removed. 'Her Majesty's confectioners...'

Sir Leon interrupted the comparison. 'We had a major disaster here only a day ago,' he said, 'and this is the first meal from our new kitchen. Lady Felice and I returned from Winchester only twenty-four hours ago, mistress.'

* * *

Far from being grateful for this intervention, Felice was on the defensive from the start. 'I don't need you to make excuses for me,' she said, attempting to out-pace her guardian along the cloister walkway at the back of the New House. Having done her duty, she was attempting a quick exit to her own abode when Sir Leon caught up with her.

'It was not an excuse,' he said, catching her arm. 'And look where you're going or you'll fall over those slabs of stone. Listen to me!'

'I don't want to listen to you.'

He held her back against the wall, making a cage of his arms. 'Listen! I was not making excuses. It was an amazing meal, considering how—'

'There! There you are! *Considering!* It was an amazing meal by anybody's standards, including hers. Perhaps you think she could do better.'

'What is it, lass? I can see you don't much care for each other, but you've only met her once before. She's harmless enough. Plenty of show, I grant, but that's only a cover. Don't take it all so seriously, sweetheart.'

'That you and she have been lovers for years? Is *that* something I'm not supposed to take too seri-ously? That she wants a room near yours? That, too? That she's spent all evening ogling you, her uncle and Marcus in turns? Truly, I don't know whether that's serious or ridiculous. What say you?'

He sighed. 'What I say is this, if you'll hear me. She and I had a brief affair two years ago, and since then I've seen very little of her except in public. Deventer has always believed I should make an offer for her, and I suppose that's why he took the chance to bring her down here with him.' He would have continued, but Felice was in no mood to hear the rest.

'Well, then, don't waste another moment here with me, Sir Leon. You've explained to me already how you have to please my stepfather. He pays you, you reminded me once. And I have some old wounds to lick, remember? Now, let me pass. I'm tired.' She pushed against his arm, freeing herself and leaping away into the darkness towards the arch where, on the stable block, a torch burned and waved crazily in the gusting wind.

Having previously schooled herself to say nothing of that to him, to refuse any kind of competition with the outrageous Levina and, most of all, to refrain from any mention of her own recent wounds, she stood for some time in the darkness shaking with vexation at her own stupidity and lack of control. If anything could be guaranteed to send him into Levina's company more quickly, it was her revelation of jealousy. And after that, how could she expect that he would come to her that night, as he had said he would?

His excuse, if one could call it that, was that Lord Deventer had wanted to talk with him and had kept him up until the early hours of the morning. It was perfectly reasonable, Lydia told her, but Felice was not open to reason and preferred to torture herself with other explanations. Coolly polite, she had thanked him for coming to tell her, making it impos-

sible for him to share an intimate caress in front of
the servants who had brought her breakfast up from
the kitchen, a bowl of porridge and a beaker of weak
ale.

Her next visitor of the morning was Marcus, who
sat beside her on the chest and scooped a fingerful of
her porridge into his mouth, his stillness suiting her
mood.

'Sleep well?' she asked, moving her bowl towards
him.

'No,' he whispered. 'Four men snoring in the same
room, all in different keys and not one of them could
keep time.'

Felice's guffaw was most unladylike. 'Oh, dear,
Marcus,' she said, licking splutters of porridge off her
hands, 'I'm sorry. I was so busy with the other two
that you were left to fend for yourself. Do forgive me.
I'll find a better place for you, I promise.'

'Last time I was here, you offered me the big chamber up there...' he pointed to the plaster ceiling
'...where I was painting your portrait. Is that offer
still open?'

On the face of it, there was no reason why it should
not be, yet there had been developments since then
which he clearly knew nothing of and which were in
a state of flux that she could not predict one way or
the other. But it was not so very unusual for people
to sleep wherever there was a space, and she had already offered it to him once. Why not again?

'Of course,' she said. 'I can't think why I didn't

offer it to you yesterday. I'd rather you used it than anyone else.'

'Thank you, m'lady.' He kissed her cheek and took another fingerful of her breakfast. 'I'll move my things across later on. My lad can stay too, I take it?'

'Does he snore out of key?' she said in mock severity.

'Soundless. I'd not employ him otherwise, believe me. And while I'm here I could finish off your portrait. I expect Leon and the amazing Levina will want time to themselves, so why don't we do the same? Would you like that? Lady Honoria was pleased with hers, I believe.'

'Yes, so you said. I'm glad. He still admires her, then?'

'Who, Leon? Well, if his attentions last night were anything to go by I'd say they'll be resuming negotiations almost immediately.' He laughed at his witticism. 'But let them get on with it. She's a determined lady, that one. Hey, have you finished with this already?'

Felice nodded, feeling her stomach revolt at the thoughts.

'Then you don't mind if I finish it up for you?'

After he'd gone to collect his belongings, she sat for a long time pondering over what Marcus had implied, not only regarding the resumption of the old love affair but also that neither he nor the other guests had been made aware of the new relationship between herself and Sir Leon, neither by hint, gesture or declaration. What was she to read into this but that he intended to keep it secret, that it was not intended to last? Like Timon.

Chapter Ten

At any other time, Felice would have seen it as essential that Sir Leon should spend most of his time with his employer, on the site, and in discussion with the master craftsmen who were not being paid to stand around idly. Whatever time was left over, he would be expected to pay some attention to his guests. But being unsure of herself as well as him, in fact being unsure of everything, Felice felt unable to see things without a strong bias, consequently overplaying her hand and making matters worse at the same time. Every look, word or smile in Levina's direction was noted; every advance in her own direction was received as coolly as before their visit to Winchester, and Sir Leon was given no opportunity to put matters to rights. His anger at Marcus's new lodging added yet more fuel to her resentment.

'What the hell d'ye think you're doing, woman,' he snapped at her later that day, 'inviting him to sleep up there? Give him half a wink and he'll be down those stairs and into your bed. Is that what you want?'

'What does it matter to you, sir, who I have in my bed? I don't care a damn who you have in yours.'

'What's that supposed to mean?'

'Think about it, Sir Leon. Your room is as close to Mistress Deventer's as mine is to Mr Donne's, so presumably you have only to give *her* half a wink and she'll be—'

'Felice…stop it! This is ridiculous. Come *back* here!'

Her efforts to escape were this time halted by Lord Deventer, who had lagged behind his surveyor to speak to the master plasterer. With a mixture of curiosity and amusement, he caught Sir Leon's words and the defiant expression on his stepdaughter's beautiful but angry face.

'Now then, lad.' He laughed. 'You told me it was working out quite well, this new guardianship. Is this a good day for it, or a bad one? Perhaps it's not suiting you as well as I believed, young lady.'

'I don't know what you were led to believe, my lord, but I was never asked for my approval of the arrangement, nor have I ever accepted it.' Boldly, she gave back stare for stare, ignoring the warning in Sir Leon's eyes. 'Sir Leon seems to believe he can order my life, but he's mistaken. I'm perfectly able to choose a guardian of my own whose interests are less complex than his.'

'Complex?' Lord Deventer bellowed. 'Doesn't sound all that complex to me. Well, never mind that now; we've more important things to settle, like clearing this mess up before her ladyship comes down.

Ye've still plenty to do in the New House, lass. It's coming together, but it'll take a while yet.'

'Thank you, my lord,' Felice said with acid sweetness. 'Your praise is as unstinting as ever, like your appreciation.' She marched off calling sharply to Fen and Flint whose loyalties were, as usual, divided.

'Unstinting?' Lord Deventer said. 'Is that good? Never did understand the lass's high-falutin' words.'

'I'm not sure that I do either, sir,' said Sir Leon, watching her go.

Levina Deventer did not appear on either of the two following days until after a light dinner in her room at midday, after which she had no difficulty in commanding Sir Leon's and Lord Deventer's attentions without even setting foot out of the New House into the messy realms of workmen. To this predictable pattern of behaviour Felice could only ascribe one thing, giving herself every reason, or so she thought, to make her appearance there at mealtimes and then to disappear on her own business.

Sir Leon had not thought fit to visit the Abbot's House on any pretext at night, and on the one daytime occasion had found her sitting for the limner in his large sunlit room upstairs. He had not stayed long, and Felice had had to strain every muscle to avoid running after him to beg him to take her in his arms.

Suppertime was a formal meal taken together in the large hall for convenience, where all the workers gathered and where the glorious Levina could entertain the whole company simply by her airs and graces.

Her loudly caustic remarks, usually at someone's expense, and her dazzling clothes were like the moon to a swarm of moths beside which Felice's quieter hues could not compete. Good manners and graciousness being the duty of every hostess, she began to wonder if perhaps the roles were being reversed when Mistress Deventer issued orders to the servers to remove some of the dishes and bring in others, to tell the musicians to play more softly so that she could hear herself speak. Felice would have stayed on, as etiquette demanded, but this time she doubted whether anyone, except perhaps Marcus, would notice her absence. The atrocious Levina's domination of the scene was getting out of hand.

She slipped away into the kitchen passage and out through the back door into the cloister, stumbling over slabs in the wrong direction and eventually coming to the door leading into the church. Dim lights burned here and there as she closed the door quietly and made her way towards them, fighting the pain in her breast. She stopped to listen, not sure whether what she heard was the wind or voices, but a fine line of light appeared under the heavily studded door on her right, the door to the sacristy and, knowing no reason why anyone should be there at that time of night, turned the iron ring to lift the latch. Silently, the door opened, the flickering light of a single candle illuminating the pale and horrified faces of Thomas Vyttery and his wife Dame Audrey.

Their combined stares compelled her to take in the scene and comment on it, to put them out of their misery. The small room had recently been cleared of its contents, ready for demolition, but the one remaining item was the cope-chest, far too large to remove until the wall was knocked down. Shaped like a quarter-circle, it stood massively on several small feet, its iron-bound lid being used as a table for its previous contents, a mountain of embroidered and jewelled vestments worn by the old abbots of Wheatley Abbey, their colours glowing richly, winking with jewels and gold thread, priceless on the continent where Roman Catholicism was allowed.

The steady glare of Thomas Vyttery's animosity was more potent this time than it had been at their first meeting when even his mastiff had deserted him, but now the candlelight showed up something she had not seen before, a terrible sadness in the pale watery stare. Beads of perspiration stood out on his brow and his hands listlessly tidied papers that had been set out before them. 'Come inside, my lady,' he said, tiredly. 'You followed us, I suppose?'

'You supposed wrongly, Mr Vyttery. There is no reason why I should follow you, but now I'm here you may find it more convenient to tell me what you're doing with vestments that should by now be in the king's treasury. I'm bound to reach the wrong conclusions otherwise. Is there a stool for me, Dame Audrey?'

The steward's wife had avoided Felice's eyes, so far, but now blinked in surprise at the request. 'Yes, of course.' She placed the stool at Felice's feet, sliding away a pile of velvet and silk stoles and a jewelled mitre thick with gold thread, as if to keep it out of her reach.

But Felice could not resist touching it. 'The gold alone must be worth hundreds of pounds,' she said. 'There must be a good reason why you've chosen to—'

'There was no *choice*, my lady,' the steward almost spat through his beard. 'There *was* no choice!' His hands shook over the papers and Dame Audrey looked away, acutely embarrassed by her husband's sudden outburst.

'Please, Thomas!' she whispered. 'Don't!'

He turned to her, snarling. 'I have to, woman! Can you not see that she knows? I expect she knew it all before she came. She looked as if she did.'

'Know what, Mr Vyttery? I wish you would tell me so that I can understand. You're a man of God, so you can hardly have been breaking the law with a light heart all these years, I'm sure. Nor your wife.'

'My *wife*!' The words came out with a venom that stopped Felice's breath and made her glance at the poor woman who stood opposite.

Dame Audrey had turned white, her eyes round with horror. 'Don't say any more, Thomas, I beg you,' she said, forgetting her previous mincing accents.

'Well, you tell her, then,' Thomas snapped. 'She's come here to find out, so she may as well have the whole story. Tell her, woman, and be damned to the lot of 'em. He's gone now, so it's hardly going to damage his reputation, is it?'

'I don't know how to start,' Dame Audrey whispered.

'Start at the beginning. Go on, tell her every sordid detail. Let's see if she'll understand as much as she thinks she will.'

'Was it blackmail? Tell me, Dame Audrey,' said Felice.

The poor lady shook her head, her face transparent against the creamy-white linen of her coif. 'You knew I'd been a novice at Romsey Abbey, my lady?'

'Yes, Dame Celia told me that.'

'See?' Thomas muttered.

'And you knew that...'

'Oh, for pity's sake!' Thomas's interruption startled them both as he turned to face them. 'From the beginning, Audrey, not halfway: the beginning is with Abbot John Aycombe, isn't it?'

'Perhaps you should tell me, Mr Vyttery,' said Felice, laying her fingertips upon his sleeve.

He looked down at them and began quietly to talk. 'When the old abbot died, m'lady, John Aycombe and myself were the next choice, but he was the old abbot's favourite. Always genial, John was, and mightily ambitious. John was elected by a whisker, though by that time we all knew that the end was in sight for the abbeys. We also knew that whoever was abbot at the time would be sent off with a good pension and enough perquisites to keep him comfortable, once he was out in the world, and that the rest of us would have to fend for ourselves any way we could.

'John made me sacristan, but he could have done

much more, m'lady. He chose not to. But then he suddenly needed my help.'

'Thomas…no!'

'We're telling her everything,' he said to his wife. 'Clever John Aycombe, Abbot of Wheatley, got a young novice from Romsey Abbey in the family way. A bright, vivacious sixteen-year-old called Audrey Wintershulle. No, it was not *me*, my lady,' he said, taking in Felice's shocked expression, 'it was John Aycombe who fathered a child on Audrey. I don't blame her. I never have done. I blame him. He knew full well what he was doing and he knew how to wriggle out of it, too.'

'Merciful heavens!' Felice said. 'Why did he not accept responsibility?'

'Because,' Thomas continued, 'by that time he'd made his plans for the inevitable retirement, even though he was only young. Audrey's parents refused to take her back once they discovered she was pregnant so she had no dowry and no home, and that was no good for John Aycombe because by that time he'd set his sights on Celia Paynefleete, who was fifteen at the time, a pupil with the nuns at Romsey. Well-connected, wealthy, friends of the former abbot and a much better catch than a Wintershulle.'

'Oh, my dear,' Felice said. 'I'm so very sorry. I'd no idea it was like that. What happened to you?'

'Celia's family took me in,' Dame Audrey said, looking down at her hands, 'but John never told Celia that he was the father of my child, and to this day she still doesn't know. He wanted nothing to do with me,' she said. 'I had nothing to offer him.'

'A child?'

'He didn't want that. It would have done his reputation no good.'

Thomas Vyttery continued the story. 'Well, whether for good or evil, Sir Paul Paynefleete, Celia's father, discovered John's misconduct at Romsey, and although Celia persuaded her father to let her marry John, he withheld his permission until a father had been found for the child Audrey was expecting. He didn't want any scandal rubbing off on to his family, you see. So John had to find somebody to marry his...'

'Thomas!'

'Yes, well. Anyway, he came to me with the proposal. Me, of all people. He didn't mind *my* reputation being tarnished.'

'But you agreed, out of charity,' Felice suggested.

'Out of greed. And necessity. Because I didn't know how I was going to live otherwise. He got me the job of chantry-priest here at the church, which paid very little, but he'd got himself the position as Paynefleete's chaplain *and* vicar, a wealthy patron, a future wife and dowry, and a pension from the crown. Not bad, eh? He offered me, if I would help him out, the treasure from the church and the abbey that we'd hidden from the king's receivers. Oh, we let them have some of the stuff, enough to keep them quiet, but we were a very wealthy abbey and only I knew what we had down there—' he pointed to the floor

'—in the vault and in that great cope-chest. He told me I could have access to all of it if I'd marry Audrey and foster their child as my own. And I agreed.

'Celia's father let us have our cottage rent-free, and Audrey had Frances there. And John Aycombe never once recognised her as his, even though he baptised her.'

Dame Audrey dabbed at her eyes, recalling the pain. 'You're shocked, my lady. Men can do this kind of thing, you see. Even the best of them.'

'*Best* of them?' snarled Thomas. 'John Aycombe's best was all show. You should know that better than anyone.'

'I think Dame Audrey meant it in a social context, sir,' Felice said gently. 'He always struck me as being totally upright. But I thought nuns were not allowed to marry for many years after the abbeys were closed.'

'There was a lot of confusion,' said Dame Audrey. 'I was only a novice, so no one could argue that I'd gone beyond the first stage of acceptance. And at that time I cared little about what happened to me, so I accepted the arrangements in return for a roof over my head. What choice did I have? But Thomas has had the worst of it by far. He made a home for me and my child. He's suffered torments over the years over this…' she indicated the piles of costly fabrics '…though he was not depriving anyone except the king's treasury. He was a young man with all of life ahead of him, yet he took me in my condition with never a word of reproach. Neither Celia nor her

brother know the truth of it; they believe John Aycombe to have been a saint, and so does everyone
else. But I've seen what he's done to my Thomas.'

From the corner of her eye, Felice saw that Thomas
was looking intently at his wife with an unusual kindliness, placing a gnarled hand tenderly over hers. 'She
looked a lot like you, our Frances, m'lady,' he said.
'Dark-haired, slender. A lovely lass, she was.'

Until that moment, Felice had been congratulating
herself on her composure but, at this, her self-
possession began to disintegrate.

Thomas Vyttery, introspective and bitter, did not
notice. 'I expect you've pieced together what happened there,' he said. 'It was John Aycombe who recommended a certain young chaplain to the Paynefleetes who then betrayed our daughter just as *he*'d
betrayed Audrey all those years before. And by that
means, my lady, we lost our finest treasure.' When
no reply came from Felice, he turned to look and saw
the tears streaming down her face. 'Nay, lass, Don't
be upset. Too late for weeping now. It's done, and
John Aycombe's gone.'

'The fire?' Felice whispered.

'Nothing to do with me,' Thomas said. 'I'd not
have wished that on any man, not even him. Now we
have to clear out of here because they're about to
knock this place down and we have to get this lot
away somehow.'

'How do you usually do it, Mr Vyttery?'

'Oh, you may as well know. There's a vault under
here full of church treasure still. Ben Smith used to

take sackfuls of it along an underground passageway to a cellar in the Abbot's House, and from there down the river to my cottage.'

'I see. And that's going to be difficult now he's… er, gone.'

'Impossible. I can't carry it, nor can Audrey. We were just checking through to see what we ought not to leave behind, but that's academic now, I suppose. You'll be telling Sir Leon and Lord Deventer, of course.'

'No, Mr Vyttery, I shall be telling no one.' Felice stood, wiping her tears with the back of her hand. 'It's no business of mine what you do with it; the secret is as safe with me as it has been with you, and that applies to what you told me about your lovely Frances. I know how you must grieve.'

'No one can know that, m'lady. By now we might have had not only a daughter but a grandchild, too, but for that man.'

And by now, I might also have been where she is.

The terrible thought reeled through her mind as she passed once more into the cool cloister and into the waiting arms of Marcus Donne who held her, racked with sobbing and unable to tell him what the matter was.

'You've been to the church…yes…I know. I waited for you. Did it not help? There…don't cry. Come, I'll take you home. Lean on me, Felice.'

She could not tell him that her fears were as much for what might yet happen as for what had already happened, that she had been a fool, that she loved a man who could never be hers.

His comfort was brotherly and gentle, his arms by no means threatening and his curiosity well controlled. He assumed, as anyone would, that the affairs of the past weeks were catching up with her, and what woman wouldn't be overwrought with Leon throwing his weight around, and now her stepfather? Quietly, he rocked her as they sat before a low fire while Mistress Lydia wondered whether she was being cynical in seeing this as the next step in the limner's cautious seduction.

Sleep came near dawn but did not stay, and Felice roused Lydia and Elizabeth to dress her and to begin their duties earlier than usual. In the New House, most of the men had drifted out on to the site, and so her hopes of catching sight of Sir Leon came to nothing as she greeted the servants, checked lists with Mr Peale and Mr Dawson, and showed her presence.

Upstairs, all was quiet except for the squeak of a new floorboard and a muffled sneeze from Lord Deventer's chamber but then, as Felice entered the small darkened closet where clean linen was kept, she heard an unmistakable sound coming from the opposite door that led into Levina's chamber. She froze, straining her ears to be sure, asking herself what the woman could have eaten to cause such a violent reaction. It came again, followed by a moan, then a voice and more retching. Morning sickness. Was it her, Levina, or one of her maids?

She tapped on the door merely as a formality and, as soon as a gap appeared, held it with one hand. 'Let me come in!' she said decisively, moving forward. No one looked up as she entered, least of all the heaving woman who knelt at a stool with her head in a basin, her blonde hair tied in a damp bundle that straggled down and stuck to her cheeks. Two young maids stood helplessly by, their expressions blankly unsympathetic. The room was in a state of chaos.

'Clear this room up,' Felice snapped at them, whipping them into action with her eyes. 'And open that window.' Quickly, she bent to Levina and eased her shoulders back, away from the stinking basin. 'Come, mistress. That's probably enough now, isn't it? Come…into bed.'

Directing the maids to remove the bowl and clean it, she half-carried the fainting woman to the bed and tucked her up warmly, tidied her hair and wiped her white perspiring face. Then she shooed the maids into the anteroom and chastised them soundly, sending one for a warm posset from the kitchen and the other for a brick from the oven to warm her mistress's feet. 'Two minutes!' she said, sharply. 'Or you lose your jobs.'

Looking at Levina's pallor, Felice could now understand the need for the heavy cosmetics, the late appearance each day, the loss of appetite. She sat down on the bed as the patient's eyes opened, this time showing wariness rather than animosity but reading Felice's concern and responding to it with a wan smile. 'Serves me right,' she whispered.

'Pregnant?'

'Yes. I've missed three of my courses. I'll not be able to hide it much longer.'

'Then why come all this way? The journey's so rough.'

'How innocent you are. That's one way of getting rid of it. And anyway, I had to see Leon.'

Felice held her breath, not wanting to hear but unable to stop herself from asking the dreaded question. 'He's the baby's father?'

The pale lips compressed, and Levina turned her head away. 'No, he's not,' she whispered. 'It would have been easier if he had been, but I can't make the dates fit when they obviously don't. We haven't been lovers for years. Friends, but not lovers. I don't even know who the father is.'

'So you wanted to ask Sir Leon's advice, is that it?'

Levina turned to look fully at Felice, showing her a ghost of the showy, noisy, ill-mannered harridan who had done her best to turn Felice's life upside-down over the last few days, demanding and criticising, trading on her own longer friendship with Sir Leon and on Lord Deventer's lusty approval. And even now she was willing to continue taking. 'No,' she said. 'I don't need anyone's advice. It's a husband I need. Leon will help me out.'

Staring, accepting the implications at a snail's pace, Felice shook her head in an attempt to clear it. 'You mean, you're going to ask Sir Leon...?'

'To marry me. Yes. He will. We've always helped

each other out, one way or another. I haven't mentioned it to him yet. Uncle Philip's been with him most of the time. In fact, it was Uncle Philip who suggested the idea.'

'My stepfather knows, then?'

'Oh, yes. He always warned me that this could happen but…well, you know how it is. Wise after the event, eh?' Her smile was watery but far from self-pitying, and apparently she expected Felice to understand not only how easy it was to become pregnant but how easy to find a solution to the problem. Her cold-blooded audacity was almost unbelievable.

'Wouldn't you rather find out who the father is?'

Levina shook her head. 'Needle in a haystack,' she said. 'Besides, I'd rather not marry any of them. Leon will be far more reliable as a husband.'

'You love him, then?'

'Hah! Love? What's that got to do with anything? No, Felice, of course I don't, nor does he love me. Never has. Men don't take a woman to bed for love, at least not in my experience. But if a woman gets caught, it's up to her to do something about it. No hole-in-a-corner midwife for me. I want a house and servants to look after me and a wealthy husband to keep me in clothes and carriages. Leon has an eye for such things, doesn't he?'

With a cold numbness creeping up her arms, Felice did her best to smile in agreement, suddenly desperate not to allow this callous creature to know of her heartache. 'He certainly does, mistress. I'd stay there a while, if I were you, and try the warm posset. It'll make you feel stronger.'

Dazed and sickened, she clutched at the heavily ornamented balustrade and took each step slowly downwards, plagued by the memory of that dark fetid room in Winchester where a young woman lay groaning and afraid. Would that be the fate of Levina if her plans did not materialise? Could a woman stand by and allow that to happen, knowing how the Vytters' daughter had expected care and found criminal irresponsibility that her parents could never have suspected? This woman's plight was here and now; her own was not yet established: there would be no question of sacrifice when Leon had never been truly hers, nor she his. And even if it were true that he had no love for Levina, his undeniable friendship for her would be enough to help her through this crisis.

Once again, Lydia was horrified, outraged and adamant that Felice should not give in to this heartless manipulation, having had good evidence from Adam Bystander that his master was behaving like a man in love. 'You cannot let her do it!' she pleaded, following Felice into the newly set-up brewery. 'Pregnant or not, she's a bitch and you've got to fight her over this. Tell him you love him, or he'll believe you don't, and then this…this *harpy* will get her clutches into him for good.'

Aimlessly moving bowls from here to there, Felice could see only the appalling dilemma of a woman who, denied help when she most needed it, could easily forfeit her life.

'Rubbish!' Lydia said, taking an earthenware jug from Felice and replacing it on the stone shelf. 'She'll not come to any harm. You don't suppose Sir Leon's the only string to her bow, do you? She may not know who the father is, but she'll have a damn good idea, believe me. You think she needs Sir Leon more than you do, don't you?'

'Yes.'

'Well, you're wrong! She's aiming for him because Lord Deventer put her up to it because he's always wanted the match. You said so yourself only yesterday. You're being mawkishly sentimental, love, and it's time *you* showed your talons, too. Oh, what *is* it, Elizabeth?'

Mistress Elizabeth Pemberton, in and out of love like a butterfly, had some news of a most inappropriate nature. 'The waggons have arrived from Winchester,' she said, eyeing Felice's tears.

'They arrived two days ago,' Lydia snapped.

'No, these have the gowns from the man on the Pentice. Shall I unpack them, my lady?'

'No,' Felice croaked. 'Leave them in their boxes.'

Lydia's unvoiced command contradicted this, and it was fortunate that Elizabeth, for all her failings, had learned to lip-read.

It was also fortunate that Lydia stayed close to her mistress for the next few hours in the expectation that something might happen to propel Felice into action. It did, but not in the direction Lydia had hoped, even though she had managed to steer her towards the small room that Sir Leon called his office with a view to pushing her inside and closing the door.

Voices reached them from the passageway causing Lydia to frown, crossly. 'Tch! He's got someone with him.'

Quickly, Felice turned away. 'Let's make it another time,' she hissed.

Lydia restrained her. 'Shh! Listen. Someone's weeping.'

'It's her!' Anger and curiosity combined to make her investigate, and unwillingly she moved forward until she could see into the room where Sir Leon stood by his table piled with papers, an account-book still open. Levina stood close to him with her forehead on his shoulder, comforted by his arms, his head bent to one side as if to catch her sobbing words. He said something to her and she nodded, and Felice could watch no more.

'Now do you believe me?' she growled to Lydia.

'No,' said Lydia. 'I'll not believe it, even now.'

But for Felice, it was the evidence she needed that she had no place in Sir Leon's future, evidence she would not have had the humiliation of witnessing, she told Lydia, if she'd followed her own advice instead of hers. Lydia was unrepentant. If her mistress lost Sir Leon, she would lose her Adam, and that would be a new and unacceptable experience for Mistress Lydia. Something had to be done.

On the top floor of the Abbot's House, Marcus Donne laid down his fine squirrel-hair paintbrush with a sigh and looked reproachfully at his lovely subject as yet another tear dripped off the point of her chin. As no explanation followed, he took a stool across to her and sat so that he could take her hands in his. 'What is it?' he whispered. 'This is the second time in two days. There's a problem, isn't there?'

'I'm sorry,' she said. 'Shall we try again later?'

'When your eyes are red with weeping? No, dear lady. I think it's better if you tell me about it, then I can see what's to be done.'

'Nothing's to be done, Marcus.'

'Ah,' he smiled. 'Don't you believe it. If it's Leon, leave him to me. Has he been severe again? I thought you two were…hush, love. Don't distress yourself. What's he been up to?'

Felice blew her nose, noisily. 'No…nothing, really. It was all a terrible mistake. Nothing. I'm being silly.'

'No,' Marcus said, slowly. 'No, there's something here I don't quite understand. Tell me to mind my own business, but has he…did he become *more* than friendly while you were in Winchester? Has he taken you to bed?'

Felice was silent, twisting her handkerchief in her fingers.

'He has, hasn't he? The swine. And now on your return there's my lovely Levina to bring him to heel, and all the while he's telling me to keep off his pitch and sending me packing when I refuse.' His voice throbbed with anger. 'I should give him a good thrashing for this. My God, I should!'

She laid a hand on his arm. 'Don't interfere, Marcus. I know you mean well and I'm touched, but he and Levina are—did you say *your* lovely Levina? You're in love with her, Marcus?'

'Oh lord, always have been. I've never bothered her. Nothing to offer on the scale that *she* needs things. I doubt she even knows. But look, if you and Leon have been lovers, you must be getting a bit worried. Did he talk of marriage to you? Has he told your stepfather?'

'No,' she said. 'He'll marry Levina. I'm sure of it.'

'And leave you to fend for yourself? Not without a word from me, he won't!' He stood up, pulling her up with him and surprising her with his uncharacteristic anger. 'Listen to me, Felice. He's not going to get away with this. This time he's overstepped the mark. It's no surprise that he's taken up with Levina again, but if he doesn't agree to marry you, I will. With or without his permission. He can't tie a woman hand and foot like this. No, it's no good protesting. I've made my mind up.'

'You cannot do it, dear Marcus. I must find my own solution to the problem.'

His voice dropped as he kissed her knuckles. 'You just have, Felice. It's me.'

'I cannot allow you to do this,' she called after him as he left her. 'I couldn't ask you to…'

'You're not asking me to,' he called back from the stairway. 'I'm asking you.'

Sir Leon was standing in the middle of the blackened ruins with a flapping plan in his hands when

Marcus found him talking with two of his masons. All around them, men were clearing rubble, sawing up charred beams and clambering along the walls while, in the distance, Lord Deventer stood talking to a black-gowned gentleman and his clerk.

One of the masons took the plan and rolled it up. 'Right, sir,' he said, looking at Marcus. 'We'll get on, then. Good day to you, Mr Donne.'

'The coroner,' Sir Leon said in answer to Marcus's enquiring glance. 'And you'll be getting dust all over you in this place, lad. Come away.' He was dressed in working-clothes—leather boots, knee-length breeches and open-necked white shirt—that set off his dark handsomeness and large frame in a way that Marcus was well able to appreciate, as a painter.

But Marcus was in no mood to be impressed. 'Yes,' he said, tersely. 'A word in private is what I have in mind, Leon, if you please. Unless you want this crowd to hear what I've to say.'

'Why, what is it? Something wrong?' Sir Leon stepped over a pile of masonry and out through the courtyard piled with salvaged materials, and on towards the river. 'Now, is this private enough for you? And if you've come to tell me about Levina being…'

'I've come to talk about Lady Felice, Leon, if you can get Levina out of your head for a moment or two. Perhaps it's time you gave some thought to her instead.'

'Wait a minute, my friend! What the hell are you talking about? For one thing, Levina's not *in* my head and, for another, what d'ye think I've been doing since all this happened, sitting on my backside? I've been out here in every daylight hour, working on plans half the bloody night, talking to Deventer about his ideas, siting new lodges that were burnt down, ordering replacement materials, with all my clerk of works' duties to cover and much of my steward's as well. Lady Felice has had her hands so full she's hardly given me the time of day, and I've no time to find out any more than that. So what's eating at you, for pity's sake?'

'I'll tell you what's eating me, you thick-headed arrogant churl.' Marcus grabbed at Sir Leon's arm and yanked him round to face him. Then, with amazing velocity, he smashed a fist into his friend's face, catching him on the jaw and knocking him backwards a couple of paces, taking him completely unawares. 'That's what's eating me, my friend,' he said, keeping his distance. 'That's for telling me to keep off your property while *you* put her in the same danger you pretend to be so concerned about. And now when the lass doesn't know whether she's coming or going, you leave her to stew while you prance about with *another* woman you've picked up and dropped at random for the past three years. It's time you heeded your own warnings, my lad, because this can't go on. You have responsibilities, or had you forgotten?'

Sir Leon looked at the blood on his fingertips and touched his lip again. 'Marcus, you're not making any sense. I haven't left Felice to stew, as you seem to believe. She won't have anything to do with me, and I've been too busy with Deventer and all this lot.' He waved an arm towards the site where already men were gazing in astonishment at the man who had just managed to get one under the surveyor's guard. 'And anyway, what's this danger she's supposed to be in? She's mine, and she knows she is.'

'She knows nothing of the kind, you great oaf!' Marcus yelled, infuriated by his friend's defence. '*I'm* going to marry her, if you won't!'

'Really. And you've told her so, have you?'

'Yes, I have.'

'Then you can untell her.'

'I'll be damned if I will! You can't marry them both, or did you think you could?'

'Both? You believe I'm going to marry Levina…oh, God, Marcus! Get a hold of yourself, lad! Of course I'm not. We've not been…'

But whatever they had not been was unexplained before Marcus took another swing at his friend in a blind fury of jealousy. This time the blow was knocked brutally aside and Marcus was hustled backwards against a tree-trunk, struggling to keep his balance. 'Why not?' he yelled.

'Why not? Ask her yourself. You seem to be developing a skill in counselling,' Sir Leon yelled back. 'She might begin to see you as husband-material at last, which is more than anyone else can, but you can forget your chivalry towards Lady Felice, my friend. I've told you, she's *mine*! And if she's having doubts about that, that's none of your concern, limner. Your profession allows you to gain women's confidences;

mine doesn't. My love-life has to wait until my patron has shifted himself from under my bloody feet!'

'Love? What do you know about love, builder?'

'More than you, paint-dabbler, but I don't splash it around so much.'

'Well then, perhaps I can show you how to make a splash.' Marcus lunged towards his friend who now stood with his back to the river on the debris-strewn banks that had only recently been covered with water. He was caught and knocked sideways by a huge fist, making him stumble and hesitate before tackling Sir Leon again. But though he faced the abbey, he was oblivious to Lord Deventer's approach or to the coroner's expression of astonishment. Madly, he rushed forward with both fists flying, but his adversary was prepared, lifting him high off the ground in a bear-hug, tossing him above his head as if he were a child and hurling him into the river to the applause of a crowd of men from the distant courtyard.

'Cool off!' Sir Leon yelled.

Lord Deventer's voice held no hint of censure. 'Well, Gascelin? So your patron gets under your bloody feet, does he?'

But although the bend in the river was not deep at that point, the current was swift and Sir Leon had no wish to prolong his friend's humiliation before an audience. However, before he could wade in, several of the men ran forward to rescue Marcus, eager for any diversion, and soon there was a thrashing group of them, pulling and shouting.

'Get him out,' called Lord Deventer. 'Time's money!'

'Yes, my lord,' one of them called back. 'But there's another body here.'

'Well, pull it out, then.'

With Marcus doing his share, fair hair darkly plastered on to his forehead, they dragged a bloated body, face downwards, up on to the bank. Still tangled around one wrist was a bulging sack, the cord of which had cut deeply into his skin. Undoubtedly it was what had held him under the water since the night of the fire.

'Ben Smith,' said one man, rolling the body over.

'So it is,' said Sir Leon. 'Come, Marcus. Give me your hand.'

'I came here to give you a hiding, lad,' Marcus said, coughing, 'not to do your dirty work for you. And you're going to lose that lovely lass if you don't look to it. She's in love with you, you know.'

'And how would you know that, limner?'

Marcus peeled off his soaking doublet and threw it down on to the ground with a loud smack. 'Well, what d'ye think *I*'ve been doing for the last few days while I've been painting her? Looking at your damned ceiling? Before Winchester and after Winchester. Think I can't tell the difference in a woman's eyes by now, my fine friend? See to it, before it's too late.'

'I intend to. Go and get some clothes on before *you* catch a chill.'

Lord Deventer moved in as Marcus squelched

away. 'Now, Gascelin, if you have a moment I'd like you to…hey! Where are you off to?'

'Business, sir!' Sir Leon called, striding after Marcus. 'Urgent business.'

In Felice's bedchamber, the vibrant new clothes from Winchester that spread like a peacock's tail across the bed had lost the appeal they'd had a week or so ago when Lady West's views had been accepted. Nevertheless, both Lydia and Elizabeth agreed that red suited her peach complexion and dark hair, quelling all Felice's arguments that it made her feel uncomfortable. 'It's not my colour,' she grumbled, as they hooked and pinned her into it. 'It makes me look like an over-ripe strawberry.'

'Stand still,' said Lydia with a row of pins between her lips. 'If the men like Levina's bright showy clothes, they'll like yours, too. If you can't beat 'em, then join 'em, love. And if they like her powder and painted lips, presumably they'll like yours even better.'

'No, Lydie! I'm not…'

'Only a dab, love, to brighten your pale cheeks. Just a quick dab.'

The quick dab became a classic case of too many cooks spoiling the broth, and yet such was the state of Felice's insecurity that she felt unable to rely on her own judgement alone, admitting to herself that, as none of her hopes and plans had worked too well so far, there was little harm in trying someone else's. So she submitted to the frills and festoons, the brooches and rings, the tightly-braided hair over padding with the silly hat on top, the collapsible farthingale made of willow-hoops that she had not worn since Winchester. She stood, scowling, while they painted her eyebrows more thickly, reddened her cheeks and lips, powdered her skin and made her almost unrecognisable while assuring her that, if it did nothing else, it would at least draw some of the attention away from that scheming callous hussy Levina.

Feeling that she may as well have held a mask before her face as have one painted on her, she took up her duties in the hall of the New House as the servers were preparing the tables for the mid-day meal where, disconcerted by the apparition before them, several of the lads crashed into each other, dropping their dishes and contents. Flint and Fen dashed in to gobble up the mess, refusing to take any notice of the strange woman who called them off and growling at one lad who dared to lay a hand on their collars.

The appearance of Thomas Vyttery did nothing to help matters, for his cowardly mastiff, unable to escape the scene, was instantly seen as a rival for the new food supply on the floor, and the fight that ensued was weighted against him from the start. Felice was in despair, hampered by the contraptions under her clothes and everything that dangled from them.

A man's deep voice cracked across the pandemonium. 'Flint! Fen! Come here!'

Without another look at the terrified mastiff, the

two deerhounds slunk away and padded, heads and tails down, to Sir Leon's side where they flattened themselves on to the floor like two grey rugs.

'What's going on, Thomas?' Sir Leon said. 'And who's…my *God*! What on earth?' He stared at Felice, aghast, his face a picture of dismay.

She knew, as soon as she saw it, that she had done the wrong thing, that she should not have given in to this absurdity, that far from finding her attractive, he found it all repulsive. There was nothing to say to him, not even in her own defence, while he stood there, taking in every detail. She whirled on one high heel and made a frantic dash for the door behind Mr Vyttery, not knowing where it led.

He dodged to one side, blinking in astonishment and remonstrating with the large powerful figure who followed with giant strides. 'Nay, sir. Leave her be! Ye can see she's upset. Leave her!'

'Get out of my way, Thomas!'

The passageway was a narrow one leading to a flight of stone stairs down which a liveried servant came, his arms piled high with white folded linen tablecloths larger than bed sheets. There was no way past him. Felice turned to confront her angry guardian, trapped between the two of them.

'Leave me alone!' she snarled at him. 'No…!' She tried to ward him off with her hands but he caught them without any attempt to persuasion or reason, holding her easily as he whipped the top cloth off the startled servant's pile, shook it out and wrapped it

round her like a shroud before she could free herself
from his grasp.

Imprisoned in this white cocoon, she fought and
twisted as she was bent forward over his knee and,
held in that position, her skirts were lifted, her great
bell-shaped farthingale untied from her waist and
dropped to the floor like a pool, her skirts replaced.

'That's a start,' she heard him say. 'Now for the
rest.'

'No…no!' she wailed. 'How dare you do this?
How *dare* you?'

He was not inclined to answer, but lifted her up
into his arms instead and, ignoring the speechless man
on the stairs, stepped over the white fabric puddle and
marched with his writhing bundle across the hall. The
same people were there who had seen them leave moments before, this time with mouths open in amaze-
ment at the spectacle of their mistress being carted
off like a side of bacon by a grim-faced Sir Leon.

He stopped alongside Lydia who had been, to her
credit, prepared to follow them. 'Mistress Lydia,' he
said. 'Take this daft thing off her head, if you please,
and collect that tent from the passageway before
someone camps out in it.'

Lydia complied, and then had no choice but to see
her mistress swung round and carried off, still protesting, to Sir Leon's room that overlooked the cloister. And while the drama was ended for those in the
hall, for Felice it was only just beginning, all the more
dramatic because he was too furious to speak and she
too furious to keep silent.

Still constrained by the winding-sheet, she was laid on the bed and held there while he began a thorough removal of the crude cosmetics that could do nothing to make her lovelier, only the opposite. Taking a handful of the cloth, he soaped her face, ignoring her protests and her tears and then, as her own features were restored, dried her more tenderly. Next, he unbraided her hair, turning her face-downwards to reach the back and teasing out each coil until it was loose and covering the pillow.

By this time, Felice's tears had run dry, though her anger had not, and now the full force of it was vented into his pillow in a rage of helplessness and unmitigated jealousy. And although she felt nothing but relief to be free of her disguise, the motivation for it could not be removed so easily. The harridan Levina was a she-wolf, did he not know that? Was he blind? Too besotted to care?

'I'll give you all the answers you need when I've got you out of this,' he said. 'And who in heaven's name told you to wear this colour? Do you not know that red's no colour for you?'

'Of course I do!' she yelped into the pillow. 'But if that loud-mouthed hoyden can wear it, so can I.'

'Ah, so that's it! Well, you're wrong. You can't.' Preventing her from turning over by a hand on her hips, he deftly unhooked her bodice and then, with his dagger, cut through the laces of her whalebone stays, removing all her casings like a shrimp from its shell. It was an easy matter after that to peel off the under-layers, one by one, until she was nakedly resisting any further peelings by holding on to his wrist behind her back in the belief that she was restraining him, not herself.

'No more,' she said, through a sheet of hair. 'Leave my silk stockings on.'

'Then let go of my wrist.'

She felt his hand explore the prettily tied garter ribbons and then continue on its own search of her thighs and buttocks, felt his tender kisses follow the path of his hand, moving upwards over hips, waist and shoulders. 'No,' she whispered. 'I don't want you. Marcus has offered to marry me. You go and marry Levina. You deserve each other.'

His sigh turned into a soft laugh as he lifted the mass of hair off her neck and allowed his mouth to roam warmly over her skin. She could see his face from the corner of her eye. 'You've got it all sewn up, haven't you, you two? Eh? Well, my fierce beauty, you can undo all your plans because mine were made as soon as I saw you, weeks ago.' His lips nibbled at her beautiful shoulders. 'And they've not changed since then.'

'Oh, I knew exactly what your plans were from the start, Sir Leon. Whether I'm a wife to please my stepfather or a mistress to suit you, I'm supposed to share my life with that monster upstairs who doesn't even know the father of her own child. Well, if you...'

'Will you shut up for a moment, woman?'

With a deft flip of her hips, he turned her on to her back and drew the hair away from her face. His kiss did more than silence her words, it reached down into her heart and gentled it, soothing its pain. 'Now,' he whispered, 'shall we leave her out of it, my lady, and speak of something more interesting? Of the first time we met, in the Abbot's House?'

'I hated you then and I hate you now,' she said, caressing the side of his finger with her teeth.

His lips twitched. 'Yes, but there was more to it than that, wasn't there? You hated the idea of being disturbed out of your unhappiness, and you hated me because I represented your stepfather. You were determined not to accept my control. And now, you believe my heart is elsewhere when it's always been yours, from that very first moment.'

She had not heard him speak of hearts and emotions before, only her adeptness at loving, which was not the same. Yet now he was saying it with such tender conviction she could hardly believe what she was hearing. 'But you couldn't have…you were so rude…so unpleasant.'

'We'd already met, remember? Look here.' He delved inside the lining of his waistband and drew out a long shining blue ribbon, now very creased, and dangled it before her.

'That's mine!'

'Yours, woman. Pulled off the end of a thick plait of silken hair one night in a moonlit garden, the same hair that you piled up on top of your head to show them all what a real woman looks like, just a few days ago. My heart nearly burst with love and pride, sweetheart, and when you're my wife, you'll wear your hair like this for me, as it is now. No paint. No more attempts to look like those wenches at court. Nothing can improve on this, my love.' His hand swept over her body, setting it alight.

'Your wife?' she whispered. 'No rivals?'

'Still unconvinced? There never have been any rivals, sweetheart. That woman thrives on mischief; I found that out soon enough. We've remained friends over the years, and I'm bound to remain polite to my patron's relatives…'

'You were not polite to me!'

'…but she knew damn well I'd not go so far as to marry her just to find a name for her brat.'

'She asked you, then?'

'Oh, yes, she tried it on. She has all the audacity of the devil, but I'm not stupid enough for that, and she knows it.'

'What about the tears?'

'You saw?'

'Some of it.'

'The tears were because I said no. Deventer had already told me of the problem, and I'd told him I couldn't help. But I've been so frantically busy since they came, love, that I've hardly had time to sleep, what with the loss of John and all. I'm sorry. I should have made you listen to me, but you seemed not to want me. *Did* you want me?'

'Wanted you. Ached for you. Forgive me, I was desperate. I was sure you loved her. Marcus told me you did.'

'Another little trouble-maker we could do without. I think we should make him marry Levina.'

'He's in love with her.'

'I know. The trouble is, he can't afford her.'

'Then speak to Lord Deventer. Perhaps he'll help.' She began to untie the cords of his shirt. 'What's he going to say about you and me?'

'He'll not be too surprised, sweetheart. He admitted he'd brought Levina down here in the hope that I'd help her out of her predicament, but I don't owe him any favours of that kind. Not in my personal life; he has no influence there. As for you, my fierce ward, he already guessed how things are between us when he saw you that first evening with your hair down, not caring a damn for any of them. He tried to change my mind, of course, but he knows that if he refuses his consent, he'll lose both of us. He's got the picture, my love.' His hands caressed as they had done at that first meeting, intimately. 'And my mind's been made up since I caught you in the garden, my sweet. I knew you must be a beauty, but I'd no idea just how beautiful until I saw you that morning with your feet in a bucket of water. And then I had you in my arms, wet and angry. I could scarcely believe my good fortune…'

'And I was afraid of you.'

'…I wanted to eat you.'

'And I loved you, I think.'

'Love me now, Felice. Be my wife. I want no one but you.'

'I do love you. I will. But what was all that talk of taming? Not *that* much of a challenge, surely?'

'To anger you. I love your wildness, your wilfull-
ness. I adore you, woman.'

The voluminous white tablecloth wrapped their
limbs, and a wrinkled hair-ribbon slid between its
folds like a reflection of blue sky on the sea, and it
was as if the sudden release of all misunderstandings
and doubts gave their loving a new direction, a never-
ending gentleness in which time had no part. All in-
hibitions dissolved as Felice gave herself up to him
in a total surrender that brought both laughter and
tears and wave upon wave of joy into her heart, now
repaired, restored and intact again. Suddenly she was
living, flying, and whole.

The notion that Marcus and Levina should solve
each other's problems found favour with everyone,
even Lord Deventer who would have done anything
to ensure his niece's future happiness. Relieved to see
Felice's glowing contentment, Marcus fussed around
Levina like a dog with two tails, caring not one whit
that Lord Deventer and Sir Leon had insisted that she
tell him the exact truth of her condition. It made no
difference to Marcus; he would take her in any condition, though the lady's uncle had made the path remarkably smooth with a generous annual allowance.

Supper that evening was an informal meal at which
Felice was allowed to dress in the new pale-blue watery silk that Sir Leon said was exactly right for a
wanton moon-spirit. And even though the grave coroner and his clerk were their guests, Sir Leon would

have her hair only loosely knotted with a crumpled blue ribbon.

The coroner wanted to know how the fire had started, but no one was sure except that one of the injured was a man who had only recently been dismissed for drunkenness. He should not have been there at all, and so far had not confessed to anything. As for what John Aycombe had been doing in the guesthouse so late, no one knew the answer to that, either.

'You say he had a beechwood box with him?' the coroner said to Sir Leon. 'Have I seen it yet?' He knew he had not.

'It's one that belongs to me, sir,' Sir Leon said. 'Nothing much in it.'

'Then what did he want with it?'

'He was probably taking it across to my new office. I can't think of any other reason. Can you, Thomas?'

'No, sir. John would have had his reasons, I don't doubt. He always did.' Deep in the pocket of his black gown, Thomas's hand closed around a fold of linen that Sir Leon had given him only that morning after their private conversation. It was soft and yielding and gave no indication of its contents, a curling lock of dark brown hair tied with a fine gold thread. There had not, apparently, been anything for Thomas to tell him that he'd not already discovered for himself.

The cloister was deep in shadow, lit faintly by a distant torch that flickered in the stableyard beyond and by a moon that had only just risen above the church roof. Already the walkways had been cleared, and the square that had once been rubble-filled was stacked out with strings and trenches ready for new beds to be laid and, at the end near the sacristy, a rectangular grave-slab had appeared which Felice had not seen before.

Hand in hand, the two lovers approached. 'Who was it?' she said.

'The sub-prior. We'll not disturb him. He was a friend of Thomas's, I believe.'

'Then we must dig carefully round him and plant rosebushes. Would he like that, d'ye think? And rosemary, for remembrance?'

'Yes, my love, he'd like that.' He took her in his arms and saw the moon reflected in her eyes. 'Do you remember sitting here? How we fought?' His kiss reminded her, sending shocks of pleasure through her that once she had tried guiltily to deny.

'I remember another fight, sir,' she said, 'when you lost something, too.' Against the pale moon, Felice held a golden pointed thing shaped like a tiny spearhead. 'This?' she whispered.

'My missing aiglet! Where did you find it? You've had it all this time, next to your heart?'

'Most of the time,' she teased. 'This has been a *most* unseemly summer, has it not, sir?'

But if she thought she would be allowed to have the last word, just for once, she was reminded otherwise. 'Unforgettable,' he whispered, his lips teasing hers, 'not unseemly. Unless you wish to argue the point?'

*   *   *   *   *

Modern Romance™
...seduction and
passion guaranteed

Tender Romance™
...love affairs that
last a lifetime

Sensual Romance™
...sassy, sexy and
seductive

Blaze
...sultry days and
steamy nights

Medical Romance™
...medical drama on
the pulse

Historical Romance™
...rich, vivid and
passionate

29 new titles every month.

*With all kinds of Romance for
every kind of mood...*

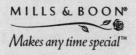

MILLS & BOON®

Makes any time special™

MAT4

MILLS & BOON®

Historical Romance™

MAJOR CHANCELLOR'S MISSION by Paula Marshall

Regency

Richard Chancellor's latest mission to catch a traitor by posing as a tutor to a respectable family was challenging enough — without the added complication of his desire for the chatelaine of the estate! While Major Chancellor was an eligible *parti*, the scholarly tutor, Edward Ritchie, was not. And although Pandora showed a predilection for his company, how would she react when she learnt of his deception?

MY LADY'S PRISONER by Ann Elizabeth Cree

Regency

Ever since her husband was killed three years ago, Julia Carrington has done her utmost to uncover the culprit. She has met with little success until Nicholas Chandler, Viscount Thayne, appears—wearing her husband's ring! Julia knows she must take action, but how can she persuade this influential man to hand over the ring and tell her what he knows? There seems no alternative—she will have to take him prisoner...

On sale 2nd November 2001

2 FREE

books and a surprise gift!

We would like to take this opportunity to thank you for reading this Mills & Boon® book by offering you the chance to take TWO more specially selected titles from the Historical Romance™ series absolutely FREE! We're also making this offer to introduce you to the benefits of the Reader Service™—

★ FREE home delivery
★ FREE gifts and competitions
★ FREE monthly Newsletter
★ Exclusive Reader Service discounts
★ Books available before they're in the shops

Accepting these FREE books and gift places you under no obligation to buy, you may cancel at any time, even after receiving your free shipment. Simply complete your details below and return the entire page to the address below. *You don't even need a stamp!*

YES! Please send me 2 free Historical Romance books and a surprise gift. I understand that unless you hear from me, I will receive 4 superb new titles every month for just £2.99 each, postage and packing free. I am under no obligation to purchase any books and may cancel my subscription at any time. The free books and gift will be mine to keep in any case.

H1ZEA

Ms/Mrs/Miss/Mr ....Initials....................................
BLOCK CAPITALS PLEASE

Surname ....

Address ....

....

....Postcode...............................

Send this whole page to:
UK: FREEPOST CN81, Croydon, CR9 3WZ
EIRE: PO Box 4546, Kilcock, County Kildare (stamp required)

Offer valid in UK and Eire only and not available to current Reader Service subscribers to this series. We reserve the right to refuse an application and applicants must be aged 18 years or over. Only one application per household. Terms and prices subject to change without notice. Offer expires 30th April 2002. As a result of this application, you may receive offers from other carefully selected companies. If you would prefer not to share in this opportunity please write to The Data Manager at the address above.

Mills & Boon® is a registered trademark owned by Harlequin Mills & Boon Limited.
Historical Romance™ is being used as a trademark.